Brood X

by DAN STOCKMAN

This edition © 2021 Dan Stockman

Published by Nickel Plate Publishing Co.
Fort Wayne, Indiana
www.nickelplatepublishing.com

Original copyright © 2013 Dan Stockman
All rights reserved.

ISBN-13: 978-1-7371186-1-9

DEDICATION

This book would not exist without the help of A.E. Griffin, the encouragement of Emma Downs and the belief of Fred McKissack, Jr.

ACKNOWLEDGMENTS

I owe a great debt to Walter Cummins, early readers such as Kristen Gregory, and especially my original reader, Sandra Cwiakala, who tirelessly waded through endless pages of drivel in the early years. Hopefully, this makes it all worth it.

A special thanks to Tazio Ruffilo for the line in Chapter 17 from his poem, "Yes, A Star Explodes Inside You."

The lyrics in Chapter 16 are from Elaina Burress' wonderful songs, "A Song for Someone" and "Paper Love," and are used by permission. Discover her music at *www.elainaburress.com*.

Chapter Eight first appeared as an excerpt in Pithead Chapel. *pitheadchapel.com*
Chapter Eight also appeared in the anthology "Gateways," published by Serving House Books. *Servinghousebooks.com*
A portion of Chapter One appeared in Petite Hound Press.

The cover was designed by Jeff Anderson.

The author photo is by Callie Cwiakala. *www.facebook.com/CallieJcPhotography*

The world owes a great debt to Charles Lester Marlatt, 1863-1954, a USDA entomologist whose landmark 1907 publication on cicadas provided the foundation for everything we know about them today. This book quotes extensively from his earlier, 1898 work on the subject.

Thanks to retired biology professor Charles Holliday, of Lafayette College in Easton, Pa., for his work on cicada killer wasps, and the University of Michigan Museum of Zoology's Insect Division and John Cooley and David Marshall of the University of Connecticut for collecting and sharing so much information on the periodical cicada.

Many thanks to Jack Driscoll, Shirley Clemens Griffin, Karyn Storts-Brinks, Jason Maxfield, Dave Grant & Co., Mr. Bob Heaton, David Dodd Lee, Mark Kohut, and Julie Crothers.

And endless thanks to Krista, Felicity and Kieran: my Everythings.

FORWARD

AS I WRITE this, there is snow on the ground, the air is bitter, and we've been under pandemic restrictions for nearly a year, time that has ticked by slowly. And yet, somehow, it is 2021 and more than a decade since I first started writing *Brood X*, more than seven years since it was first published, and an incredible 17 years since 2004 − the last time Brood X cicadas emerged from the ground. Minutes pass slowly, years are gone in an instant.

So much can happen in 17 years: Our daughter was born in 2004, just a few months after the insects emerging this summer tunneled into the ground, and now has just two years left in high school; our son was born in 2006 and is in high school himself. It's mind boggling: When Brood X emerged in 2004 to live their few short weeks above ground, our daughter was in utero. Now, as the offspring from that crop prepares to emerge, she has her first job, is learning to drive, and is already thinking about graduation. Our children have gone from newborns to toddlers to children to amazing young adults, and through all of that, the cicadas of Brood X have slumbered underground, slowly growing and transforming, waiting for that day in early summer when they will emerge for just weeks of light and air before dying. Seventeen years after that − in 2038 − their offspring will emerge and start the cycle again. Where will all of us be in 2038?

Brood X's characters, Andy and Ashley and Scarlett, of course, haven't gotten any older since 2013 and never will, but the rest of us will continue to age. It took Andy a long time to learn how to seize the moment, and it can be difficult for all of us. But as Andy finally found, it's not impossible, and when we do it can change us in profound ways.

So seize the moment. Take advantage of the fleeting time we have together. And if it seems your moment will never come, remember what the cicada has known for millennia: The moment never comes until you're truly ready.

—Dan

BROOD X

ONE

"The periodical, or seventeen-year Cicada is especially remarkable in its adolescent period, during all of which time its existence is unsuspected and un-indicated by any sign, and the perfect regularity with which at the end of these periods every generation, though numbering millions of individuals, attains maturity at almost the same moment. To those unfamiliar with its habits, these sudden recurrences not only startle but often excite the gravest fears…"

—"The Periodical Cicada," by C.L. Marlatt,
U.S. Department of Agriculture, 1898

AWAKE. No, he couldn't be awake, because there was someone near, and that could not be. It's a dream, he thought, only he knew he didn't dream. Not anymore. For him, sleep was simply darkness, but the darkness was gone, and yes, he *was* awake, and there was someone there, in the bed, next to him. How? He tried to think of an answer, but the sleep was closing in around him again, along with a sound, slowly rising, so slowly that at first he wasn't aware of it, and then he was aware but with the realization that he had been hearing it for a while now. Wait, a sound? Yes, one, single music note, humming in the air, a note that stayed exactly the same, even as it changed. Wait, no – it wasn't changing. The pitch was the same, but the tone was changing, or maybe his perception of it was, as he sunk into the sound and the darkness of sleep again.

Sleep. Sleep like a womb that not only surrounded him; but a sleep where the sound was part of the embrace, too, his very cells resonating with it. And She was there, now, too – not the body outside, laying next to him, the woman he barely knew, but Her. Her, the almost forgotten. Her, out of the shadows. Her from places his mind no longer dared wander to.

The Song. He had forgotten the song. Or thought he had. After all these years, it had been pushed so far back into the crevasses of memory that it could not haunt him anymore, until now, suddenly, it was back. Of course it was. He knew it had never really left – he had just forgotten

1

to think about it, the way he had forgotten to think about Her.

Or had he already been thinking about it for days? Didn't it come back the other day, when he heard the bugs in the yard, the loud ones – what are they again? He and Ashley were seventeen that summer. In the dream, she was back with her canvas shoes and blue eyes, and the little sighs in her voice. He could hear her voice even over the Song, the note that resonated in the air until other notes could be heard in harmony with it, growing until it became all consuming as it reverberated in the spaces between his bed and the walls of his house. He had forgotten her voice, too, hadn't he?

He woke up for real now, and sat up. He turned his head toward another noise, this one intruding on the Song, a rumbling. Silver moonlight seemed to flood his little bedroom and the sleeping form next to him: Scarlett was snoring.

Scarlett. The woman. He hadn't forgotten her, but was confused for a moment by the dream. Because suddenly, there was Scarlett – whom he barely knew – sleeping next to him. And snoring, her face nearly buried under a pile of curly brunette hair, but the moonlight was so bright he could still make out her freckles, until she stirred and rolled over and the snoring stopped. She was wearing his t-shirt, and her breasts were untamed beneath it as she rolled over. He would not be forgetting those anytime soon. Still, their perfection was as mysterious as her arrival. How the hell did she get here, anyway? Here in the moonlight, in his bed, in his t-shirt, in his arms until they each fell asleep and rolled over, both more used to sleeping alone than with anyone else anymore.

A woman in the bed that was usually occupied by ghosts.

He listened to Scarlett breathe and remembered the sound of her knocking on the door – he could hear it perfectly, the door's gray aluminum in need of replacement for a couple of summers now, but it was easier just to put up with it than to get a new one, wasn't it?

He was amazed at the way the moonlight made Scarlett's hair seem to glow, but was not sure what she meant. Everything has just changed, he thought, and he dreaded the emotional investment those changes would require.

Still, he would be a liar to say he hadn't wanted things to change, and one thing Andrew J. Gardner was not was a liar. But just because he wanted his life to change didn't mean he had done anything to make that change happen. In fact, he had done seemingly everything in his power to avoid change, of any sort. But here it was, as if the universe had just toggled from one state to another: There was his half-naked neighbor sleeping next to him, and change had come to his life whether he was looking for it or not.

He watched her breathe and remembered exactly how it was before she arrived, how the air moved, how the floor felt beneath his feet, how the room echoed back the sounds of his daily existence. How his '92 Grand Am, like always, had seemed to moan as the car heaved itself up the little rise from the street and into his driveway. Man, he remembered driving that thing off the lot – fire engine red – the day after he graduated from Indiana. He had felt like a king driving that Pontiac back home to Fort Wayne, a college degree in his back pocket, a serious girlfriend in the bucket seat next to him and the whole world laid out before him.

Buying an obnoxiously red car had made sense at the time. Perfect sense. Now, Andy thought as he turned off the too-loud, rough-running engine, it looks exactly like every other piece of crap car on the road. Only mine is 11 years old and has about a million miles on it. He slammed the door shut and even that sounded like it hurt the car. The serious girlfriend he thought would erase the past had turned into his wife and then into his ex-wife. The degree got him stuck in middle management at a mid-sized cabinet company in the middle of nowhere. And the whole world that had been laid out before him? Somehow it had narrowed to little more than his job, his car and his living room. On his way home from work he saw at least seven cars exactly like his. For all he knew, General Motors was still cranking out red Pontiac Grand Ams by the trainload for other suckers to define themselves by.

Even as he lay in bed, somewhere between awake and asleep, he could feel the shame he felt looking at his stupid car just hours before, knowing he would never buy another until he was forced to, because it was easier to be ashamed of it than, well – it was just easier to be ashamed.

He had gotten out of the car and saw the grass in his little yard was long again. It was June, and the stuff seemed to be on steroids. He swore he could mow it every other day in June and still wouldn't keep up. But having to mow the grass again was so depressing he turned back to the damn flaming red car in the driveway in front of the little white house, tucked in a little neighborhood by the river.

He had once loved this car, he thought. Then he tried not to think about it. Now he hated it. He hated the way GM pretended its crappy V-6 engine was sporty, hated the way the black interior was always about 100 degrees inside and hated the way he had to shift the manual transmission all the time when the plain truth was the car – a Pontiac, for crap's sake – was just a grocery-getter with bucket seats and a stupid paint job. Mainly, he hated the fact that he had ever loved it.

"Damn car." His voice sounded stupid in the middle of the yard with no one around. There was never anyone around in his neighborhood, it seemed, because everyone was at work all the time. When they weren't, they were shut up inside their little houses, just like him. His was a one-story, like about half of the other houses there, and was painted white, also like about half the other houses. Its one unique feature was the front door, which fronted an entryway that sat at an angle to the rest of the house and had some fieldstone on it, setting it off from the tired white aluminum that covered the rest of the place.

If some people grow to look like their spouses over the years, Andy had grown to look like his house – not neglected, exactly, but tired and perhaps in need of some sprucing up. He had never been tall, but he had been skinny once and that made him look taller than he really was. Now, the pounds had begun to add up over the years and while he was far from fat, he certainly wasn't skinny anymore. His hair was no longer thick. His eyes were still bright if he cared to look at them, which he didn't, and his posture usually made sure no one else did, either. Mostly, he was tired.

He walked up the steps to the porch and saw the morning newspaper still laying in the long grass. He thought about reaching down to pick it up but couldn't imagine anything inside that could honestly change things and walked in without it. He hadn't read it that morning when it got here, and yet somehow he had survived another day at Yoder Cabinet Company. Maybe he could survive a few more hours without it. He was a regular newspaper reader, but lately, he just couldn't do it. Screw it.

At the door, the robin in the bird's nest built over the porch light didn't even bother to fly off when he approached. He wasn't sure whether it was because the bird had gotten used to him these past few weeks or because he was just not that intimidating. A few years ago, he took down the nest whenever birds built one there, but they usually re-built it the next day, so when he realized that they abandoned it as soon as the babies left the nest, he started leaving it alone until they were done. There was no way he would leave it there year round, but letting it stay a few weeks so they could raise babies didn't seem like it would hurt anything. They obviously felt safe there, and it was kind of nice for a couple of weeks watching them raise their little family. They seemed happy.

He walked in, leaving the door open and shutting only the screen. Work was over, and he could look forward to a relaxing evening of – well, there was television. And he'd have to eat something at some point. And the grass needed mowing. Tomorrow, he would go back to work, overseeing people making cabinets. Perfect.

He cracked open a beer and sat down with the remote. How did it come to this? It seemed like there was nothing but possibilities when he left Bloomington. True, there was the divorce, after Susan left him, but that was a while ago now. Well, eight years to be precise. Now he was 34 and just seemed to be in a holding pattern. Work, eat, sleep, work. And for what? There was his little house, but it just seemed to be one project after another and the equity he thought he'd be building up? It turns out it wouldn't really seem to start to add up until about 20 years into his 30-year mortgage.

And on the couch was a basket of laundry that needed folding. Crap.

He sat down, grabbed the remote and started folding. Undershirts, socks, t-shirts, button shirts for work, more undershirts, more socks, more undershirts, more button shirts he would have to hang up so he wouldn't have to iron the damn things. More clothes to get dirty so he could wash, dry and fold them again. Eventually tonight, he would tire of being awake, and he would go to bed alone. He would wake up alone, get ready for work, and eat breakfast by himself. He would go to work, where he was surrounded by people, but no real friends. Then he would come home, and eat dinner alone. It was easier just not to think about it, really.

At least SportsCenter was on, but – surprise – the Cubs were still not in first. They had been in first in May, but that was May and this was June, and well, they were the Cubs. They're kind of in a holding pattern, too, he thought. The fact that their holding pattern was approaching the century mark did not give him hope. It was only June, and already he just wanted the season to be over.

As the baseball roundup continued to blare out of the TV he realized that nothing really made him happy anymore, not even the good things. He loved holidays and family gatherings at his parents, but while he was there all he could think about was just getting it over with. His little sister Sally and her husband and two kids were great and they loved their Uncle Andy, but he got tired just thinking about them. He went out with the guys now and then, but that took effort, and the whole time all he could think about was "why am I doing this?" The answer – that he had nothing else to do – didn't help matters at all. And once again, he found himself just wondering when it would be over.

One basket of laundry was done, his beer was gone and he was thinking about getting another one when there was a knock at the screen door. Not just a knock, but a voice. Scarlett's voice.

"Hello, Andy? It's Andy, isn't it?"

Andy stood up to find Scarlett standing at his door holding a package of bratwurst and a bag of hotdog buns. She was a neighbor he had seen around a few times. He had even given her car a jump back in January when the temperature hit single digits, but he had never really gotten to know her. Not that he wouldn't have liked to, but she always seemed busy, either going out with friends or doing stuff with her little girl, and so he stayed in his house and occasionally wondered about her.

"Hey," he said. God, I sound stupid.

She looked like heaven standing there. How did this happen?

"Hey, look I got all this stuff I was gonna grill out and realized I don't even have a grill," Scarlett said. She was skinny, and had mounds of dark, curly hair but bright eyes. Green maybe? She moved around a lot, and up on her shoulder, just peeking out from her white blouse collar, was the top of a tattoo. She had on stylish black pants and a white, button blouse like professional women wear to work.

She had remembered his name.

"Wait, you didn't realize you don't have a grill? How does that happen?" Andy laughed.

She laughed too. "If you let me in, maybe I'll tell you."

Right. He was still talking to her through the door. Dumbass.

"Yeah, sorry, I'm— Hey, you wanna beer?"

"Of course. And yes, I used to have a grill, but my ex took it, and I don't grill out much so I guess it's been gone, like, what, two years now? And I never even knew it. I guess I just always assumed it was there and then, you know, it wasn't."

He led her through the little living room that he suddenly realized was dominated not by the fieldstone fireplace he had been so proud of when he bought the place, but by his stupid TV. Not too many fires at the ol' Gardner place these days. The furniture was decidedly 1990s Post-Married Man: Not the impractical stuff of Early Bachelor, but rugged enough that it would never fly for Just Married. Of course, like most things he owned, the furniture that he once thought had said "I'm my own man," now seemed to say, "I sit down a lot."

Between the living room and the kitchen was the dining room, which should have been renamed Home Office, since there had never been any real dining there since he owned it. While most of the walls had a few pictures he had taken as a hobby in college, the dining room was dominated by a big blank space, waiting for a built-in hutch he hadn't quite gotten to building in yet. Maybe next year.

In the small kitchen, he gestured toward the table for her to set her stuff on and stuck his head into the refrigerator to grab the beers.

"So then I was like, well, heck, there's that nice guy with the jumper cables – thanks again, by the way, you totally saved me that day – and I've seen him grilling, and it's more fun to eat brats with someone else anyway. I'm talking too much, aren't I?"

He finished opening the second beer and handed her the first.

"No, you're probably just drinking too slowly," he said, and raised his bottle in a slight toast.

Now she smiled. Damn that was a nice smile. And she had freckles. He understood why she always seemed busy – she was busy standing still. He would have to work to keep up with her.

"So listen, that day with the jumper cables, it was a little crazy, so let's make it official," he said, offering a handshake. "I'm Andy Gardner."

She smiled again, like she was surprised that he actually had a little style.

"Scarlett King," she said, shaking his hand. She shook like she shook hands often, but her hand felt small in his.

"And yeah, you're right, bratwurst really sucks when you're alone," he said, grabbing the brats and a box of matches and leading her toward the back door to the patio where the grill was.

"Well, yeah, they do actually. But you know it was just so dang nice out today, and I was like, you know what? I need to grill. You can't let a day like this go to waste," she said. "So I was at Scott's and these big fat ol' bratwursts just called my name."

Andy looked at her as he raised the lid on the grill. He was probably staring, but he didn't care. It was like she never stopped moving, and it was amazing to watch.

"Well, I'm glad they did, because I was looking forward to an incredible meal of, I dunno, like Totino's frozen pizza or something," he said.

And then they were looking at each other, smiling stupidly, until both seemed to realize it, and Scarlett started moving again, and he started lighting the grill again. It was like living in a house for several years and suddenly discovering a Porsche had been in the garage the whole time.

"Well, you got any chips or anything? We can make an actual meal out of this."

"Yeah, top of the fridge," he said, forcing himself back in gear. "Help yourself, and look around and see if there's anything else you want, and I'll get the grill going. There might be a half an onion or something in the bottom of the fridge we can dice up. And there's mustard and stuff in there."

Scarlett walked back inside, and Andy lit the burner on the grill and then started cleaning the grate with the wire brush he kept out there, scrubbing all the baked-on crap off it down into the blue flames and lava rock below. Where did this girl come from? Forget that, he thought, you've got to remember not to sound as desperate as you actually are.

You've got to fly casual here. And whatever you do, do *not* try to get her in the sack. That will drive her out of here faster than anything, and she'll never come back.

The grill cleaned, he closed the lid and headed inside, where Scarlett seemed to be making herself right at home.

"All right, I found chips, the onion and all the condiments," she said, pointing to the counter. "But without going through all your cupboards, I need a cutting board and we'll need plates and stuff."

"And more beer," he said, grabbing two more out of the fridge. He didn't want to seem like he was trying to get her drunk, but her bottle was empty so he figured the only gentlemanly thing to do was get her a full one. "You must be thirsty. Here's the plates, cutting board's down there and here's the knives. You want to do the honors?"

"Sure," she said, grabbing the biggest, wickedest looking knife he owned for the little half-onion. "Now, I haven't really grilled much – obviously – isn't there some special technique to cooking brats?"

Andy opened their beers and sat down at the little kitchen table while she diced.

"Well, I like to get both sides of the grill good and hot, throw the brats on one side and then turn that side either on low or totally off. With brats, I usually go totally off," he said. "That lets them cook without the grease catching fire and burning the outside. If they're big fatties like these, I'll switch sides when I turn them, so they're always over some nice hot lava rocks. It takes a little longer, but it's worth it."

"That makes sense," she said, finishing the onion and tipping back her beer. "But you still get all the flavor from the grill and stuff, right?"

"Oh yeah. And, you know, you can always put them right over the fire if you want to char the outside a little," he said. "You know, cook some of the grease off. I'll do that with hamburgers or whatever if they're not very lean."

"It's the old stereotype of men and fire, eh?" There was that look again. He liked the way her freckles framed her eyes and seemed to make them even more green and alive. The funny thing is, he thought, most girls who have freckles hate them. They have no idea.

Scarlett walked outside, and he walked over to the stereo and set it to shuffle, then turned it up so it was just a little too loud inside. He wanted it to be just background music outside – as hot as this girl was, he really liked talking to her and didn't want to screw that up. Seriously, he thought, whatever happens, I actually do like just hanging out with her. Weird.

Outside, Scarlett had ensconced herself at the picnic table with her beer and was looking over the backyard.

"So how long have you had this place?" she asked as he sat down. "And how pathetic is it that we're neighbors and are just now getting to know each other?"

"Yeah, it is, pathetic. I've been here about seven years," he said, remembering how he had bought the little white house about a year after Susan had left. "I was trying to make a new start, build up some equity, give me something to work on. Now, though, it just seems like it's nothing but projects I have to do. It seems like I'll never have any real equity, and there's always something fix."

"Yeah, try it some time when you don't know how to fix anything," Scarlett said. "Every little thing, it seems like I've got to hire it out and they charge you like they're re-marbling the Taj Mahal. Did you grow up in Fort Wayne?"

"Oh yeah," he said. "In fact, my parents still live over on Kensington. Do you know that neighborhood? Over in Lakeside?"

"The one with the boulevard? There by VA hospital?"

"Yeah. That's where I grew up. They still live in the same 75-year-old house over there. My sister still lives in town, too."

Kensington Boulevard featured an actual boulevard of grass and trees down the middle of the street. His house was about the same age as theirs, but while theirs was stately; his was just old. Their house was considered historic. His was, well — not. "I like this area, but I miss the sidewalks," he said. "There was always someone walking their dog or pushing a stroller. Here, no one walks unless they're actually going somewhere, like to the store. They even have a porch swing."

"Yeah, it's kind of all business here," she said as he got up to take the brats off the grill. "I tried to join the neighborhood association when they started one a few years ago, but it only lasted about three meetings. Everyone was either at work or exhausted from work."

"That's right, I saw you there. I forgot about that," he said, dishing up the brats. "I was there, too, while it lasted. So when did you get your place?"

"Well, Mike and I bought it about six years ago, but one day he just up and left, so I got a lawyer. He couldn't be bothered to show up, so I basically got everything, including the house," she said. "That was about two years ago. The one thing he got was three week's visitation a year and a few weekends. That's where Abby's at now."

Just then, the Black Crowes started twanging through the windows, and Scarlett laughed and said she had partied with the band once.

"Really?"

"Yeah, back in school," she said wistfully. She leaned back in her chair and Andy tried not to notice that her blouse separated at the buttons. Her bra was dark green, like her eyes. "You know, back before I got married, had a kid, got a divorce. Before, well, before everything. So what about you? Why aren't you married?"

Andy winced. It was stupid, but even after all these years he was still ashamed to say he was divorced.

"Well, I'm not anymore," he said. "Divorced about eight years go." Then he paused. Scarlett was still for a change, just watching him talk, so he did. She's divorced, too, what was he afraid of? "Man, I can't believe it's been that long already. Or maybe I just can't believe I'm 34 already. Anyway, we were married three years. No kids, she left. I don't know," he said.

He didn't know why he was talking to her about this – maybe it was just that whenever he talked, she looked at him – or that she actually seemed interested. And for once it didn't feel like someone was judging him. Someone was always judging him.

"At the time, you know, it was the most horrible, gut-wrenching thing ever, and now it's like I can hardly remember it. Almost like none of it ever happened," he said. "It's even hard to remember being married sometimes, like I can't even remember the good times. A lot of times I meet people I don't even mention it, because it's like, I don't know, like it was all just some weird dream. That's why I bought this place. Trying to, you know, move on or whatever. I don't really know if it worked, I guess."

"Yeah, it's the same for me, except for my little three-year-old reminder," she said between bites. She used her napkin a lot. "The nice thing is, I can kind of concentrate on her being my good times and not think about it all."

Andy had seen Abigail playing in the yard. A darling little chunk of a kid. Big, fat cheeks and a head full of curls like her mother, only hers was angel blonde. And he had to hand it to her mother: Scarlett was skinny, but she could eat. He liked a girl that wasn't afraid to put down a couple of brats if she was hungry. She could drink her beer, too.

With the brats and chips gone, they put the stuff away and threw away the trash, then grabbed more beers and went back to the patio.

"So why'd you get married in the first place?" she asked. "Wait, is it OK if I ask stuff like that? I don't want to be like, you know–ᵗ"

"Yeah, it's fine," he said, taking a long pull on the fresh beer. Thankfully, he had bought decent beer for a change instead of the Miller Lite he usually stocked. "I don't know. Why does anyone get married? We were dating in college and it seemed serious, and well, I guess we were graduating and – I mean, we never thought about it like this, but in hindsight I guess it's true – it was either get married or break up. So we got married. Moved here and got jobs. And then, you know, reality set in. Turns out we were both looking for the fairy tale and Happy Ever After and when that didn't work out, there wasn't really anything left. What about you?"

"About the same, I guess," Scarlett said. "I got my social work degree at Ball State and moved here to work at Community Action. Met Mike at the bar, and well, you know, it seemed like a fairy tale for a while, but well, it sure wasn't. We thought having a kid would make up for it, but all it really did is drive the spike into it. One day he disappeared, and the rest is history."

The sky was still bright, as they talked and drank, but dusk seemed to seep from the trees until it hung from the branches like a fog. The deep green grass turned gray.

"I guess we've both kind of been there and done that, eh?" he said.

She was quiet a minute. She was leaning forward, holding her beer in both hands. He was, too.

"Yeah. Been there and done that," she said, not moving. "You try not to think about it, I guess."

"It's kind of hard not to think about it though," he said. "When there's just, I don't know, nothing."

"Yeah, after Abby's asleep it gets... Hey, listen, you don't mind if I smoke, do you?" she said, pulling a bag of loose-leaf tobacco from the little purse he hadn't even noticed before.

"No, of course, not – especially if you roll me one," he said. "Wow, you really roll your own? That's serious."

"Well, yeah, it's a huge pain but it's just soooo much better than the regular ones. You will not believe how smooth this is," she said as she expertly guided the tobacco onto a paper and somehow turned it into a perfectly shaped cigarette. "It's called Bali Shag – this is the Red – and it's amazing. And it's actually cheaper this way, too."

"Nice," he said as she handed him the first one, then started rolling a second. "I quit smoking like 10 years ago, but I never stopped loving it." He looked at the cigarette Scarlett had rolled admiringly, then put it up to his nose. "Wow, that even smells better."

"I know, it's like, 'Damn!' right? I should quit, too, but when they're this good, how can I?"

She pulled a white Bic out of her purse and handed it to him, but when he took it from her he accidentally grabbed part of her hand and then held it too long, awkwardly. They both seemed to realize it at the same time and he pulled his hand away quick then, and lit his cigarette, then handed it back. He tried to put it out of his head, and as she lit her cigarette, he noticed her longish nails, but they were working nails, painted dark pink.

She was right, the tobacco was incredibly smooth, and the nicotine buzz was almost instantaneous as he inhaled deeply and blew the smoke out into the gathering gloom of the yard. Why did he ever quit smoking?

"So why'd you move back to Fort Wayne?" she asked.

"I had worked out at Yoder Cabinets during the summers when I was home from IU, so when I got my degree I moved into management," Andy said, then took another hit off that amazing cigarette. "Susan was from Valporaiso. When she split she went back there, and I stayed."

The shadows had moved out from the trees and into the yard now, and the sky looked as if someone had twisted a dimmer switch when out of the silence came an incredible sound.

The noise was electric, like some huge short-circuit or a massive, live wire carrying millions of volts of electricity. It held a single pitch for a few seconds, then dropped a step for a half-second, then immediately returned to the original pitch. It did this over and over, like a vinyl record playing and someone sticking their finger on the turn table every few seconds, slowing it, and then immediately letting up, over and over.

And it was loud, louder than Andy's piece of crap car, louder than the music from inside, louder than Scarlett's voice.

"What the hell is that?" she said, barely audible over the noise.

Just as she spoke, another version of it began, this time on the other side of the yard, doubling the volume and making it stereo as the two sounds called to each other, the dips in pitch making an irregular rhythm.

"Hey, it's cicadas!" Andy said over the din. "I always forget about them. They're those, you know, those bugs that come out every summer."

"Oh God, that's right," Scarlett said. "What a noise!"

The noise was vaguely familiar, but not the way he remembered it from last year, like an old friend you haven't seen in years – immediately comfortable and familiar, but changed in unexpected ways. Now that he thought about it, didn't cicadas usually do those short noises, like when you shake a maraca or something? This seemed more like the drone of bagpipes.

Whatever it was, it was impossible to ignore and impossible to concentrate on anything other than its electric mayhem.

"You wanna go inside?" he yelled.

"Yes!"

As they grabbed their beers and fled the patio, dozens more insect voices joined the chorus, raising the noise level to near-deafening.

As the storm door closed behind him, the volume dropped

dramatically, but he turned and closed the wooden door as well, then turned the deadbolt out of habit and turned on the patio light, leaving only the noise of the stereo playing a little too loud. Maybe he'd go out there later after Scarlett left and have a beer and listen to the bugs.

Then he turned around, and Scarlett was facing him. Her beer was on the counter. So was her purse. But her blouse was half-unbuttoned, and she was unbuttoning the rest of it, not looking up at him, just looking at the buttons like she had to – needed to – get them undone as fast as she could. Her fingers seemed awkward, and she had started unbuttoning at the bottom.

And then her shirt was on the floor and he took her in his arms and the awkwardness, for both of them, was replaced by something more like relief.

Outside, another cicada joined the chorus. And then another. And another, until their electric screams filled the blackness.

Was that the sound he heard in his sleep? Was that the Song? He didn't know. He didn't know why Scarlett was here or what it would do to him. He didn't know why he never missed Susan, at least not in the way he had missed Ashley – still missed her sometimes, if he thought about it. He didn't know why Scarlett showed up the same time the cicadas did, or why he wasn't sleeping. All he knew for sure is that they shrieked through the night, until the shadows pulled back into the trees as the sky lightened, and the sun rose fat and sluggish over the low, muddy river.

TWO

"The young ant-like larva, hatching from the eggs, falls lightly to the ground, and quickly burrows out of sight, forming for itself a little subterranean chamber over some rootlet, where it remains through winter and summer, buried from light, air, and sun and protected in a manner from cold and frost. It lives in absolute solitude, separated from its fellows. In this manner it passes the seventeen years of its existence in a dark cell in slow growth and preparation for a few weeks only of the society of its fellows and the enjoyment of the warmth and brightness of the sun and the fragrant air of early summer. For four or five weeks the male sings his song of love and courtship, and the female busies herself for a little longer with the placing of eggs. At the close of its short aerial existence, the Cicada falls to the ground again, perhaps within a few feet of the point from which it issued, to be there dismembered and scattered about, carpeting the surface of the ground with its wings and the fragments of its body. Such is the life round of this anomalous insect."

—"The Periodical Cicada"

Andy awoke to the strange sensation there was a body next to him and remembered, after eight years, the way it felt, smelled and sounded to have someone sleeping near you. It's crazy how much you forget, he thought, and then realized she wasn't asleep at all. Scarlett was not only awake, but was getting out of bed and stripping off his t-shirt.

"Look, I'm sorry, I know this sounds bad and all, but I really have to go so I can go to work," she said. She stopped and looked at him as he stared at her. This was all a little fast, and the fact that she was wearing only dark green panties made it even more difficult to concentrate on what she was saying. Wait, she's leaving? "You have to go to work, too, and admit it, the sooner I get out of here the sooner we can avoid talking about it and start concentrating on making everything awkward."

He laughed, and she started searching for her clothes, some of which were as far away as the kitchen. "All right," he said, "but don't you at least want a cup of coffee?"

"Hell yes I want some coffee – like a big jug of it," she said as she pulled on her pants. "But I seriously don't have time. I'm barely going to

14

have time to stop at Starbucks. Thank God there's one on my way."

As he lay there watching her, he tried to remember everything, every detail, every moment, every thought of the night before, because it was going to be gone, and chances were good it was never coming back. He had imagined himself a sponge while they were together, saving water for the coming dryness.

"So you're leaving? This is, uh, like a role reversal or something, right? Like karma coming around to bite me on behalf every guy that's ever fled at first light, isn't it?"

She started working the buttons on her blouse and gave him that smile again.

"Oh, is it really that terrible?" she mocked, pinching his cheek.

"No, it was pretty damn wonderful, actually," he said. "All of it, I mean. Not just the— you know. All of it. The brats, the talking, the… well, all that was great right up until the cicadas started."

"Wait a minute," she said between shoes. "It was terrible after that?" She laughed, and her eyes seemed to scrunch up and get even more beautiful when she laughed.

"Yeah, just awful. The worst I've ever had! And now you're leaving me on top of it all…"

She grabbed the pillow and mashed it into his face, both of them laughing like crazy.

Then she pulled it away and kissed him on the forehead. He wondered if that was the way she kisses her little girl.

"Go to work, you loser," she said. Damn those green eyes. "Seriously, call me after work or something, OK?"

"Yeah, right."

"No, really, or I'll call you. We can talk."

And then she was gone.

He sat on the edge of the bed. The house was suddenly, incredibly, silent. What the hell just happened? One minute, before she got here, life was normal – empty and pathetic, but normal – and then it was not. And then – poof! – she was gone again. How does that happen? It's like, like—

It was like something that had happened to him once before, but he couldn't put his finger on what, exactly. Of course, his brain wasn't working right. He needed coffee, for one thing, and for another, well, there was last night, and there was Scarlett.

He got up, made coffee, then instead of sitting down with the morning paper, went out the back door to the patio. He couldn't think about the world and politics and everything right now. He needed to just sit in the sun with his cup of coffee and think a little. The sun was glorious. Just warm enough on his skin, his coffee steaming in the cool morning air. Was it always this nice in the morning? Why didn't he do this everyday? Hell, there were even birds.

Seriously, if mornings were like this all the time, they wouldn't be so bad, he thought. Given that he had now used his patio twice in less than 24 hours, he figured it was the most it had been used in, well, a good long time. He was going to have to use it some more.

He stretched, feeling the sleep in his muscles, but it felt good, like he had just had a good workout or came in from a good run.

Who was he kidding? He didn't run. Still, it was Friday, and the weekend suddenly – for the first time in ages, it seemed – had some promise.

He thought of waking up next to Scarlett and remembered the weird dreams he had had while sleeping in the few short hours before that. Nothing coherent, just bits and pieces, small scenes and emotions. None of it made sense, but then, not much in reality was making sense either, so what was the difference?

He looked out over the long grass of the back yard and tried to imagine the way it had been last night, dark and alive with the shriek of unseen insects, like they were shadows hiding on the periphery, just waiting for a chance to reappear. And he realized that despite the rush Scarlett gave him, there was also a dread somewhere, a fear that it was all an illusion. The same way that when the cicadas were screaming they seemed all-encompassing, and then they were gone, leaving only silence. Would Scarlett be the same way? Hell, she was already gone. Would she ever be back? Was she even ever here in the first place?

He finished the coffee, then went inside to get ready for work.

He had snagged a parking spot in the lot across the street from the Cathedral so at least he didn't have to drive around looking for some place to park on the street. That was about the only drawback to coming here instead of going with his parents to St. Jude. Not that St. Jude had any more parking, really – the people who think Catholicism is all about guilt obviously know nothing about the parking issues – but at least the street parking there was close. No, the real benefit to the Cathedral, besides the stunning beauty of its 150-year-old architecture, was anonymity. He didn't have to put on any fronts here. He didn't have to tell people he was doing fine. He didn't have to tell his parents or his parents' friends that nothing was new. He didn't have to look around St. Jude and remember taking First Communion there, or Confirmation, or anything else. Thankfully, when he had married Susan the wedding was at the church she grew up in over in Valparaiso, so at least he didn't have that to deal with. Still, it just seemed like such an emotional commitment to go back to St. Jude that he just hadn't been able to do it for the last several years, so he found himself among the faceless crowds at the Cathedral. He could be alone with his thoughts there, or alone with God or his thoughts about God or whatever it was he did there. He wasn't always sure, but he was always there.

As he found a pew and knelt on the kneeler, he had to admit that the architecture was totally worth coming here, regardless of what a mess he was. He still had no idea how they built something so large, so tall, and so incredibly beautiful in the mid 1800s. And he liked the quirks, too, like the fact that the ornate Stations of the Cross that lined the nave were carved in Germany, so it appeared that Christ was crucified in Bavaria rather than the Middle East.

The Bishop's homily that day was about hope, and though his eminence's train of thought wandered off the tracks a few times and took a few detours on its way to the destination, the message seemed to be that all hope lies in God.

"It sure doesn't lie in me," Andy thought, and then stopped. It was true. Of all the things that seemed to be wrong in his life, at the bottom line seemed to be that: He had no hope. As the Mass moved on toward Communion, he realized that the malaise, the inability to get emotionally involved in anything, the dead spin that had taken over his life was just that he was without hope. There was Scarlett, of course, but that was more … Things seemed to be a little brighter in the three days since she showed up, and he wanted things to work out, but he didn't really expect that they would in the end. He was surprised it had gone this well, so far, seeing as how he had called her like she asked, and was just as fun to talk to on the phone as she had been in person. And when he had asked her out on an official date, for that night, no less, she had agreed instantly, and they had had a great time at Club Soda, drinking martinis and eating dinner. Still, did he honestly have a hope that they had some kind of future together? He couldn't imagine that they would. Was he just depressed? No, he knew depression. Knew it inside out, and this wasn't it. This was just, just … living without hope. Not that everything was terrible or that he couldn't go on. That was depression. He could go on. Things weren't terrible. They just … were. And they always would be.

It felt a little better knowing that hope was what he had lost somehow, but it also disturbed him. No hope? None at all? But he honestly couldn't think of anything he was hopeful about.

Except for one thing.

"This is the Lamb of God who takes away the sins of the world," said the Bishop as he held up the holy Body. "Happy are those who are called to His supper."

Then the congregation responded.

"Lord, I am not worthy to receive You, but only say the word and I shall be healed."

That was his one hope. That someday – certainly not today, and probably not tomorrow, but someday – someday God would say that word and he would be healed.

He didn't know when He would say it or why He seemed to be waiting so long. And though Andy couldn't feel it, he knew that if he was here at the Cathedral every Sunday, waiting for that word, that he must somewhere, somehow, still have some hope that it would be said. Without that word, of course, there really was nothing to be hopeful about. And he knew he was unworthy of that word, though he couldn't fathom what he had done to deserve it being kept from him for so long. But something deep inside of him still believed that at some point God's gaze would fall on him where he knelt at His doorway, and He would feel pity, and He would say the word Andy had waited and waited to hear for such a very long time. And at last, he hoped, he would be healed.

"Hey you."

Andy seemed to wake up at the words. He had been walking with the crowd down the aisle at the close of Mass, staring mostly at his feet, when he heard Scarlett's voice.

"Hey Andy," she said again from the pew where she was standing with Abigail. They had been sitting about ten pews behind him the whole time.

"Oh hey, I didn't even see you there," he said. "And hello, Ms. Abigail. Welcome back to Fort Wayne." The girl smiled shyly.

"Yeah, we saw you, but, you know, we couldn't really shout at you."

He stepped out of the crowd into the pew in front of them so they could talk.

"Do you come here a lot? Or..."

"No," Scarlett said. "We should. You know, we try to, but it just— you know. Plus, when we do it's usually the 5 o'clock, just because it's so much easier with her nap and everything. Then today, after we just got back last night, I just felt all homey and wanted to go, if that makes any sense."

"Yeah, it does. Like comfort food, for lack of a better..." he said. "Hey, speaking of food, you guys wanna get some lunch? We can go out. Especially since I wanted to take you out last night and you turned me down."

She smirked, but there was a smile behind it.

"Did you know that, Abby? I tried to buy your mommy dinner, and she said she was busy. Probably washing her curly hair."

"Yeah, because driving to Gas City and back was WAY more fun than letting you take me to Chappell's for seafood," she said. "What do you think Abigail, should we go out for lunch with this guy?"

The little girl smiled. "Hot dogs!"

"Oooo, I think we have a Coney Island fan here," Andy said. "I can do Coney Island. Whaddya think?"

"Yeah," Scarlett said. "Let's do it."

Fort Wayne's Coney Island Wiener Stand was such an institution that it was the only place in town where you could get away with parking in the middle of the street – Main Street downtown, no less – while running inside for a carryout order, as long as you left your hazards on. People wouldn't even beep, they would just change lanes and go around, probably thinking to themselves how good a carryout order sounded about then.

The place was closing on 100 years old, and hadn't changed much in those years. On the back wall hung a neon sign that said "OUR BUNS ARE STEAMED" and the steamed-up plate glass windows up front where they made the dogs was proof enough. The place was packed at lunch, packed at supper, had lines down the street during the holidays, and they didn't even have French fries.

There were two parking spots on Harrison, so Andy pulled into one and Scarlett pulled into the other. They were near the back door, so they went in that way.

"You know, I've lived here almost my whole life, and I still love the fact that you can go in the back door and no one cares," he said, as he held the steel door open for them.

The door led right into the kitchen, where a guy in his late teens was stirring a batch of coney sauce, while on the counter lay a 50 lb. bag of onions waiting to be diced.

"Hey," the guy said in greeting as they traipsed through his work space.

"I know," Scarlett said. "I'm still not used to that."

They snagged a table on the wall and were almost immediately ordering. Scarlett took hers with everything – chili, mustard and onion – Abigail got a plain dog, and Andy got his with everything, extra chili and light onions. For drinks, there were miniature bottles of Coke all around.

At the table behind them, two guys were talking loudly.

"See, fiction is a guy walking around in a bear suit. Meta-fiction is a bear writing a story about a man in a bear suit," one said.

"Sure," the other guy said. "But if you deconstruct it, it's really about how man oppresses bears and has now co-opted the bears' image for his own entertainment."

"So what did you think of Mass?" Scarlett said. "I just love the Bishop. His train of thought wanders like a drunken sailor, but you just can't help but love him."

The place was long and narrow, with high ceilings and old wood floors that creaked.

"Yeah, he's really great. And the whole hope thing I really related to," Andy said. "More and more I think that when we try to create our own hope it just, you know, turns to garbage."

"I didn't feel like he was saying that so much as he was saying that there's like misplaced hope, that like the things we hope for – 'I hope I get a new TV' or 'I hope I get a new job' – that those things are things that don't last," she said, helping Abigail with her straw. "That, you know, there's like what we think of as hope and then there's hope for things that matter, like eternity. Things that, you know, I probably need to work on a bit."

The waiter – another guy in a Coney Island t-shirt – set down steaming plates of hot dogs slathered in coney sauce. They smelled like heaven.

"You and me both," Andy said. "As I was sitting there, though, I realized, that eternal hope or whatever, that seems like about the only hope I've got going right now. Not that I deserve it or anything, but, you know, I have hope it'll happen."

Scarlett wrinkled her nose as she chewed. "You don't have any other hope?"

Andy swallowed his bite. Man these dogs were good. "That sounds bad. I don't mean I'm like, hopeless or something. Just that, you know, things are what they are. They don't really seem to change," he said. "Not that everything's terrible, it's just, hope that everything will be sunny and wonderful just seems, I don't know, misplaced."

"Can I have ketchup?" Abigail asked.

"Sure, honey," Scarlett said. "I don't know, Andy, that sounds pretty depressing."

He found himself shaking his head. "No, I'm not really explaining it well. It just– well if God has a plan for everything anyway, then why worry about what's going to happen? Just like worrying doesn't change things, maybe hope doesn't change things, either. If He wants everything to be great, it will be whether I hope for it or pray for it or not," he said. "Not that I don't want it to be great. Or that I think it can't be or won't be. I just, you know– I guess mostly I try not to think about it."

"I have to go potty," Abigail said, to Andy's relief. What was he saying? He sounded like a Calvinist or something. A depressed Calvinist.

"OK," Scarlett said, wiping her hands on her paper napkin. "Let's go, honey."

The old lawnmower heaved and groaned through the long, heavy grass, the wheels leaving behind long, track-shaped clumps of wet clippings. Andy had gotten about two passes around the edge of the front yard and was about to start working his way back and forth in horizontal stripes when he almost ran over the newspaper from three days before.

He stopped the mower and sat down on the front steps with the paper to catch his breath.

The war in Iraq, the presidential election, the city council, blah, blah, blah, he thought, scanning the headlines. Then he saw a brief on page 6A that caught his eye.

"Cicadas return after 17 years," the little headline said. Holy shit.

Brood X, the three paragraphs explained, was the largest brood of seventeen-year cicadas, and this was the year they were emerging. The brood was so large that some places in the Midwest would see as many as 1.5 million insects per acre, scientists claimed.

And then, the story closed with a hammer right between his eyes: "The last time Brood X appeared was 1987."

Nineteen eighty-seven. Oh shit, he thought. Oh fuck.

And it all came back to him, every detail, every emotion, every thought he had tried to bury and forget about for seventeen years. The summer he thought he had put away forever when he married Susan. The summer that stayed at the edges, hidden from sight, but was never really gone. That dread with Scarlett he couldn't quite place. The weird dreams the first night she showed up. Yep, that was it. One sentence about some damn bugs was all it took to remind him. Time may heal all wounds, but that doesn't say anything about the scars.

Of course, it wasn't that summer with Ashley that did him in, he thought, it was the fall and winter *after* Ashley that damn-near killed him. The endless months after it all ended, the years of, of— fuck if he knew what that was, besides some kind of sheer, unadulterated living hell.

Shit, he thought. Brood X. That's just perfect. And here Scarlett just comes walking into my life from out of nowhere. Sound familiar? Goddamn it. Ashley had shown up the same time the bugs had and up and disappeared at the end of the summer. Now, seventeen years later, the cicadas were back and Scarlett just shows up at his door. Perfect.

He took the newspaper inside and pulled the entire page 6A out of it. He folded the page in half and set it on the kitchen counter, then threw the rest of the paper in the recycling bin.

He stared at it for a minute as it lay there, just staring up at him in black and white. There was just something so permanent, so authoritative about things printed in the newspaper. Like those damn bugs weren't real until he saw it there in The Journal, next to an ad for Zesto's Ice Cream Stand. They're real all right, he thought. They're more real than ever, now. And now the truth of it just sat there on the counter, like it was daring him not to believe it. You'll see soon enough, it seemed to whisper, just as darkness starts to fall and those bugs start screaming.

Unbelievable.

He grabbed a beer out of the fridge and chugged it. Just pounded the damn thing until his stomach hurt. He set the bottle down, steadied himself, then did the same thing with another one. Still the little newspaper story stared back at him, only now it didn't seem to cut quite as deep. No, that's not true, he thought. It cuts just as deep as it did in 1987. It's just that there's two beers' worth of salve over the wound. Yeah, salve was the right word. A clear, gooey covering that obscures the wound – makes it blurry if you stare at it – but doesn't really change a thing underneath.

He stared at the newspaper page for a minute more, then he went back out to the yard and started the mower. He didn't stop again until the grass was cut, front and back, and he was soaked in sweat and covered in hot, sticky grass.

After mowing, he grabbed a pizza out of the freezer, cooked it and tried to eat it without thinking, washing it down with many beers.

Only later, when it was dark and the cicadas were ringing in the air around him on the porch, did he let himself think. What had ever happened to Ashley, anyway? For a question he obsessed over for years, he had pretty effectively managed to bury it for the past 12 or so, he thought. Could he find her? What if he did? Did he even want to?

When the phone rang, the caller ID said it was Scarlett and he let it ring while he went back outside to the patio. When he finally went to lock the front door to go to bed, he stood outside for a minute and looked toward Scarlett's house. Behind him, the bird nest was dark and silent, the shape of the mother bird hulking over the babies protectively, and the cicadas seemed louder than ever, crying out into the night.

But what they were crying for, he had no idea.

THREE

"The larger digger wasp is the natural and perhaps the most destructive of the insect enemies of the adult Cicada. In fact, no more curious and interesting illustration of the wars with take place in the insect world is afforded than the sight of one of these wasps seizing its victim and silencing and paralyzing it with a sting, which, while throwing it into a comatose condition from which it never recovers, does not actually kill it, but leaves it an unresisting, living prey for the delicate wasp larva. The fact that some tragedy is being enacted is often brought to the attention of the observer by the sudden cessation of the regular song of the unsuspecting Cicada. The song ends in a sharp cry of distress, and if one is in position to witness the struggle, the wasp may be seen grasping its victim and endeavoring to take flight, the quick thrust of its sting having almost immediately quieted the Cicada."

—"The Periodical Cicada"

He's got his head down, watching the front wheels of his dad's lawnmower roll down the tracks laid down in the grass by the pass before, every line perfect as he turns the thick, wet grass of June into the perfectly manicured lawn that his parents – and the neighborhood – expect in front of their house.

As Andy follows the self-propelled Craftsman mower across the yard, he notices the dozens and dozens of holes in the dirt, each about the size of his pinky. Most of them are near the where the grass slopes down to the sidewalk, but a few of them are in the flat parts, and some of those have little cones built around them, like an ant house on steroids. His mom is convinced the holes are from something she calls "ground bees," whatever those are, but he thinks she's nuts.

But it's when he reaches the driveway and turns the mower around for another pass that he sees the feet. They're on the sidewalk and they're sockless, in white canvas shoes, with little flowers drawn on them with magic markers. Without even raising his head he can see that the feet are slender, and attached to ankles – beautiful ankles somehow – and just above those are Capri-cut jeans that are tight against clearly female calves. Until that point in his life, he had had no idea ankles could be

23

beautiful.

Even after seeing only shoes, ankles and calves, it's getting hard to concentrate on the mowing, and he raises his head slightly. Sure enough, the legs continue higher, and the jeans are still tight, and – Good Lord! – they wrap around feminine hips. He's halfway across the yard now, and the feet have stopped walking at the property line, near the hedge between his house and the Herberts' next door. The feet are facing him.

He raises his eyes a little further, only to see a white t-shirt punctuated by a black Nike swoosh and two shapes underneath that make his head swim. The face has got to be ugly, he thinks, barely daring to look up further. It's got to be.

But it's not; not by a long stretch. Her long, honey-blonde hair reaches just past her shoulders and her eyes are blue. And she's standing by the hedge, watching him mow the lawn.

He kills the engine and he's staring.

"Hi. You need some lemonade or something?" she asks.

"Uh, yeah, that sounds great," he says, then takes the opportunity to – openly this time – look her up and down. "Are you... hiding some somewhere?"

She smiles, and all becomes right with the world. Her head leans back slightly and her mouth opens in a small giggle that sounds like a sigh.

"No, I just thought if you wanted, I'd make you some," she says, then shifts into her sales pitch, which includes cocking her head to the side slightly. "Especially if you'd mow my lawn, too."

Her stance relaxes as she laughs at herself, and Andy's laughing too now. Some of her hair seems almost straight, and some of it has long spiraling curls like tendrils that hang down.

"That's pretty slick," he says. "OK, I'll bite. Where's your lawn? Lemme guess, it's giant, right?"

She actually seems to be nervous. She's hiding it well, but it's like she's shy, he thinks. Or maybe she's just afraid he'll sweat on her – a real possibility. Her face seems almond shaped, with a nice nose and that little smile with just a hint of overbite. Her eyebrows are darker than her hair, making her blue eyes even bluer.

"No, it's not giant. It's tiny, actually. It's right around the corner," she says pointing. The skin on her arms is not tan, but it's not fair, either, and she's got some muscles. She's standing with her feet very close together. "But we just moved in and we don't have a mower, and well, I thought maybe I could bribe you into helping out."

She doesn't seem to care about the sweat or the grass that's already stuck to him. She must really need her lawn mowed.

"Oh, and I'm Ashley, by the way," she says, suddenly looking formal

24

and sticking out her hand. "Ashley Hudson." When she talks, some of the words seem to come out like little sighs, the way her giggle did.

"Well," Andy says with an exaggerated bow and a wave of his arm, encompassing the yard, the nearby houses, and the boulevard, "welcome to the neighborhood. I'm Andy. Andy Gardner. You just moved here? Where from?"

He wipes his hand on his jeans before he takes hers and shakes it. Her hand feels small, but rough.

"Muncie," she says in a little sigh. "And about a million places before that. My mom and I kinda move a lot. Anyway, we're here now."

"Yeah, my parents never move. They've lived here for about a hundred years I think," he says. "They'll probably die here."

She smiles again. "That's not so bad in some ways. It must be nice to have roots. And it's a nice place to be."

Andy looks around. She's right about that – Kensington Boulevard was one of the nicer neighborhoods in town. It's no Forest Park or Old Mill Road, but the houses are stately, probably historic, and well taken care of. And it has a real boulevard – though the old people in the neighborhood call it a "park strip" – running down the middle of the street. About 15 feet wide, it's a grassy strip lined with shade trees, dividing the road into two one-way streets running parallel. With the trees lining the street in each front yard, it sometimes looks like a movie set for the Perfect American Neighborhood. And now the Perfect American Girl is standing in the middle of it, asking him to mow her yard.

"All right, let's get mowing," he says, and starts pushing the mower onto the sidewalk.

"Wait, what about your yard?" she says, with another little sigh. "Shouldn't you finish this first?"

Andy looks at the front yard and realizes he's only half done. And the back yard is at least three times as big – it will be almost an hour before he can get over there. Screw that.

"No, I'll come back to it," he says. "It's not going anywhere."

As they talk while he pushes the mower up the sidewalk toward Vermont Street, he realizes that, unlike most girls who look like she does, Ashley is actually nice. To be fair, maybe those other girls are nice in general, but not to him, so what's the difference? But Ashley actually seems like someone he could hang out with. And he likes how, even though she's beautiful, she seems to have her own style – like the flowers she's drawn on her shoes.

"So what year are you in school?" he asks. Oh please, oh please.

"I'll be a senior, at least I hope," she says. Yes! "I've changed schools

25

so much it's hard to tell. Some places make you test into your grade and stuff. I can usually do it, but it sucks, and it makes you worry you're going to get put back a grade, you know?"

"Awesome – we're both Class of '88 then. Man, changing grades just because you moved would suck," he says. "So what's with all the moving?"

"My mom's in the military," she says, then seems to wait for a response.

"That's cool," he says. "So she's stationed here now?" There's a National Guard fighter wing out at the airport, maybe she's with them.

Ashley laughs at him. "No, I'm teasing you, dummy. She's not in the military."

"Oh. Wait, what?"

"No, my dad took off when I was little, and mom's been raising me ever since. So basically we go to wherever she can get a good job. This time it's Kelly or something. I think they make brakes for cars or something like that."

"Yeah, OK," he says. "Over on State, right?" They're at the corner now, and Ashley's pointing at the little tan house sandwiched between the big corner houses on Kensington and Anthony. It's a two-story, but small by comparison, and sits on the alley that runs behind the other houses. She's right about the yard being small, he thinks. It's like a postage stamp. "Did you guys buy it?"

"No, we're renting. And mom got the guy to knock a few bucks off if we handle the yard and stuff," she says. "Only thing is, we have no way to do it, really."

"Well, I guess you do now," he says.

He mows while she makes lemonade, or more accurately, lemonade-flavored Kool-Aid. As it usually does, his mind wanders as he pushes the mower, though there's not much time to get lost in thought. The yard is really small, and seemed even smaller because of the tall houses so close around it – there's the house on Kensington, its stucco sides and Mediterranean architecture are cool, but from below it seems about five stories tall, especially since the second floor has what appears to be a sleeping porch that juts into the back yard, looking down over the alley and Ashley's place. On the other side is the house on Anthony, another two story that seems to loom over him. Then there's Ashley's house, standing like a two-story wall between the backyard – further enclosed by a wooden privacy fence – and the street out front. And while most houses in the neighborhood are painted with some character, Ashley's is just flat brown. Brown sides, brown trim, brown eaves – all the same flat shade –

making its utter blandness the only thing remarkable about it.

Much of the front yard is not even grass, just dirt after the grass was trampled down by the last renters. They didn't seem like bad people, Andy thought, but they hung out in the front yard a lot, just sitting around, like they were waiting for a ride or something. Kensington was not the kind of place where people just sat in their front yards. That's what the giant front porches were for. His even had a porch swing on it. But not here. The "porch" was really just a couple of cement steps. It didn't matter, because now – he couldn't believe his luck – it was Ashley who was living here, and suddenly a summer that was going to be just another endless parade of mowing the lawn and scooping ice cream at Atz's had new promise. Screw the college fund, I've got something to spend my money on now.

He finishes the back and kills the mower, and Ashley's at the door.

"Come on in, have some lemonade," she says.

"Thanks," he says. He's trying to be polite, but it's almost like she doesn't want him to be polite – like she just wants him to chill out and stop trying to be so nice. She flops down on a bright red beanbag, about the only furniture in the living room besides a big old couch. There's a tiny sunroom on the other side of the room, but it's really only big enough for a TV cart or maybe a love seat. Today, it holds an empty TV cart and an old lawn chair he parks himself on. The TV sits on the floor nearby.

The house may have once been pretty nice, and it still had some style, but it's clearly been a rental for a long time and just seems worn somehow. The front half of the house is basically the living room – one side opens to the staircase, the other to the kitchen, both openings are plastered arches that have somehow survived the decades. The pale blue walls are bare. From the sunroom, Andy can see the kitchen, which has a beat-up table and chairs, with a couple of boxes on the table. Some of the cupboards are open.

Ashley's sprawled out on the bean bag, her legs wide apart but not facing him, and she's sucking down the lemonade, looking around at the walls and cracked ceiling.

He chugs his and sets down the glass, a big plastic cup that says 7-Up on the side.

"Thanks, that was aweso—" he starts, but he's cut off by a huge belch as Ashley sets down her own cup. He wants to die until he realizes it wasn't him that burped.

"Beat that," she says. Who is this girl?

"BWAAAAARRRRRKKKK," he belches in reply, just topping her in volume and length.

She smiles at him with a new respect. "*Nice*. You wanna see my room?"

Hell yes, he thinks.

"Sure."

They clamber up the wooden steps. The staircase is steep and narrow, but there's a little window halfway up that looks over the alley toward Kensington. The upstairs is basically two bedrooms and a bathroom. The front half is one big bedroom with a sitting area set off from the rest of the room by another arch. The back half is the other bedroom and the bathroom, which has a door that opens to the outside, but Andy can't remember whether there was anything back there for it to open out to. Ashley's room looks out over the backyard, down the alley and over the backyards of about four other houses. It's a bed, dresser, and four or five boxes. Someone at some point has painted the walls dark blue.

"I'm still unpacking, obviously," she says. Again with the little sighs. "You wanna help?"

"Sure." God, is that all he can say? Sure? What a dork.

She grabs a box and starts handing him clothes.

"Shorts and pants, bottom drawer," she says.

"Like this?"

"Yeah, whatever. Hey what kind of music do you like? Shirts, second drawer."

"You know. Everything. Bon Jovi, the Bangles, Huey Lewis. Whatever's on, really," he says, trying to stack the clothes the way she might want them, but who knows how she wants them? She doesn't seem to care. "I don't mind country but I don't listen to it much. I'm not like some people that just hate it, but it's fine."

She opens another box. "Here. Underwear, top drawer."

"Wait, me?" Their hands are both on the stack of panties, but he's frozen.

"What, they're just underwear. Don't you wear underwear?" she laughs, then takes the pile back and grabs the top pair of panties, silver, and starts stalking him with it like she's going to rub it in his face. "Ooooo panties!" she cries.

"All right, all right," he laughs. "I just didn't want to be like, you know, all staring at your underwear and stuff if you didn't want me to."

"I *didn't* want you to stare at them Andy, I wanted you to put them in the drawer," she says, then hands him a bra. "Oh my God, stop touching my bra you pervert!"

He instantly drops the tangle of white spandex and straps and God-only-knows what until he realizes she's shrieking with laughter now at his red face and stammering apology.

"Andy, it's just a bra," she laughs. "Don't you have a mom? Doesn't she have boobs?"

"Well, yeah I guess, but…" he says. "You know, it's like, well I don't know. What if you don't want me to, I don't know, see what size it is or something?" The more he talks the more he realizes how stupid he sounds. What *size*, Andy? They only hang off the front of her, idiot, there's not a person on the planet with eyeballs who can't tell you what size they are. Hell, you're already standing in her room, putting away her panties and holding her bra. Roll with it, you idiot. "Or what if it's, I don't know, like leopard skin or made of leather or something? Or, like, barbed wire?"

Now her smile is as wide as the little lace and spandex creation he's holding up.

"Sorry to disappoint you, but no barbed wire," she says, and the "wire" is the little sigh this time. "Leather yes, barbed wire no. And here, maybe these socks are more your speed."

The socks come by the handful, but he's on a roll now.

"I don't know, I think I'd like to go back to the underwear if we could," he says.

"Yeah, I bet you would, you sicko. Looking at a poor teenage girl's underthings. You should be ashamed," she says.

"What, you're not even going to model? I'm clearly new to all this type of gear. Maybe I need someone to show me how it all works." He's saying things to her he couldn't ever have imagined saying to a girl, ever. And she likes it.

"Oh, I never model for the staff," she says in a fake British accent, then straightens her posture. So that's a 32-B, he thinks, not that he was looking. "Remember, I just hired you to mow the lawn."

"Yeah, how did that deal work exactly? I thought I was hired to mow the lawn, and here I'm also unpacking your room? What's the pay for that?"

"The pay is you got to rub your grubby paws all over my panties and look at my bras," she says. "That isn't enough?"

"Oh, don't worry, I didn't just *look* at your bras. I rubbed my grubby hands all over them, too. That must have been the overtime pay."

With a few clothes to hang in the closet – Ashley and her mom clearly travel light – the boxes broken down and a radio put on the dresser, Ashley Hudson is officially moved in, and they sit down on the bed to take it all in as "Living on a Prayer," soars out of the yellow plastic boom box, the back of the thing slightly golden and warped from the heat it has put out over the years. He'd never met a girl like this. Hell, he'd never met anyone like this.

Is she easy? he thinks. I mean, she let me see her underwear – is she like a slut or something? It doesn't seem like it. She's just, I don't know, free somehow. Like I wish I could be sometimes. I don't even see my sister's underwear, not that I want to, but…

"So what do you do here in Fort Wayne in the summers?" she asks. "You have a car?"

"No, but I can usually borrow my mom and dad's. Mostly I work a couple days a week up at Atz's. That's the ice cream place. When I'm not there, I just hang out around the house I guess. Sometimes I ride my bike on the trails along the river."

"Is Atz's cool?"

"Not really," he laughs. "In some ways it is, but mostly it really isn't. I can't really explain it, but it's sort of cool in how un-cool it is. Basically, it's like all high-school kids that work there, so that's sort of cool, except some of them are, you know, whatever, but all the customers are like a hundred years old. And so the whole place is like really old fashioned, but not really in a good way. So it's like, kind of cool in a dorky, old-people who say crazy stuff sort of way, but…"

"Wow, you really know how to sell it," she says, and she's laying down on the bed now, one knee up in the air, her arms over her head as the breeze comes in through the busted up mini-blinds on the window. Man, he could get used to looking at that.

"Yeah, well, the nice thing is it's only a couple days a week and it gives me some spending money so I can buy gas if I get the car and go to the movies or whatever," he says, then rolls the dice. "I can take you up there some time. To Atz's I mean. Or, you know, whatever."

The screen door downstairs slams before she can answer.

"Ash honey? I'm back," a voice comes up the stairs.

"Yeah Mom, up here," Ashley yells at the top of her lungs. Andy never yells like that.

Andy immediately stands, but Ashley stays where she is, sprawled on the bed. "Shouldn't we go down there?"

"For what? I was thinking I'd put my AC/DC poster up on that wall," she says, pointing. "And maybe Randy Travis over there." He sits back down.

Soon, they can hear her coming up the stairs.

When the woman appears in the doorway, Andy immediately sees she looks much older than she really is. Skinny, but not in a good way, with hair dyed blonde somewhat recently, but hair that has seen better days, regardless. She's got a blue work shirt with "Kelly" on one side of the chest and "Frank" on the other. She looks tired. Andy stands.

"You must be either Kelly or Frank," he says. "I'm Andy."

"Yeah honey, I'm Frank," she says and for a moment – just one – Andy can see Ashley's smile in hers. But her smile fades quickly. "No, I'm Barbara, Ashley's mom. It'll be a couple a days before I get my shirts. Looks like you got moved in, Ash."

"Yeah, and Andy mowed the grass for us. He lives around the corner."

Barbara is holding a little purse, like the kind he's seen women use at the bowling alley for cigarettes, vertical with no straps. Sure enough, she opens it and pulls out a box of Capris and a plastic lighter from the gas station.

"I thought the grass looked nicer. You want to stay for dinner, Andy? We were going to celebrate and get some pizza delivered."

Damn, that would be awesome.

"Oh man, I'd love to, but I actually have to finish mowing my own lawn," he says. "I was only about half done when I got interrupted by something." Ashley smiles.

"OK, well if you get bored later just come back over," Barbara says, working a Capri out of the box and starting down the hallway. "We'll be here, and it's nice to meet the new neighbors."

Andy sits down on the bed; Ashley's still lying where she was before.

"So what was Muncie like?"

She twists her hair around a finger.

"It was all right. For a while."

"Only for a while?"

"You know. It started out good, but, well…" she pauses until she hears her mom's bedroom door shut. "My mom has a way of, I don't know. Getting into situations."

"Oh." He's probably supposed to know what that meant. He doesn't.

"Anyway, it all worked out, 'cuz now we're here."

"Yeah," he says.

"You have any brothers or sisters?"

"Just a little sister, Sally. She'll be a freshman this year," he says. "She's OK, I guess. No, I mean, she used to be OK, but now it seems like we fight all the time. I don't know. She's in dance, and now that I can drive, my Mom makes me drive her to dance all the time. Are you in anything? Like sports or whatever?"

"Me? No," she says. "Any time I'd start getting into something, we'd move, so I don't really bother with it anymore. Plus, with studying and everything, you know, it's not really worth it. I guess I just hang out with people whenever I can."

"Well," he says, glancing at her body one more time for inspiration, "maybe you can hang out with me once in a while."

She sits up and raises an eyebrow.

"Are you busting a move on me?" she says, and he notices she sighs a little when she says "move."

"No, I was just— "

"OK," she says, and lays back down. "I'll hang out with you once in a while."

"Yeah?"

"Yeah. Especially if you mow my lawn."

That evening, after finishing the lawn and having supper with Mom and Dad and Sally, he walks back to Ashley's, wondering if it's stupid to just show up again. It's nice and cool inside, where his parents have the air on, but outside the evening air feels warm and muggy. Halfway there, he runs back home and back inside to get the scissors, then cuts eight or ten tulips from the flower garden in the front yard. Halfway there again, he realizes he's taking flowers to a girl he just met. Oh God, I'm the biggest dork on the planet, he thinks, but his thoughts are interrupted by a piercing, shocking sound from the tree branch right above his head. Almost instantly, the sound is doubled as another cicada in another tree takes up the song. Then another, and another.

The hell with it, he thinks. I'll just say the flowers are to welcome them both to the neighborhood, and if I sound like a dork, well they probably won't even hear me over all these bugs anyway. Or I'll say they're from my Mom.

He turns the corner at Vermont and sees Barbara sitting in the old yellow lawn chair, now moved to the front yard. Even from here he can tell she's got a cheap beer in one hand and a Capri in the other. Sitting on the porch is Ashley, who immediately jumps to her feet and waves to him. Nothing after that even matters.

"Hey," he says to the both of them. "I stole some welcome-to-the-neighborhood flowers from my Mom's landscaping."

"Oh, that's great, Andy," Barbara says, flicking an ash that looked to be about an inch long. "See if you can find something to put them in, Ash."

Ashley returns with probably the biggest travel mug he's ever seen, with a giant Marathon logo on the side. It must have held a gallon of coffee — he could have brought twice as many flowers and they'd still fit in there.

"So you guys get all unpacked and stuff?"

"We're getting there," Ashley says.

"Actually," Barbara says, "you're a big, strong guy. Do you think you could lift the TV up onto the TV cart in the living room? I got it inside from the car the other day, but I tell you, I'm beat after working today. This job is a lot more physical than my last one, and they've got me on tens for a while."

Andy doesn't know what tens are, and he's not big and strong, but he's certainly strong enough to pick up a TV.

"Yeah, not a problem," he says. "You want me to get it right now?"

"Just some time before you go," Barbara says, but she's not really looking at him. She's looking out toward Anthony, where the evening traffic is going by, some of it slowing down for the light at Lake, some of it speeding up heading north, away from the city.

He looks at Ashley, and feels the pull of the dusky living room. "I'll just get it now so I don't forget."

He's thinking Ashley will get up and let him in, but she doesn't move, so he opens the door himself and walks in. The air inside is even warmer than outside; no wonder they're out on the lawn, he thinks, then remembers he didn't mow around an AC unit, because there wasn't one. It's getting dark inside, but as he walks over to the TV, he notices most of the stuff in the kitchen is put away now. The TV is more awkward than heavy, after he gets it on the cart, he plugs it in, then sees a cable hookup on the wall, so he attaches that, too. He has no idea whether they have cable or not, but if they do, the TV's ready for it now, he thinks. He walks through the shadows, wishing Ashley had come in with him so they could share a little moment in the dark, and then wonders who he's kidding. You just met her, you idiot. There are no moments to share.

"OK, you're all set," he says, sitting on the step next to Ashley. "I didn't try it out, but it's up there and all plugged in and junk."

"Thanks a lot, Andy," Barbara says, still looking toward the traffic. She sounds tired.

"Yeah, thanks a lot," Ashley says, and suddenly her hand is on his arm, waking every nerve ending from his shoulder down.

"So Ashley tells me you guys will be in the same class," Barbara says, and Andy can see the end of her Capri glowing in the gathering shadows now.

"Yeah, over at North Side," he says. "It's a pretty good school."

"Do you know any place she can get a summer job?"

It was funny how sometimes it seemed like she talked like Ashley wasn't even there.

"Oh yeah, that shouldn't be a problem," Andy says. "There's a bunch of places right up Anthony that hire in the summer. You can walk there from here."

"That's great," Barbara says.

"Yeah great," Ashley says, and this time the sigh is not just in her words.

They listen to the sound of the cicadas rise and fall, just as the traffic noise rises and falls with the changing of the lights down at the intersection. But more is changing than just the traffic signals, Andy thinks.

"Well, I'm really glad you guys are here," he says. "Really glad."

FOUR

"As one approaches a colony of these insects, a peculiar roar, not unlike the noise of a factory or a distant reaper, falls on the ears, and this becomes louder and more intense as one draws nearer, having at times when standing in the midst of a colony an all-pervading and penetrating effect. The individual notes are somewhat obscured under these circumstances, but in the lulls the characteristic sounds strike the ear and the peculiarity is never to be forgotten, especially the mournful falling note at the conclusion of each effort. Some instinct seems to prompt the singing in unison, and as it rises at such moments the intensity and volume of sound has a startling and weird effect."

—"The Periodical Cicada"

Emma Dunne got into the passenger seat of the Grand Am and closed the door.

"You ready?" Andy asked.

"Of course," Emma said. "You know I love your parents."

That was Emma – they had been friends in high school and when he came back from IU they picked up right where they left off. Of course, it was impossible not to run into someone you know in Fort Wayne. For a big town – at 250,000 people it's bigger than Orlando – it's really just a small town where everybody knows everyone. Emma was married now but still managed to be a buddy. Of course, it helped that she was entertaining – you never knew what she was going to say – and had her own sense of style. Today, she was wearing black leggings under a red plaid skirt and a big grey sweater with a brooch of a cat made of red rhinestones. Her hair was combed straight down in a kind of bob. Some girls he knew got married and you never saw them again. Not Emma.

"So what's going on this weekend?" he asked as he backed the car into the street.

"Well, the husband is sick so I've been running around taking care of everything, and in the middle of it all I had a Tupperware party."

"Tupperware? They still make that stuff?"

"Oh yeah, it's huge," Emma said, making a face. "You wouldn't

35

believe it. They're going to have a big Tupperware conference at the Grand Wayne Center. Crazy, is what it is."

The road wound along the St. Joe river here, a tall concrete floodwall on one side, houses that used to flood on the other. Emma had become a sort of comfort food for him – totally safe. She was married, so that was off the table, she never judged him, and she was always fun.

"Andy, when are you going to stop being afraid of your parents?"

Whoa. "What?"

"Look, you always invite me to these things and I'm always happy to go," she said. "I am. I mean it. And it's great because my family never does stuff like this. But you shouldn't be taking me to distract your parents while you crawl into the woodwork."

"That's— No. I don't..." he said, but as he steered toward his parents he knew she was right. Emma was always right. "It's only a couple times a year, just when, you know, I can't really deal with... you know."

"More like five or six times a year."

He turned left at the Tennessee Avenue bridge and thought about that.

"At least the food's good, though, right?"

She laughed. "Yeah, the food's awesome," she said. "Plus they always have good wine."

He wasn't going to tell her this, but why not?

"And maybe next week I'm bringing someone else," he said. "I just wasn't quite ready to ask her to meet my parents for the first time."

"What!?!" Emma shrieked. "You're seeing someone? Who is she? Why didn't you TELL me?"

The big, Sunday family dinner was a tradition at Andy's parents and they did it almost every week. Starting about four o'clock, Andy and then Sally and her family would show up, and soon the old house on the boulevard would feel as warm and full as it did when he and Sally were kids.

"Oh, hi Emma!" Andy's mom greeted them at the door, and always acted like Emma was one of her own.

"Hi Paula, dinner smells great already."

Sally's husband Steve looked up from the couch where the ballgame was on. He was a nice guy, but Andy still couldn't believe Sally married a White Sox fan. What was she thinking?

"Uncle Andy!" the kids yelled and did their best to tackle him. Derrick and Danielle were five and three already, and they were strong if you weren't expecting their flying leaps.

"Hey Mom, where's Dad?"

"He's in the basement, looking for some wine to go with the roast. I told him a Rhone but he never listens to me."

"Well Emma's here so I hope he brings up extra."

"Ha-ha, Andy," Emma said. "Can I help in the kitchen, Paula?"

When they were finally around the table and grace had been said, Paula sprung the trap. Andy had just reached for the gravy.

"Andy and Emma, you remember little Charlie Savage, don't you?" she said, passing the rolls.

"Oh yeah, I used to baby sit him," Emma said.

"I read in the paper that he's working at the Boston Globe now," Paula said.

"Well, sure," Andy said. "He probably just knows someone there from when he went to Harvard."

Damn. He walked right into that. But his parents played it cool.

"Well, you do make a lot of connections at a school like that," his dad said.

"Yeah," Andy said, staring into his plate. They didn't say anything else, but they didn't have to: He was supposed to have gone to Princeton. Was, being the key word. Everything was set. It had been Princeton for, well forever. Pre-ordained. His parents could read the newspaper announcement in their minds: "Andrew J. Gardner graduates with honors from Princeton University…"

Only, Princeton never happened, had it? After Ashley, he just … couldn't. He had a full-ride to IU if he wanted it and would have had to take out a few loans to cover the difference at Princeton, so he told himself it was the smart choice, the practical decision to stay closer to home. No sense in taking a big, financial risk. Backing out of Princeton and going to IU was just somehow …easier. Princeton was far away and IU was, well, comfortable.

The table conversation moved on without him while he pushed the food around his plate, basically eating nothing but the gravy with a few potatoes for show while silently cursing Charlie Savage. Until Paula dropped her next little bomb.

"Do you ever hear from Susan anymore?" she asked.

"No," Andy said, and reached for the wine, then filled the glass to the rim. "No, Mom, I don't hear from my ex-wife anymore. We're divorced. We don't really talk a lot, you know?"

What the hell, he thought, and then drank about half the glass of wine. What's gotten into her today?

"I was just asking if you'd heard from her, is all." Even Sally's kids were quiet now.

"No," he said, feeling a shell building up around him, a shell that hardened the more everyone stared. "No, I haven't heard from her in about four years."

"Damn," Andy said as soon as Emma was in the car and had closed her door. "You know, if I do hide behind you, it sure didn't work today."

He started the car and then just stared at the gauges for a minute before putting it in gear. "I mean, seriously."

"Andy, they're just …"

"Disappointed in me? You can say it. Everyone knows it."

At the intersection, he had to fight not to just mash the pedal to the floor and squeal the tires out of there.

"They're not," Emma said. "They're disappointed that you're not happy and they don't know why. They want you to be happy. If you're a manager at a cabinet place and live in Fort Wayne, they're fine with that if that's the choice you made and you're happy with it. But you're not, and you know it and they know it and they don't know how to fix it for you anymore. More than anything, I think they're sad that you're disappointed in yourself."

"Who says I'm not happy?" he said. "I'm not unhappy, at least. I just, you know, am. And I'm not disappointed in myself. I made these choices. After Susan left, I could have gone anywhere. I could have gone back to school, like Charlie did. Didn't he go to Yale or something? I could have done that. This is what I chose, so I don't know why people can't just get off me already."

He pulled up to the intersection by the Tennessee Avenue Bridge and wondered what it would be like to go straight and just head out of town instead of taking Emma home. It'd be like old times, cruising around in his mom's car, with nowhere to be and nothing that mattered except finding something to do and maybe a place to sneak a smoke or two.

But that wasn't going to happen, was it? Emma had a husband to go home to. He had a house, and now a sort-of girlfriend to consider. Damn.

"Seriously though, when are they gonna forgive me?" he asked. Usually, it was nice that Emma was married. But now, it was like it put some wall between them that she was not allowed to cross. He didn't know what it was he wanted from her, but he suddenly realized that whatever it was, she couldn't give it to him anyway.

"When are you going to forgive yourself?" she asked.

He turned the car north and started toward Emma's house. He didn't say anything. He didn't have to, because there was nothing to say.

Forgiveness was …

"Well, listen, thanks for putting up with me," he said. "I appreciate it."

"Oh Andy," Emma said. "Tell me about this girl you're seeing. Is she a slut?"

When he awoke, he realized he was sure of something. Absolutely damn sure: There was no way in hell he could go to work that day. It may not sound revolutionary, he thought, but he realized it was the first thing he was positively sure of in seventeen years. Seriously, since that awful Labor Day in 1987, he hadn't been sure of anything.

Should he finish school or just bag it and join the military? Go to college? Where? Choose a major? Get married? Get divorced? Hell, he hadn't been able to make a decision in nearly two decades, and the few really big ones he had made – marriage and divorce – had left him frozen, afraid to make another one, for the last eight years. Like that damn Grand Am in the driveway – he could certainly afford a new car. Hell, he could pay cash for a new car out of his savings. But the emotional investment it would take to pick out a new one was just impossible.

But this thought that had exploded in his head – that he was not going to work – was like waking up after seventeen years and finally – finally – realizing the stiffness in your arms and legs was because you had been paralyzed all that time. His brain – maybe his soul, too – had been paralyzed.

That morning, he was completely sure he could not face another day of cabinets until he figured out this Ashley thing. And honestly, if it cost him one freaking sick day to get his head right, was that really the worst thing in the world? Hardly. It was a baby step after seventeen years, but it was a step, and he was going to take it.

After coming out of the bathroom, he picked up the phone and called in. He hated to lie, but what had to be done had to be done.

"Yeah, I can't do it today," he said into the receiver, which was certainly true. "Let's just say I went from bed straight to the bathroom." Which was technically true, also, since it was the only thing he'd done since getting out of bed. "Yeah, thanks man."

Jeeze, if calling off work is really that easy, no wonder so many people do it. Heck, I should have taken a lot more mental health days, he thought, easing himself into a cup of coffee and out onto the back patio.

Once again, the morning was perfect – just enough sun to warm the skin, but still cool enough to let the steam rise off the joe. At least he didn't have to worry about Scarlett this morning. It wasn't that he didn't want her around, it was just that when she was here it was impossible to think about anything else. That wasn't such a bad thing, honestly – heck, maybe it was the best thing in seventeen years – but still, to have a little thing like a news brief in the morning paper feel like being hit in the gut with a sledgehammer was a wake-up call.

"You need to deal with some shit, my friend," he said out loud. Indeed.

Seriously, he needed to figure out Scarlett, too. She was great. Amazing. He liked just being with her, just talking. The sex was fantastic, too, of course, but he was trying to not let that be a factor. It's just that it was hard to figure out what was happening. One day she just walked in and bam! Are they dating? Is it casual? He wasn't hung up over these things, but they seemed to nag more with this whole Ashley thing out there. Mostly, he just wanted to figure out what the hell was going on.

As the sun rose over the yard he reasoned that maybe he just needed to clean out some cobwebs in the ol' mental attic. Go in, take an inventory, get rid of what you don't need any more, and move on. Travel light. Heck, while you're at it and you've got the day off, clean out the basement, too.

If his brain needed a mental cleaning, the basement needed a literal one. Not that it was messy, but he knew what was down there: Boxes. Boxes of crap that needed to be sorted out and triaged the same way the thoughts in his head did. There were things down there he'd rather not deal with – just like in his head. Maybe both could be taken care of at the same time. In fact, his basement was a lot like his head, now that he thought about it. I mean, it's not like Ashley just went away, he thought. You didn't really forget her. You just packed her away and she was still there the whole time. Just like the crap downstairs. It's not gone, it's just in storage, waiting for … well, for who knows what?

And seriously, what the hell was this Ashley thing, anyway? OK, true, he had been close to suicide the year after she left, but that was something he didn't think about, didn't talk about, didn't dwell on. He was past that. He was past that a long time ago. Hell, that was 16 years ago. No point in even bringing it up, really, except to acknowledge it and move on. OK, and true, maybe that had affected a lot of things down the road. Like with Susan – would he really have just married her if it hadn't been for that summer with Ashley? Or would he have actually made a decision and done the right thing, the thing no one else seemed to be willing to do — which was admit the truth that while they were a cute couple, that's about all they were. Being a cute couple will only get you so far in life.

So what's going on that seventeen years after the fact, Ashley is all he can think about, except when Scarlett's around? And then there's Scarlett.

For one thing, he thought, the sudden Ashley obsession is not fair to Scarlett. Not that we're like a couple or something, but seriously, you meet her and almost immediately start obsessing over your high school girlfriend from almost 20 years ago? If you met a chick who talked like that you'd think she was psycho and get the hell out of there.

He took a drink of coffee.

"Am I psycho?" he wondered. Maybe I've been psycho all this time and I'm just now realizing it.

As his mind wandered, he noticed the patio was covered with translucent brown shells in the shape of cicadas. He bent down and picked one up – sure enough, it was the exact size and shape of a cicada, only without wings, and of course it was empty and had a crack right down the middle of the spine. Like someone had encased a cicada in plastic, then freed it by cracking it open and letting the creature inside crawl out, back into the world.

He remembered being a kid and watching a cicada come out of its skin on the bark of the maple tree in the back yard one time. It was a slow process, and he would eventually wander off to do something else, but each time he came back, the ghostly white bug would be further out of its brown shell, until it was completely emerged. Eventually, the white faded into the alien colors of all the other cicadas, and the old skin fell off the tree, useless and discarded.

There were basically two rooms in the basement beneath his house, the laundry room and storage. The laundry room was a sort of clean, well-lighted place, he thought – a good place to triage. Stuff to keep, stack over here by the washer, everything else goes out with the trash. No yard sale, no donations to St. Vincent de Paul, just get it out of your life and get it out now. Haul it out to the curb and thank God that Fort Wayne had no limit on the amount of trash you could put out. Just toss it out there and let the garbage man deal with it. Poor bastard.

The first few boxes were easy: winter clothes, a spare set of dishes, Christmas decorations. Stuff that he needed and made sense to store part of the year downstairs out of the way.

After that it got a little tougher. These were boxes of things he meant to use. Wanted to use, planned to use. But the fact is he never used them. There was the box of softball gear, for one thing. He had played on a couple of rec leagues a few times, but since the divorce it hadn't really seemed worth the bother. It was all good stuff and probably could have gone in a yard sale, but then he would have had to have a yard sale. Or worse, he could put it in his parents' garage sale. He could just imagine his mother: "Andy! Why are you getting rid of all this good softball gear?

Aren't you playing softball anymore?" Screw that.

There was the giant backpack, which he got on extreme clearance at a sporting goods store's going out of business sale. He was going to use it to go back-country camping. Never happened.

Same thing with his golf clubs. Maybe this will be the year, he thought. Right.

Into the pile they went. There were boxes of magazines – gone. One with old newspapers and his gown from graduation. Gone. One with his collection of 1983 football cards. Football cards? What the hell was he thinking? Gone.

Then there was stuff from when he and Susan were married. Much of it was the same as the other – crap tucked away thinking it would be needed someday, when the reality was it would never be needed, not by anyone, certainly not by an ex-husband eight years after the fact. There were entertaining dishes, platters and snack trays. A spare set of glasses. Seriously?

Gone.

Between breaks, lunch, and a stop to make about a dozen trips hauling boxes out to the curb, it was almost 4 o'clock when he found it.

It was a box of stuff from high school: Old notebooks of journals he had to keep for a creative writing elective, his junior letter for showing up for track one season, year books and report cards.

And a pendant.

More to the point, it was half a pendant. He held it up and was surprised at how cheap and flimsy it looked compared to the way he remembered it. There were parts of the pendant and the chain where the fake gold finish had worn away from when he wore it for most of a year.

It had originally been a break-apart pendant, where a golden heart inscribed with "I Love You" was broken in half and the pieces each attached to a separate necklace. That left half saying "I L Y" and the other "ove ou" until they were rejoined. He had gotten it out of the gumball machine at the convenience store and gas station across the street from Atz's that summer. It took him about $4 in quarters to finally get one – in the middle was an incredible run of brightly colored rabbits feet – but when he did, he knew it was perfect: Just cheesy enough that Ashley wouldn't take it too seriously, but heartfelt enough that she would know he really did mean it.

They each wore them a few times, mostly for fun, until she disappeared, and then he wore his every day. Well, every day until he had to stop because he just couldn't deal with one more reminder. Eventually, it went into a box when he went to IU, a box that went to his parents' basement for four years until he came back and got married.

Then it went to he and Susan's basement, then it went to his own basement. And now, the box was open again, maybe for the first time since.

He thought about putting the necklace on for old time's sake, but instead just slipped it into his jeans pocket.

He sealed the box. Stacked it carefully with all the others he was saving. Hauled the boxes in the discard pile out to the curb. He was heading back inside to sweep up when he heard it – had it been there before? No, it was definitely new: The robin's nest by the door had peeping noises coming from it.

He finished up in the basement, went outside, and lit the first one out of a pack of cigarettes he had bought on a whim the day before but hadn't even opened yet. The sun was hot, and so was the tobacco smoke on his dry throat. It was no Bali Shag, for sure, and while the nicotine was soothing, in the end, he had to admit, it just made him feel more lonely than ever.

The sun was about to set and he was back on the patio. He had chilled out a little, had a beer, made and eaten dinner, and watched a guy in a junk truck take about half the crap he had hauled out to the curb.

That was another of the things he liked about Fort Wayne: It still had junk men. He had read about them in other cities, but always as a forgotten relic of the past. Well, somehow they hadn't been forgotten here and you could put cash money down that if you put something metal out by the curb there'd be someone within a day or less throwing it on the back of an old pickup with busted springs, headed for the recycling yard.

Maybe that's what he needed to do – some mental recycling. Take the junk rusting away in his head, melt it down and make something new. Throw out Ashley and get back Scarlett somehow in return. Now there'd be a trick.

The question was how to pull it off. Because simply deciding to move on didn't seem like it was going to do it, at least not in reality. After all, he had pretended to move on for years and all it took was one little reminder to erase all the progress he thought he had made.

As if to make the point, the cicadas started up, quickly filling the evening air with their incredible sound. And that really was the point, wasn't it – when those things started howling, there was no ignoring them. And for some reason, Ashley was still howling and he could no longer ignore it.

He reached into his pocket and pulled out the pendent and looked at it for a minute. It was hard to believe it was seventeen years ago.

And now? Seventeen years later he was still somehow screwed up, and he didn't know what to do about it.

Was he just lonely? Maybe he was just reaching for something, anything to pull him out of a decade-long funk — any straw to grasp and the nice girl he knew when he was seventeen happened to be a straw. It was a pretty convenient one, for sure: It wasn't like she had dumped him, she had simply disappeared, so he was free to write her future any way he wanted. And the truth was he wanted her to still have her half of the pendant. Hell, he didn't just want her to have it, he wanted her to be wearing it and thinking about him.

As the shadows grew and the cicada symphony rose and fell, the idea seemed to make more sense. Finally, he thought, those psych courses he took at IU were paying off: Of course he was pining for Ashley – she's perfect, at least in his mind. She'll never be inconvenient or bossy and she'll never be anything less than a fairy tale, because she'll never be anything except that perfect seventeen-year-old he spent a perfect summer with. She'll never say no to sex, she'll never be late getting home, and she'll never, ever nag you.

Meanwhile Scarlett could, in fact, be perfect, but as long as you're comparing her to Ashley all you'll ever see are the warts.

Suddenly, the cicadas stopped, all at once, as if some sound had alerted them to a predator nearby. In the silence, he could hear the traffic on the bridge as it crossed the river, until, almost tentatively, a lone cicada started up again. Soon it was joined by a growing chorus, and before long the entire orchestra was back at full volume.

So the issue seems to boil down to this, he thought: Scarlett's great, but you'll never be able to find out how great until you stop comparing her to this impossible standard of Ashley's ghost. And Ashley's ghost will always be an impossible standard as long as she's just a ghost.

And the only way to bring her back to life…?

Nah, he thought, tipping back his beer and lighting up another smoke. That's too crazy.

But the thought returned.

The only way to bring her back to life – warts and all and finally put it all behind him – is to find her.

The nicotine coursed through his blood as he thought about it, like cool water numbing him from the inside out. Could he find her? And what if he did? The possibilities seemed endless.

If nothing else, he could put it to rest and move on with his life.

He'd take a few weeks off work – Lord knows he had enough vacation time coming – and hit the road. Track her down. Knock on her door. Find out what the hell happened. Tell her how it's been all these years without her. Let her know – even if she's moved on – that he never forgot about her. It's not like he hasn't moved on. After all, he had been married three years. Got a divorce. Bought a house. They'd probably both laugh about the whole thing.

He didn't know if it would work, but compared to Scarlett, he seemed to be living a life of regret. And as long as Ashley was out there like some giant question mark, he would continue on that way.

"That seals it," he said out loud, but this time he didn't feel stupid doing it, maybe because he couldn't be heard over the fog of insect noise anyway.

No regrets.

FIVE

"The gift of song is found in the male insect only, and the true sound apparatus consists of two small ear-like or shell-like inflated drums situated on the sides of the abdomen. These drums vibrate by the action of powerful muscles, and the sound is modified by adjacent smaller disks – the so-called 'mirrors' or sounding boards – and issues as the peculiar note of the species, which once heard is never likely to be forgotten."

—"The Periodical Cicada"

"Double mint in a waffle," Laura says.

"Got it."

Andy grabs a new scoop out of the scoop well and moves over to the cooler with the mint chocolate chip in it, grabs a waffle cone and starts scooping the ice cream, packing it into the bottom of the cone first, then stacking it up on top until it's the perfect double scoop. Perfect, he thinks. Just like Ashley.

By the time he's done scooping, Laura has the woman rung up, and the lady is counting out pennies. Women, he's noticed, just love to count out pennies and nickels so their change will either be bills or, at the very least, some combination of quarters. Does Ashley do that? Probably not, he thinks. She's not wound that tight. She flies casual.

"Andy? Andy?" Laura says.

"Huh?"

"Double chocolate? Like I said?"

"Sorry."

He grabs another scoop, and looks at the clock. Only another hour, and then he's out of here. Maybe Ashley can come over. They hung out at her house yesterday, and at his house the day before that. Chocolate's clear on the other side of the ice cream bar that wraps in a U shape around the front part of Atz's building. The walls are an off-white, and the ceiling, if anyone bothered to look up, is off-white. Everything is off-white, except the carpet, which at one point was probably green.

Chocolate, chocolate, chocolate, he thinks as he scoops. I wonder if

Ashley likes choco—

"Andy!"

"What? Geeze, I'm scoopin' here!"

"She doesn't want chocolate anymore. Aren't you listening? She wants butter pecan. Goll."

"Fine," he says, and chunks the chocolate back into the bucket and then tosses the cone before grabbing a new one. Whatever. You know, Ashley's hair is kind of butter colored…

There are moments when he realizes that if he thought about it, he would have to admit that he eats, sleeps and breathes Ashley, but for the entire week he's known her, he has steadfastly not thought about it. Instead, he just thinks about the way she looks, the way she talks, the way he loves it when she ties up her hair in a pony tail and he can see her neck and the wisps of hair that veil its pale skin. He loves the way he's the only guy in town who knows what she looks like when she ties her hair up in a pony tail.

"OK, so what's her name?" Laura says.

"Huh?" Laura's one of those girls that, at school, he and his friends never refer to individually, only as part of her little group — a group they call The Bitches. In most company, they call them The Cheerleaders, but everyone knows who they're talking about and what everyone who's not one of Them thinks of them. At Atz's though, away from her friends, Laura becomes almost human at times. Almost.

"Look, either you're on drugs or you've got a girlfriend," Laura says, dropping her dishrag and walking over to him. "You might as well tell me because I know you're not on drugs."

"Yeah? How do you know?" He's smiling, but it's clear what he really means and her Barbie-doll exterior falls for a minute.

"Look, I know we're not friends at school. I know we hang out with different people. I know it's all a big, stupid game and that I play it just like everyone else. I know that, Andy. But I *do* know who you are. I know you," she says, and leans against the ice-cream cooler. "And yeah, when school starts again, we'll probably go back to our little groups of friends and it will be just like before, but it doesn't mean we have to do that all summer. And it doesn't mean I like it."

She has brown hair, and brown eyes, and underneath all the makeup, if you really look, you can see they scrunch up a little at the corners sometimes.

"Her name's Ashley, and she just moved here," he says. "She's not like— I don't know. She's not like anyone."

"Yeah? Where's she from?" Laura actually sounds interested in what he's saying.

47

"I don't know. Muncie or something. All over, really – they move a lot, I guess. But, I don't know, I can just, talk to her," he says. "Plus she's totally hot."

They're laughing then, and for a second he thinks maybe Laura's all right, and then he remembers how the last time he had a girlfriend, girls seemed to come out of the woodwork wanting to be his friend. Until she was gone, at least, and then they scattered like rats. Feast or famine, he thinks. Wait a minute – does that make Ashley his girfr—

"Excuse me!" It was an old lady at the counter. Oh great. "Can I get some service here? Or is it time for 'Teen Chat' or something? I'd like some ice cream."

Laura turns around to face the woman, and even from the back, he can see the plastic façade return to her frame. "Sorry about that, what can I get for you?"

"Andy, is Ashley staying for dinner?" the voice comes from the kitchen, where Andy's mom is mixing bleu cheese crumbles into hamburger so his dad can make bleu cheese burgers on the grill when he gets home.

Andy only has to raise his eyebrows to her to get the response he's hoping for.

"That'd be great Mrs. Gardner," Ashley calls back from the living room, where they've got photo albums spread all over the place. "I'd love to."

Ashley's turning pages in Andy's Baby Book, as they both laugh at the pictures of him as a baby, an infant and a toddler, especially the one of him in a yellow raincoat, green rubber boots and a red fireman's hat.

"What?" he says in mock indignation. "I was like 5. I wanted to be a fireman. Come on!"

"You were a very cute little fireman," Ashley says, with a little sigh.

"Yeah? And what about now?"

"Now you're just a fireman!" she laughs, and he wonders if there's a way to bottle up that laugh, to save it somehow for later, just in case it's gone someday. But then he sees her eyes and thinks there is no way there will be anything but forever. No way.

"Yeah, well, listen, I was wondering if you'd want to go see a movie with a plain old fireman sometime," he says, and then it's out there. Not that there should really be any doubt, but now it's out there now and the question has to be answered.

But it's like her laughter never even stops as she looks at him. "Of course. Why wouldn't I?"

Why wouldn't I? He can think of about a thousand reasons why, but none of that matters because she would. He could drown in those blue eyes.

"Because it's 'The Chipmunk Adventure'," he says.

"Oh, well in that case, maybe not," she says, grabbing another photo album, and then punching him – hard – in the shoulder. She's wearing shorts today. *Shorts.*

"Well, I was going to take you to a porno at the adult theater down on Broadway, but we're not 18 yet, so I can't unless you've got fake IDs for both of us," he says. "So you're going to have to settle for the Chipmunks."

Just then Sally comes downstairs.

"Are you guys really going to see the Chipmunk movie?" She's only three years younger than Andy, but it seems like she's about 10 years younger sometimes. "Can I go?"

"Sure," Ashley says. "Andy'll even buy you popcorn."

"No, you can't. And no, we're not going to see the Chipmunks. We're going to see 'Beverly Hills Cop 2'," he says, then turns to Ashley. "If that's all right with you?"

"Man, I kinda had my heart set on the Chipmunks," she says. "And you don't want your little sister tagging along on your big, important date?" She's looking at his elementary school photo album now, mostly pictures of him in a Cub Scout uniform and a bad home-haircut.

"Oh, I didn't realize it was a big, important date," he says. "I thought I was taking you."

Sally plops down on the floor in front of them and grabs an album. She treats Ashley like the big sister she's never had.

"How can it be a big, important date when you're practically boyfriend and girlfriend anyway?" Sally asks. Oh crap.

But Ashley's still game. "Yeah, Andy. What's so important about this date, huh? Am I going to get my first kiss or something?"

That sends Sally from the room and into the kitchen. "Mom! They're being gross!"

They can hear Mrs. Gardner from the living room. "That's what teenagers do, honey. You should know this – you are one."

But now a new question was out there, and this time it was his turn.

"Your first kiss? Your first kiss from me, maybe, but I'm sure it's hardly your first kiss."

She doesn't answer. She just turns to him and puts her hand on his shoulder. He can feel his pulse everywhere in his body, as she leans in close. They're sitting on the couch in his living room in the late afternoon and his mother is just around the corner in the kitchen and this girl is beautiful and she likes him and now she's—

"You'll just have to find out," she finally says, and closes her eyes,

49

leaning in even closer. He can feel the warmth of her face on his as he leans in and then, for a tantalizing second his lips brush hers and he can feel her legs touching his and he is suddenly aware of the crown molding in the room and just as she starts to press her lips against his there are heavy footsteps on the wooden porch outside and the sound of a key in the lock and his breath suddenly comes in heaves as they both sit up and the light in the room seems starker as his father walks in — home at last from a long day at work.

"Hey, kids," he says, oblivious to the splendor he just postponed.

"Hey, Dad."

Ashley looks up and smiles, then returns distractedly to the photo album.

"Hey, Mr. Gardner. Andy was just about to kiss me."

Wait. What?

But Andy's dad is just as unfazed as he hangs up his keys and walks toward the piano to set down his briefcase. He usually wears a tie to work, but it's summer and he's switched to a polo shirt. The advertising agency he works at downtown is pretty casual, but aside from the summer months, he wears a tie anyway. Something about looking professional and setting a tone or something, even though he hates wearing ties.

"Andy was going to kiss you? I doubt he even knows how, Ashley," he says. "You're probably going to have to teach him."

Ashley smiles as if she is the Devil herself.

"Yeah," Andy says. "They didn't teach us that in Cub Scouts."

Dad walks toward the kitchen. "You staying for dinner?"

"Yeah, Mrs. Gardner asked me," she says. "She says you're grilling burgers."

As they get the living room to themselves again, they can hear Mr. and Mrs. Gardner and Sally talking about dinner, but all Andy can think about is the near-kiss. And the fact that she said yes to an actual date. And how, when he walks her home tonight, and says goodbye on her porch, there won't be any interruptions.

It's nearly dark by the time he walks her home, and as they walk along the sidewalk they occasionally crunch on empty cicada shells.

"What the heck are we stepping on?" Ashley says. "I'm freaking out here."

"They're just cicada shells. They come out every summer, but this is the most I've ever seen. I'm surprised we don't hear any yet," he says. "You know, that really loud, crazy noise you hear in the summer, like radio static or something? That's cicadas."

On the locust tree in front of the Herberts', Andy sees something moving on the bark.

"Here, look at this," he says, pointing. "Here's one coming out of its shell."

About four feet up the tree, there was what looked like two bugs, joined like Siamese twins – though instead of twins, one was brown and nearly translucent, and one was ghostly white, even in the fading daylight. The white cicada, about an inch and-a-half long, was crawling out of its old, brown shell.

"What's it doing?"

"My dad says it's molting when they do that," Andy says. "It's shedding its old skin, and then it's like a different kind of bug. See, it's got wings now, and there's no wings on the old shell."

"Weird. I've always heard those things, but I don't think I ever looked at one before."

She stands and starts walking toward her house again. Now the sound of the insects begins, and it spreads through the trees on the street like crazy.

As they walk in the shadows, it feels like he can tell her anything.

"It seems like there's a lot more of them this year. The cicadas, I mean," he says. "And you know, I've never met anyone like you."

"Is that good?" she says.

"Yeah, it's good. It's pretty amazing, actually," he says, then stops and just looks at her. "You're amazing."

She smiles, and then takes his hand. Her skin is rougher than he expected, but Andy feels like his head might touch the tree branches 10 feet in the air.

"Hey, I was thinking, since you don't have a bike, we should go to some garage sales," he says. "I bet we can get one for like ten bucks. And then when we don't have a car, we can still cruise around."

"Hey, that sounds great," she says. "Oh, I forgot to tell you – I put in a job application at that grocery store by Atz's. What's it called? Roger's? Anyway, it sounds like I'm probably going to get in like in the deli or something."

"Sweet – then you can take me out," he says. Again with the Devil smile.

As they walk, the empty space in his stomach seems to grow with each step closer to her front porch. Will she? Won't she? What if he really doesn't know how to kiss? He does – thanks to Danielle O'Claren back in freshman year after the football game once – but still.

They reach the corner at Vermont, and as they round the Stancius' yard there's only one house left before Ashley's. Even from here, Andy can see Barbara isn't home, thanks to the giant 1978 Ford Thunderbird she drives. The thing is metallic green, and looks like someone took a massive steel rectangle and added a white roof for the passenger compartment, then covered the whole thing in chrome. Plus, one of the springs or something is broken in the back, so back of the car on the driver's side sits low to the ground, while the front passenger side seems to point in the air.

Ashley's mom works hard, that's true. But she seems to party hard, too, and the idea that someone's mom would just be out on a school night is a foreign one to Andy. Still, the freedom it affords Ashley is a major bonus. Already, he's heard his parents talking about Barbara in hushed tones when they think he's not around. They clearly love Ashley, and they clearly love him hanging out with her, but they seem to give each other knowing glances whenever the subject of her Mom comes up. Luckily, it comes up about as often as Barbara is around.

And then they're there – on the front porch, and Ashley's unlocking the door before turning around playfully.

"Thanks! Goodnight!" she says, and then jumps inside the door, leaving him stranded on the front porch. He considers fleeing, but already knows better, and within a second she is back on the porch and somehow – how did she do that? – she's in his arms and her lips are on his and he can feel her entire body pressing against him and her tongue and the way she breathes and he's caressing her hair and smelling her neck and all of it is heaven as the cicadas raise their chorus to the darkened heavens, their song rolling up in waves the way his heart rises and the moment draws out the way a singer holds one note – one beautiful, trembling, heartbreaking note while the refrain swells around it but that note continues, high and alone above the harmonies beneath until at last, it breaks, and the song is done, except in the memories of those who heard it and were there and were forever changed by the hearing.

It's Saturday, and Ashley's at her first day of work in the deli at Roger's grocery store. The store is like two doors down from Atz's, but it doesn't really matter when you're working, does it? She could be right next door and he couldn't see her. Still, if they ever get out of work at the same time they can walk or ride home together. But it doesn't look like that's ever going to happen. Whatever.

She's at work and he's not and it's Saturday, and Saturdays in June in Fort Wayne mean garage sales. He hits three of them before he finds one with a girls' bike that's not for little kids. He puts the kickstand down on his own bike and walks over to where it sits near tables loaded with crap being pawed over by women with enormous purses and loud children. It's a 10-speed, blue, and looks to be in good shape. The big thing in bikes now is BMX bikes, which are fun, but not actually practical. Those are good on the trails down by the river, with their big, knobby wheels and single gears, he thinks, but they're no good at all for getting around town when your mom wants to run errands instead of letting you have the car.

The gears and brakes look good on this one, and the tires look fine. He shouts to the lady running the sale. "Hey, do mind if I try this out a little bit?" She's got a tiny dog sitting on her lap, maybe the ugliest he's ever seen. "I'll just ride it right out front here."

The lady looks him up and down. "You're not going to steal it, are you?"

"No." What would she do if I said yes, he wonders.

"All right, but stay where I can see you."

Geeze, he thinks. It's a garage sale bike, lady, not the gold at Fort Knox.

He pushes the bike out from behind a table of hideous clothing and weird looking dishes, then hops on and aims for the street. The tires flatten as he rides past his own bike and out into the street, but the brakes work good. Since they both flatten about the same amount, the tires are probably just low from not being used, he thinks. He has to peddle hard to make up for the low pressure, but he works the gears to make sure they change OK. He circles back and rides up the driveway to where the lady's sitting with her dog, counting out the change for a bag full of used underwear.

"It's twenty bucks," she says.

"Yeah. The tires are flat though."

She shifts the dog. "I don't know nothin' about that. It was my daughters'." Perfect, he thinks.

"Yeah, the derailleur in back looks a little dicey, too. Was she really cranking on it?" He's making stuff up now, but the lady clearly doesn't know a rear derailleur from a front fork. "Will you take ten?"

"Ten? No, not ten," she says, and turns to help someone else.

"No problem. I was going to have to spend almost $20 on tubes and tires for it anyway," he says. "Someone else can spend $40 on it only to find out it needs a $50 de-railer, too."

The seed of doubt planted, he starts walking toward his bike. Then a Hispanic guy who was about to buy a clock has second thoughts. "You sure this works?" he says. "You said it works."

"Yes, it works, I promise," she says, then calls out to Andy. "All right, I'll take ten."

Yes.

On the way home, he realizes it's actually more difficult than you would think to walk two bikes at once. Somehow, when you're walking your own, it's nothing to push your bike one-handed. But when your other hand is on another bike, for some reason neither one wants to cooperate and you find yourself fighting them every step. But it doesn't really matter, because when Ashley gets home from work she's going to find that he just bought her a bike.

He's so excited about it he forgets the weirdness of last night. They had gone on their "big date" to the movies and then stopped at Atz's for shakes afterward so she could check the place out. But when they got to Ashley's house, Barbara wasn't home.

"You wanna come in?" she said.

"Yeah, if it's all right," he said, looking around. "Where's your Mom?"

"Out," she said, then sighed as she closed and locked the door behind them. "She's probably out finding Mr. Right."

"Mr. Right?"

"Yeah, only somehow they always end up being Mr. Wrong," she said as she lead him upstairs. "Actually, not even Mr. Wrong. More like, Mr. Felony Conviction, or Mr. Deadbeat, or Mr. Hey Girlfriend, Your Teenage Daughter Sure Looks Hot."

Andy grabbed her hand then.

"I'm sorry."

"Don't be. It's not your fault," she said as she flipped on the light in her bedroom and flopped on the bed. "Mom has a way of getting herself – well, us really – into situations."

"Situations?"

That was when she reached under the mattress and pulled out the biggest knife Andy had ever seen. It was some kind of Rambo knife, with jagged teeth on top of the huge blade and black metal handle.

"Let's just say she doesn't always make the best choice in men, so we end up moving. Quickly. Without, you know, leaving a lot of forwarding addresses, if you know what I mean."

Holy crap.

"And that thing?"

She was already putting it back under the mattress, but Andy could still feel it in the room.

"Let's just say that if I would have had it in Muncie, we wouldn't have had to move," she said, then smiled that crazy, half angel-half devil smile. "Why, do I scare you?"

"Yeah, you scare me in a lot of ways," he said, laughing.

54

"I can tell. I think you were almost as scared just now as you were of my underwear when we first met."

Now it's his turn to try the crazy angel-devil smile.

"I'm not scared of your underwear anymore," he said.

"Really?" she said, pulling him close, and then with one swift move rolling him off the bed onto the scuffed hardwood floor. As he lay there, stunned, she looked down off the bed at him and laughed like it was the funniest thing she'd ever seen.

"I seriously can't believe you bought me a bike," she says, her hair flying behind her in the breeze and the purr of the gears on their bikes like music in the summer air. She had changed out of her work clothes and into shorts and a t-shirt, but not showered before coming over, and she smelled a little like the deli's fried chicken as he led her out to the garage, promising a surprise. He loves deli fried chicken.

He had spent the afternoon spiffing the bike up. He even checked the tires for leaks – sure enough, they were just low on air — and she hugged him when she saw it.

"I can't believe it," she said, with a little sigh on "believe."

"It was only ten bucks," he said. "It's not a big deal."

But, of course, it was more than just a $10 bike. It was the promise of spending the summer together. It was a commitment. It was them. Together. And now they're cruising down Edgewater, tall houses on the right, the Maumee River on the left, Andy on the left, Ashley on the right, the breeze on their faces and the entire summer laid out before them. The river is lined with trees – tall ones – locusts and sycamores and ash, and they seem to reach 100 feet in the air, with the canopy way up high, making the shade below airy and light.

She looks amazing on a bike, he thinks, shifting gears to keep up with her, and she's got a big, goofy grin on her face, just like he does.

Ahead of them, sitting on the hood of a blue car, is a girl in black tights, jean shorts, a long, black jacket and dark sunglasses, smoking a cigarette. Her long, straight hair looks unnaturally light against all the black clothing, and she's listening to a Walkman.

"Hey, that's my friend Emma," Andy says. "You'll like her. She's really cool. I've known her since … well, I remember we got in trouble in second grade because we wouldn't stop talking in class. So we go way back."

Emma doesn't even look at them as they pull up and stop, but instead takes a long drag on her cigarette and blows it out like a movie star. Finally she turns toward them and takes her headphones off.

"Hey Emma, this is Ashley," Andy says. "Ashley Hudson. Ashley, this is Emma Dunne. She's in our class at North Side."

Emma tosses her lit cigarette into the street, where a little pyre of smoke rises from the pavement.

"I'm not going by 'Emma' anymore," she says. "Call me Emma Louise."

"Um, OK. What are you listening to?" he says. She always listens to the coolest music. She was the first person in school to listen to the Violent Femmes, and had introduced Andy to bands he never would have even heard of otherwise. As soon as they became popular with everyone else, though, she said they were "old" and moved on to something else.

"It's 'Breakfast at Tiffany's'," Emma says. "You wanna hear some?"

"You're listening to a movie?" Ashley asks.

Finally, Emma's façade cracks. "Yeah, I thought it was going to be really cool to say to people, but it's actually mostly stupid when you do it," she says. "Unless you have the whole thing memorized, which I do, but then why listen to it? So I don't know."

"And why are you smoking right in front of your house?" Andy asks. "You've got like fourteen brothers and sisters, and if you get busted your mom'll kill you."

"True, but they're all off doing things," Emma says. "What are you guys doing? Just out riding?"

"Andy bought me a bike," Ashley says. "So we went out for a spin."

Emma looks over the bike. "What, no bell? Seriously, you bought her a bike?"

"It's just a garage sale bike. I got it for ten bucks," he says. "But now we can do stuff when I can't get the car. Which is like, always."

"I hear that," Emma says. "Try getting a car when you have as many kids in your family as we do. At this rate, I'll be able to use it when I'm like 40. So what are you two kids doing this summer?"

Ashley's down off her pedals, straddling her bike as they stand in the street.

"Working at Atz's again," Andy says. "Same old thing."

"I'm working in the deli at Rogers'," Ashley says. "I just started."

"No, I mean for fun."

"Whatever. What are you doing?" Andy says.

"I don't know. I was supposed to work at the library downtown, but I really don't want to," Emma says. "I'm probably going to have to anyway, though. You guys wanna smoke?"

Ashley immediately says yes; Andy hesitates. She smokes?

"Don't worry, I don't really smoke," Ashley says to him. "But it's fun sometimes. And if you breathe really deep it gives you a huge head rush.

Try it."

Emma gives them each a Marlboro Light, clearly stolen from someone somewhere, because Andy knows she only smokes Virginia Slims – when she can get them, at least – then lights each one. He watches the girls to see how they do it.

Ashley's right: He can just kind of breathe normally, and it's like not even smoking except that you look and feel totally cool. Or you can really suck it all the way in and feel like your head is floating off its shoulders.

"So are you guys dating, or what?"

He loves Emma because you never, ever know what she's going to say. But at the same time, you never, ever know what she's going to say.

Ashley looks at him.

"Well, we did have a big, hot date last night. He took me to a movie," she says. "And I thought he was going to feel me up afterward when we were making out, but he didn't. He's kind of shy."

Andy feels a cold place in his gut, a place that just gets bigger and bigger. But Emma laughs and looks at Ashley like she's just found her new best friend.

"Better luck next time, Andy," Emma says. "Ya big, dumb virgin."

SIX

"In escaping from the soil the pupa burrows directly upward, but not always in a straight line, and under normal conditions emerges directly, leaving a small round hole about the size of a man's little finger. While it is generally true that they do not pierce the surface at all until they are ripe for transformation, they seem to have a frequent habit of penetrating nearly to the top of the ground some time before they actually issue and remain usually within their burrows or sometimes emerging, but concealing themselves under logs, stones, etc., awaiting the proper moment to come forth. Usually throughout the month of April they are to be found thus near the surface, as has been recorded by many observers."

—"The Periodical Cicada"

It was Saturday, and he had slept in. Lord knows he had deserved it after the mental and emotional gymnastics he had put himself through the day before. But he had also slept the sleep of the righteous – for the first time since he could remember, Andy Gardner had slept without tossing and turning. Deep, untroubled, peaceful sleep.

Waking was a revelation: A new purpose, a new determination. He was going to find Ashley, for good or ill, and get on with his life, come what may. First, would come coffee. And then, maybe – why not? – a decent breakfast for a change. Shower, dress, and hit the library.

The library was really about as far as he had gotten in his planning, but it was something. He had thought about going over to the school to see if there was any information he could get, but he figured the privacy laws nowadays would probably prevent that, and there wouldn't be anyone around on a Saturday in June now that school was done.

Besides, the library was a bigger step than one might assume, because Fort Wayne didn't have just any library: It had the Allen County Public Library, holder of the second-largest genealogical collection in the country — second only to that of the one held by the Church of Latter Day Saints in Salt Lake City — and the largest one that was public. He didn't know what was in a genealogical collection or how to use it, but he figured the tour buses full of old people that were always out front must be there for a reason.

If people came from all over the country to the Allen County Public Library to find people, then that was the place to go to find Ashley.

It was his first time in the library since it had been renovated, and it was amazing. For one thing, there was a huge lobby-like area stretching almost a city block that seemed close to three stories high with skylights down the whole thing. The floors were terrazzo and the space was finished in a light-grained wood that looked to Andy like maple, contrasted by black, textured steel railings. Walking through there – past the giant, revolving globe of the Earth that had been in the library ever since he could remember – felt like, well, it felt like being in the center of something. Like if there was one, single, central focus of the entire downtown, this space was it. The rather plain library he had known and loved as a child had become Fort Wayne's beautiful town square.

From the atrium, the children's section appeared to be bigger than most entire libraries, and had things to climb on and nooks for reading, computers and a playroom. Further down there was a giant computer lab and a Periodicals section that looked like it had every magazine he had ever heard of, and many he hadn't. There were Public Access television studios, a mini art museum and a coffee shop. There was a whole department of movies you could check out, and another one full of CDs.

Finally, there was the Genealogy Department, which seemed to be like its own library, with its own front desk. Since he honestly had no idea where to even start, that seemed like the place to go.

Behind the curved, maple counter, a woman bent over a computer screen. She looked to be about his age, except that she had a tiger-skin pillbox hat perched on top of her head, and wide, rectangular glasses with tiny rhinestones on the tips. Her prim, black sweater covered a lava-pink tank top cut low. It could only be Emma Dunne.

"Hey there Andy!" she said. "What brings you down here?"

"Hey, I didn't know you worked in this department." He instantly relaxed, and leaned against the counter. Even if this was pointless, it had just gotten fun.

"Oh yeah. Mostly I'm down in the Juvenile Department, telling kids not to wipe their butts on the books, but sometimes I'm up here. Whatchya lookin' for?"

It's crazy how people age, he thought. Sometimes she looks exactly the same as she did in high school, only older. Well duh.

"Can you help me find someone? Someone who's not dead yet?" he asked. "I don't know how any of this works. At least, I don't think she's dead. Can you do that? Or is this department just for, like, family trees and stuff?"

"Oh no, we can find almost anyone. Well, usually. Sometimes," she said, moving a pile of folders from one basket to another. "A lot, actually. I'm not being very helpful, am I? Whatever. Who do you want to find?"

"You remember Ashley Hudson?"

Emma paused, and the tilt of her head with that crazy hat on top almost made him laugh.

"The girl you dated that one summer? Yeah, I remember… Whatever happened to her?"

"Well, that's the question."

Emma came around from behind the counter. "OK, well, what do we know about her? Tell me everything."

Can she just leave the front desk like that to help someone? he thinks. This could take a while.

"Well, her name is – or at least it was – Ashley Marie Hudson and she'd be our age, and I know she moved away from Fort Wayne. That's it."

"You try Google?"

"I've tried nothing. You are the very first step in my search," he said. "Nice hat, by the way."

She instantly turned back around to the front desk.

"OK, let's try the computer first," she said, walking over to where the whole thing started when he first walked in. "You never know."

She types a few words and almost instantly has to turn the computer's flat-screen monitor around so Andy can see it from his side of the counter.

"Image results – any of these her?"

"Nope."

"'Ashley Hudson's on Facebook.' Are you on Facebook?"

"Me? No."

She clicks on the link anyway, bringing up a blue and white page with a picture of some girl he's never seen before. "This her?"

"Nope."

"Here's an Ashley Hudson who's a college wrestler."

"Seems unlikely," he says. Girls wrestle? College girls? He may need to revisit that page later.

"On the rowing crew at Northwestern State?"

"At our age?"

"Hmmm, yeah, this is going nowhere fast," Emma says, and turns the computer around, then comes out from behind the desk again. "OK, we're going to have to get serious now. You really have no idea where she went?"

"None."

When she emerged from behind the counter he could see she had on tight jeans and pink boots with high heels that matched her tank top, and as she began leading him past stacks of books and filing cabinets and what appeared to be another front desk and toward an entire room of microfiche readers, he touched her arm and stopped her.

"Hey, I'm sorry about all that mess at my parents' house," he said.

"Don't worry about it," she said. "And I meant what I said. I know it seems like they're being intrusive and petty and dredging up the past, but they're just worried about you." He wondered if she wanted to continue and say "we all are," but she didn't.

"How are you doing?" he said. "Seriously? You're always there for me, and I'm never, I don't even ask, really, I just—"

She stopped and looked at him.

"I'm good," she said. "My life got a little crazy there for a while before I got the husband, but I'm good. And why are you looking for Ashley after all these years? Do you need a kidney transplant or something?"

When he didn't answer, she turned and entered the stacks, and found a shelf with rows of "Who's Who in American High School Students."

"She was a good student, right?" she said, pulling out one labeled 1987-88.

"Yeah, I guess. She left right before school started so…"

Emma flipped through the pages, then found what she was looking for: Ashley Marie Hudson, Marshall High School, Marshall, Michigan. Cum laude.

"Bingo," Emma said. "She moved to Marshall. You know Marshall?"

Marshall? He knew Marshall – that wasn't the thing. The thing was that after all these years, after she went from being real into vapor, like she had never happened, she had moved somewhere else, went to school, met friends and had a life. Her life had… continued.

"Yeah, I know it," he said. "It's there by Battle Creek."

Emma slammed the book shut and put it back on the shelf. "Follow me."

She went down two more aisles and up another to one filled not with book shelves but cabinets, and began looking at the names on tiny file drawers. The main areas were as brightly lit as the rest of the library, but these stacks were strangely dark, and it took a second to get used to the change. "Why are you looking for her again?" she asked.

"It's kind of a long story, but the short version is she just disappeared and now I can't get it out of my head until I figure out whatever happened to her," he said. "It probably makes no sense, but there it is."

Finally, she stopped in front of a section of shelves where the drawers were labeled "Marshall Chronicle."

"Well, for whatever it's worth, I really liked her. I was sad when she left. But mostly," and she looked right at him, "I was sad about how badly it hurt you."

"Oh, it wasn't…"

"No, it was, Andy. I know. You didn't say anything, but I knew," she said.

"You know, I miss the way you and I hung out all the time," he said. "I miss that. When it's not all drama, and just fun. I think somehow everything becomes drama these days."

"Well let's hang out some time, then. In the meantime, here's what I'm thinking," Emma said. "You know she moved to Marshall, right? And that would have been her senior year? Well Marshall is a tiny little town with a tiny little newspaper, right? Well tiny little newspapers print freaking everything that happens. You can't fart in a town like that without getting at least a brief in the paper, and if it's a really slow day and the wind is right, you might make the front page. So if she got a scholarship or was top of her class or anything like that, it's probably in there. And if it is, it probably says where she's going to college. Even if she wasn't top of her class, they probably print something about every graduate anyway."

As she said this, she began examining the dates on the drawers. "What year do we need?"

"That's brilliant," he said. "Uh, like 1988, spring. Wouldn't that stuff come out in like April or May? Like right before graduation, right? Wait, will we have to look at every single paper?"

She pulled open a drawer to reveal a long row of cardboard boxes, each one carefully labeled with about a month's worth of Marshall Chronicle microfiche.

"Well *we* won't have to, but yes, *you* will. The good thing is you probably only need to look at April and May, and it's a small paper, so you're talking about like three, maybe four pages total for each day. Here it is," she said, handing him a box. "I bet it will go faster than you think. You know how to use this?"

"Yeah, I'm good."

"All right, let me know if you need anything." She got about four steps away before she turned back to him and stopped. "Andy? Are you sure you want to do this? I mean, it was a loooong time ago. And, just, it's hard to see, if you do find her, how that works out, really. I'm just wondering, is all. Are you sure?"

"Oh yeah," he said, shaking his head. "It's totally casual. Just, you know, trying to figure out what happened and all. You know, just— I was curious, I guess. Curious, right?"

"Yeah, I guess," she said. "Sometimes moving on is good, too. Sometimes."

As they stood there awkwardly, he remembered that they had dated once – just one date – but it was too goofy. What was that, like, sophomore year? They were already friends and hung out all the time, so it seemed like a natural, but when they actually went out, it felt all weird, like they were acting. In fact, she might have even said something like that, like "I feel like we're in a play about two people dating." It was even weirder at her front door, until finally she had ended the scene by kissing him on the cheek and then slamming the door in his face, and neither one ever brought it up again. Huh, he thought, weird that he would remember that all of the sudden. What is this, flashback week? I gotta get my head straight.

The room full of microfiche readers was huge, and there were at least 20 other people in there, but it was even darker than the stacks, making the people inside just shadows in front of the glowing machines.

He found an empty machine and had already begun threading the film through the reels when he realized it was no ordinary microfiche reader – it was connected to a computer, so he could scan the image, print it out on a regular computer printer, or even save it to a disk or email it.

Less than an hour later, he had it. The Marshall Chronicle had indeed published an entire special section – four pages – on that year's graduating class, creatively entitled, "Class of '88." Ashley was in the Top 10:

"Ashley M. Hudson: No. 5, Honors Society, Cum Laude, Youth Advisory Council. Daughter of Barbara Hudson, 396 S. Mulberry Street, Marshall. Plans to attend Western Michigan University, Kalamazoo. Major: Undeclared."

Western Michigan? All those years, and she was just a few hours away, he thought. How many times did I wonder where she was, when I could have driven there in like three hours? Man.

He looked at a few more papers, but didn't see anything else. Still it was enough to get started.

But what then? Did her mom stay in Marshall? Did she go back there? If they would print anything – including the plans of every single member of the graduating class of Marshall High School – they probably print college graduations, too. Sure enough, there were a couple listed in that same Saturday edition: One girl had graduated from the University of Minnesota and was going to be a pharmacist in Findlay, Ohio. Man, they will print anything.

So he spent another hour going through the April and May editions from 1992 and then 1993, too, in case it took her five years to graduate, but there was nothing. If she graduated, she had no reason to have the news printed in the Marshall Chronicle, which meant she was no longer from there. Figures.

He put the reels of film back into their boxes, carried them to the return bin, then walked toward the front desk, his head reeling. What now?

"So how'd it go, Perry Mason?" Emma asked as he approached her station.

"Uh, good I guess. You were right – turns out she went to Western Michigan, up in Kalamazoo," he said, leaning against the counter and fingering a plastic mat that read "Allen County Public Library." "But that's all I can find. Now what?"

She stopped typing and rolled her big gray eyes toward that tiger-skin hat and squished up her face as she thought.

"Well, I'm pretty sure we don't have the Kalamazoo newspaper here in the collection. We have a few Michigan papers, but not that one. Even if we did, that's like a normal-sized paper, so looking through two months of them would take hours and hours," she said, then brightened, and almost seemed to hop a little. "You know what you could do? If you can go there, you know, go to Kalamazoo, you can go to the student newspaper on campus. They might have an electronic archive you can search, and if they don't, the campus library might. You might even be able to just ask around if you know what her major was. Heck, you might even get one of the reporters there to try to find her for you."

Go there? Something seemed to click.

"You know what else? While you're there, you could check with like the Alumni Association or whatever. They always do like alumni magazines and stuff that are full of things like, 'Bob Evans, business major, 1995, started a chain of restaurants and is now fabulously wealthy.' That would be huge."

Yeah, he could just go there. Make a road trip of it. Maybe take some time off work, heck he could take a few weeks off and just go wherever the trail leads him.

"Yeah," he said. "I could go there."

Emma shrugged. "Yeah, why not? Just go."

"Yeah, why not?" he said.

Why not?

If the Sunday family dinner was an important tradition for the Gardners, the Fort Wayne Philharmonic concerts were even more so, even if they were four times a year instead of weekly.

As far back as he could remember, Andy's parents had taken him and Sally to the symphony, and that had never changed. His dad was always trying to convince Sally that she and Steve should bring their kids, but they never did. For Andy, it was about the only time he got to wear his one suit, but this time he had a surprise for them.

As he walked toward the Embassy Theatre, he could see his parents staring the minute they spotted him. Of course, they weren't staring at him: It was Scarlett, stunning in a little black dress and on his arm. She looked perfect – heels that seemed a mile high, legs that seemed to stretch upward to her chin, a dress with a neckline that seemed to stretch down to her waist, and green eyes that shone under the marquee lights. And just when you were convinced she was the Philharmonic type, you spotted the tattoo on her shoulder, concealed just enough by the strap of her dress to make it that much more enticing.

"Mom, Dad? This is Scarlett King," Andy said. "Scarlett, these are my parents, Chuck and Paula."

"A real pleasure," Andy's dad said with a little too much sincerity. "Thank you for joining us."

"Scarlett, that dress is amazing," Paula said. "Where did you find it?"

Just then, Sally and Steve walked up.

"Where's the kids?" Chuck said. "It's important they go to things like this, Sally."

"Dad, this is like our one night out," she said. "Believe me, they hear lots of classical music."

Andy's dad turned back to Scarlett.

"And how about you, Scarlett? Are you a big Gustav Mahler fan?"

"I am," she said – to Andy's relief. "But I'm really more of a Rachmaninoff girl."

That got his attention almost as quickly as the little black dress.

"Rachmaninoff?" he said, pulling out the pack of season tickets, then taking her arm and starting for the door. "What is it about his works that stir you?"

That left Andy and his mother stranded on the sidewalk amidst the buses from the retirement homes dropping off old people under the marquee, so he took her arm and headed in. She smiled.

Suddenly, an evening with his parents didn't seem so bad.

Andy's parents gushed about the concert as the crowd surged through the lobby, but Scarlett was grabbing his arm.

"I'm hungry," she said. "Feed me."

Under the marquee, Andy's dad, who usually fussed over Sally, turned instead to Scarlett.

"Scarlett, I hope we'll be seeing you at a Sunday dinner soon?"

"Thank you, Chuck, that sounds wonderful," she said, extending her hand. "Maybe Andy will get around to asking me."

Sigh.

"Don't wait for him, my dear," Chuck said. "You can be my guest."

"OK, Dad, you've made you're point," Andy said. "We're going to get something to eat."

"Man, that sounds great," Sally said. "But we've got a sitter."

After his parents and Sally and Steve left, Andy turned to Scarlett.

"All right, Diva – where are we going?"

"You're going to laugh, but what I really want is Powers."

"Powers Hamburgers? Really?" Powers, like Coney Island, was another Fort Wayne institution. The place was a glorified hamburger stand, with seating for about 10 people, but they made the best sliders anywhere. One visit to Powers and you would smell like onions for days. "We're going to stand out a little dressed like this," he said, taking her arm.

"Oh, I know. But I need to have this dress dry cleaned anyway, so hopefully the onion smell will come out. It's worth it."

He leaned in to her curls and put his nose near her ear. "Mmmmm..." he said. "Onions..."

"You're a weirdo," she laughed.

It was only two blocks up to Powers, past the Botanical Conservatory and the federal courthouse, and the night was warm, with a cool breeze wafting the smell of hyacinths from the outdoor gardens. When he held her hand, she squeezed back.

Inside the little hamburger stand, the seats were largely empty except for two guys in blue workshirts and navy blue hats, on a break from somewhere. The smell of grilled onions was both intoxicating and overpowering. The lady behind the counter didn't give their clothes a second glance. "Here or to go?"

After ordering, they sat down in the one booth, and Andy looked at her. Even now, Scarlett seemed to be somewhat of a mystery.

"So tell me about growing up, your parents, what it was like being you," he said. "I feel like I hardly know you at all, even though, you know..."

"Well, half a life is kind of a lot to share in a few weeks, so maybe you don't know much about my past, but it doesn't seem like there's that much to tell," Scarlett said. "We lived in Marion; my dad worked at the GM plant and mom stayed home. I was a cheerleader, if you can believe it."

Andy tried to picture her in a cheerleading uniform, clapping in unison and chanting rhymes. He could see how it might have once made sense for her, but not today.

"That is a little hard to believe, actually."

"Yeah, well, it happened. I'm not necessarily proud of it, but I'm certainly not ashamed, either. It was fun at the time."

"See, I'm pretty much trying to forget everything I've ever done in my life," Andy laughed. "I'm all about being ashamed."

They both laughed, and the lady from behind the counter appeared with two steaming plates: four hamburgers for Scarlett and four cheeseburgers for Andy.

"Do you think that's why you avoid making decisions?" Scarlett said, not looking up from the mustard she was squirting on her burgers. "Like, maybe subconsciously, you're afraid that whatever you decide will be something you'll regret later?"

"Maybe," he said, taking the mustard. "Do you have any regrets? I mean, you seem so free and, I don't know, willing to cast your fate to the wind. Does that ever come back to slap you?"

"Sometimes. But that's the risk you take, Andy. And you have to take risks sometimes. I regret marrying Mike, obviously, but look at the payoff: I can't imagine life without Abby. She's part of who I am and that's incredible."

"You're both pretty incredible, actually."

"You know, you're going to make some bad decisions along the way. It happens. It's part of life, you know? But then you fix it and move on. I just figure, for most decisions, what have I really got to lose? My feelings get hurt? I'm disappointed? So what?"

Andy picked up a burger and started munching, the caramelized onions turning a simple, tiny cheeseburger into something extraordinary, and thought about what Scarlett had said. What did he have to lose? For the last seventeen years, it seems that he always had *everything* to lose. Maybe that was part of the problem: The stakes were always too high.

"So," he said between bites. "Tell me about Mike. He just took off, but then came back and demanded visitation?"

Scarlett finished her bite and took a drink of lemonade.

"Yeah, honestly, and I'm not trying to sound like the bitter ex-wife here, but he's not dealing with it well. It's like, not bi-polar, really, but it's like he goes back and forth between wanting everything – including our marriage – and wanting nothing to do with any of it. Like some days I swear he would take me back in a heartbeat and others I think he'd just as soon beat the crap out of me."

"Wait, does he— ? Has he ever—?"

"No, nothing like that," Scarlett shook her head. "But he is drinking more and more – which scares me with Abby, though he promises he doesn't drink around her at all. It's just that he's so angry. Like I've never seen anyone that angry."

"Angry at you?"

"Well, it seems like that, but he's probably more angry at himself than anything. He's the one who couldn't deal and left. So he's really got no one else to be angry at."

She took a thoughtful bite, then continued.

"The weird thing is, I'm angry too. Like irrationally angry," she said. "I don't even know why, but the instant I see him now, I just go into a full-on rage. It doesn't make any sense."

But Andy was stuck on Mike being angry at himself. It was bad enough when you took things out on others. But when you turned it on yourself, there was really only two ways for it to go. One slowly ate you away until it felt like there was nothing left. Andy knew all about that. The other, though, was like a bomb, ticking away the seconds, with every one taking you closer to the inevitable.

"I don't know," Scarlett said, looking at her burgers. "Things could be fine, or at least well enough, between us, but then I go off the handle and say things that rile him up. The worst part is, I know I shouldn't do it because it's poisoning whatever relationship Abby has with him. Maybe that's why he's so angry — because something in me just insists on torturing him. Even I don't get it."

"Hey, I meant to ask you. What was with that newspaper page in your kitchen when we were there?" Scarlett asked. "It looked like you had saved it for something, but there were no stories, just little— those little three-paragraph news nugget things."

The noise of the cicadas in the early darkness was intense, but they found after a while that they could talk over the buzz around the new charcoal grill in her backyard. Soon, the rise and fall of their stereophonic pitch was like a soundtrack to their words as they drank beers and digested the hamburgers Andy had grilled on her shiny Weber.

"One of the items was about the cicadas," he said. "See there's regular cicadas, that you get like every year, right? Then there's these ones that only come out every seventeen years. And this is the year."

"Is there any difference between them? Besides the seventeen-year thing, I mean?"

"I don't know. I just know a little bit about these seventeen-year ones," he said. Do I ever. "See, there's a bunch of different batches of them, called broods, and like every year or couple of years one of the broods hatches. But this one, the one that's coming out this summer, is the biggest. It's monster. They were saying that some places will have like a million cicadas per acre. It's called Brood X, or I guess Ten or whatever. That's why they're so loud – this is practically historic."

"Holy crap," Scarlett said, and took a long pull on the beer. "A million an acre? That's a lot of bugs. So these same ones came out seventeen years ago?"

"Something like that. No, I think they were laid as eggs seventeen years ago, then hatched and lived underground for seventeen years and now they're coming out to lay eggs for the next batch," he said. One fantastic bug orgy for a summer, he thought, and then seventeen years of being buried. Jesus.

"So when I was like a freshman in high school, these guys were just being born, and ever since, they've been underground, waiting to mate and lay eggs?" Scarlett asked. "Hey, you want a smoke? I could use one. So where were you seventeen years ago?"

"Well, yeah, see that's kind of the thing," he said as she handed him one of her amazing hand-rolled cigarettes. He wasn't going to tell her, but those green eyes were burrowing into him, waiting for an answer. "I was seventeen, just finished my junior year, and there was this girl…" He took a long drag, then blew the smoke out toward the hi-fi orgy in the yard. "We had this amazing summer, and then one day, poof, she was gone."

He laughed, but Scarlett didn't. So he went on, talking like some idiot. "I know, right? Crushed my will to live and all that, yada yada. Anyway, it was like she showed up with these crazy seventeen-year cicadas, and then disappeared at the end of the summer when they did. And I never saw her again."

Scarlett stopped staring at him long enough to take her own long drag on the smoke, and then looked at him again.

"What was her name?"

"Uh, Ashley. Ashley Hudson," he said. "Why, you know her?"

"Oh my God," she said. "Oh. My. God! That is why I love boys. It doesn't matter what kind of horn-dog, one-night-stand loving asshole they are, they never, ever get over the first girl they have sex with. I'm not saying you're a horn-dog whatever, but she was your first, wasn't she?"

His only answer was another drag on the cigarette.

"I knew it! And you never, *ever* got over her, did you? See, that's why boys are so sweet. If you wonder what women like about men, that's it. Right there. Mmmph."

She sucked on her own cigarette in triumph. "That's very sweet, Andy."

"Yeah, I know, I know, it sounds all puppy love and stupid and, you know what? It is. I know that. It's just— And I'm not saying you're— I just. Hell, I don't know. All I know is she showed up one summer, made everything, just – well, she made me. I mean, it was like I was just a collection of parts before and then she created something out of that. And then, she just, I don't know, she … evaporated."

"Wait a minute. And then seventeen years later I show up? Is that what you're saying?"

"Yeah, something like that," he said, looking down at the cigarette. "I don't know. I don't, OK? All I know is that nothing was the same after her. Until now, at least. Maybe it was whatever you were saying because she was my first love or it was just all in my head, or whatever, but—"

"So what happened to her? People don't just disappear. She broke up with you or what?"

He got up to get two more beers out of the cooler Scarlett had set on her patio. "No, I'm telling you she disappeared. Her and her mom lived around the corner from us – my parents – right? They were renting this house. And then on Labor Day, the day before school was going to start, I go over there and the place is cleaned out. Empty. Just – gone."

"Well," she said, tipping back her beer. "I don't plan on evaporating any time soon. I have a daughter and a mortgage."

"No, I wasn't trying to say that," he said. "And I'm not trying to put anything heavy on whatever this is between us or anything. I was just trying to figure out all that crap I was talking about that day at Coney Island, about not having any hope, and then I remembered this, and it all kind of fell into place."

She sat back in her chair and just looked at him.

"Wait a minute. So never mind that you got married and divorced, you think that everything sucks because of this girl that disappeared seventeen years ago?" She sat up, and then sat back again.

Now he sat back. He wanted to cross his arms, but knew it would make him look defensive.

"That does sound kind of stupid, doesn't it? I guess all I'm saying is that summer fucked me up somehow, and it seemed to fuck everything up afterward. From getting married to …everything. And all I know is that I'm tired of everything being fucked up. It seems like the one thing in my life that hasn't been screwed up was the last few weeks since you showed up. Or, at least it wasn't screwed up until I started talking tonight."

Over the drone of the cicadas came yet another cicada sound –

instead of a long note that dipped in pitch every few seconds, this was short notes in pairs, like a pair of maracas, easily cutting through the din.

Scarlett stubbed out her smoke and looked at him again.

"Is there anything in your life you don't regret, Andy?" she said. "You're great, and this is great and I'm not saying everything's not great, but it just seems like you are one giant ball of regret. I think the only thing you don't regret is letting me in that day, and sometimes I'm not even sure about that."

When you're really sailing, you hardly feel the wind, because you're traveling with it. But when the wind suddenly dies, and the sails fall slack, it's like the whole world has stopped, not just you. Or maybe it is just you, and the entire planet continues to spin around you while you are dead in the water.

"No, you're probably right. I regret not trying to find her, I regret letting it do what it did to me, I regret, well, pretty much everything that's happened in my life afterward. I regret getting married — hell, I regret getting divorced, even though there was no choice. Maybe I do regret everything," he said, "except letting you in. I don't regret that."

At least, he didn't regret it until he read the damn newspaper that had been laying in his yard for like three days, like a land mine just waiting for some dumb ass to step on it and blow his own legs off. And even then, it wasn't so much regret as it was just that well, it made this whole thing complicated. Pain he understood. Pain in the midst of those eyes surrounded by soft brown freckles surrounded by mounds of brown curls, surrounded by—

"So I'm the first good thing in your life in seventeen years?" she laughed. "Thanks for laying that burden on me. No pressure, Scarlett, but by the way, if you're not perfect I'll probably kill myself…"

Now he was laughing, too.

"And don't forget the bugs," he said. "I believe that if you read between the lines properly I probably called you a seventeen-year cicada. You ever seen one of those things?"

"No, but if they're anything like they sound…"

He put out his smoke. "You got a flashlight?"

When they finally found a cicada – following the sound should have been easy, but instead it was like trying to find a single jet engine in a darkened symphony hall full of them running full blast – the thing stared back at them with its giant red eyes on blue-black skin. And it was big. Huge, for an insect, really – an inch and-a-half long, with a fat head and giant wings.

"The eyes look like those candy dots that come on the strips of paper you lick off," Scarlett said.

"Oh man, I remember those," he said, holding the light on the startled and now silent insect. "And look at those wings – they look fake, like if you decided, 'OK, I'm going to take some Styrofoam and plastic and make insect wings,' that's what they'd look like."

They watched the cicada for a while, then walked back to the patio.

"Is there anything that eats them?" Scarlett asked. "I sure as hell wouldn't."

"Oh yeah, birds and stuff do. Anything that eats big bugs, I guess," he said. "When I was growing up, the dog next door would eat so many of them it would throw up."

There was one other thing that preyed on cicadas, he remembered. But he tried to push that out of his mind, and didn't mention it. He didn't mention it when he said good night the first time, and he didn't mention it when he said good night the second time and walked back home, down three doors and across the street, the streetlight creating a weird, yellow-orange halo on her unruly curls as she stood on her porch watching him go. No, the real enemy of the cicada was something he didn't want to think about at all.

SEVEN

"The phenomenon connected with the transformation of the periodical Cicada from the pupal to the adult stage is a very interesting one and always fills the observer with considerable wonderment. When these insects emerge from the ground it is usually with a rush, and a lively scramble ensues for each elevation near the point of their emergence. Trees, bushes, weeds, poles, stumps, fences; in fact, everything upon which they can get above the level of their recent homes is ascended. The instinct which has caused them to burrow to the surface of the ground still drives them in the same direction upward, and they seem to make up for their long subterranean periods and their weeks of waiting near the surface in activity when the time has finally arrived for their emergence."

—"The Periodical Cicada"

"Let's go to Mo's," Ashley says. "We can dance there."

Andy has to think for a minute to remember where Mo's is.

"Isn't that a bar? Can we even go in there?"

"Yeah, it's that place across the river from Foster Park," Ashley says. "I found it the other day when you were at work."

It's Sunday afternoon, so Andy can use the car, but they're still on his parents' front porch, in the porch swing, deciding what to do. It doesn't help that it's raining, and their usual fallback activities of just riding around or going to a park are out. Still, he's on the front porch swing with Ashley, and she's wearing lavender corduroys and a purple plaid button shirt and the sight of her lower neck is driving him crazy. He has spent a lot of time kissing her neck but feels like he's just getting started on getting to know the territory. He can't even think about trailblazing some kisses onto the new ground below her collar, but damn if it doesn't look inviting. Outside the porch, the rain falls lightly, but it's through a weird light from the sun coming through rain clouds. There's thunder, but it's far off in the distance, and even the rain is sporadic at times. They hold hands as he moves his legs just the minimum to keep the swing going. Turns out, even doing nothing with Ashley is better than doing something with anyone else.

"So what are you going to do with your life?" he says. "You know, long term?"

"I dunno. College, I guess, but I hadn't really thought about it. I don't really know if I can. We probably can't afford it, you know?"

Andy seems much more worried about her future than she does as she points her toes in the air while they swing.

"What? You have to go to college. Haven't you applied anywhere yet? You at least took your SATs, right?"

"Oh yeah, I took those in the spring. But, you know, I didn't know where to send the scores or anything because it's not like I've picked a college or anything. I don't even know what I want to do."

She's taken her shoes off, and she has long toes, with the tiniest hints of blonde hair on them. Her toenails are purple.

"Oh man, my parents have had me doing campus visits since freshman year," he says. "They've got it all mapped out for me, it seems like. You know, they act like it's all up to me, but it's pretty clear what choice they think is the 'right' one. And the 'right' one is Princeton, in New Jersey."

"At least you've got someone to do that for you," Ashley says. "I'm not complaining, but, you know, long-term stuff is not really my mom's best talent, you know?"

It hurts a little that she didn't say anything about the fact that in just over a year he would be moving to New Jersey, but he lets it go.

"Yeah, hey listen, I know this sounds weird, but you know who you should talk to? Mr. McFrederick at North Side. He's one of the guidance counselors, and I know that sounds really lame because most guidance counselors are like 800-year-old people who don't know how to talk to kids, but Mr. McFrederick is not like most guidance counselors. He's really cool."

"OK, yeah, whatever," she says. "If you say he's cool, he must really be awesome."

"Why, because most of the adults I know are complete geeks?"

"Well, yeah," she says. "But you know, I meet a lot of geeks who are cool, too."

It sometimes frightens him the way Ashley is so fearless. She explores the city when he's not around. She meets people. She talks to them. Heck, she charms them and they want to do her favors. They walk in to places and she seems to know everyone there, and they act like they've just been waiting for her to come back. Good-looking girls just don't do that. Even at Mass, she seems to fit right in, though she's not Catholic. She had gone with his family again this morning, and he had spent most of the hour attempting to concentrate on the sacraments and trying not to remember how amazing she looked in those lavender pants walking the six blocks to church. Even the priest knew her somehow, greeting her by name as they left the sanctuary, while Andy, who had gone there since birth, seemed to be an afterthought.

"You know, you scare me some times," he says.

"What?"

"Just the way you're not afraid of anything. The way you'll just walk up to people and talk to them. The way you'll do anything. I can't do that," he says. "At least, I couldn't before. Now, well, I'm still scared, but with you I do it anyway."

Of course, it also thrills him that she enjoys such freedom – the way roller coasters both scare and thrill. And the rewards don't hurt at all: When they're done gushing over her, they look at him. And they realize he's with her. And Andy Gardner, who had always felt invisible before, is suddenly The Man.

"Who says I'm not scared of anything?"

"You don't act like it."

"Just because I don't act like it doesn't mean I'm not," she says, and turns to face him. "I was scared to walk up and talk to you the first time we met."

"Why? I was covered with sweat and grass clippings. Plus, you know, it's just me."

She looks down at their enmeshed hands.

"You don't get it do you?" she says.

"Get what?"

She leans to him and puts her mouth up to his ear, then hesitates just for a moment as every nerve in his body seems to stand on tiptoe and the hair on his neck seems to be electrified.

Then she whispers. "I'm falling in love with you, Andrew James."

He wants to look her in the eye. He wants to tell her he has loved her since the moment he first saw her. He wants to say he loves her elbows and the freckle at the corner of her mouth, and the way she never looks in mirrors. He wants to say things that are profound and meaningful and find some way, some words to express the emotions he feels. But she holds him still, her mouth still in his ear, her breath hot on his neck, and so he squeezes her tight, hoping that will somehow convey the feelings a book full of words could not. Finally, he pulls back and looks at her, but it looks like she's about to cry.

"Hey, what's the matter?" he says. Oh God, what did I do now?

Then she's back in his ear.

"I'm just scared," she whispers. "I'm falling in love with you, and I'm so scared."

Mo's is far from busy as they burst through the door out of the rain.

Andy's never been here – he's not sure if they even legally can be here – but Ashley's leading him by the hand, and he would follow her anywhere.

The entryway is painted black, like it's a backstage area or something, though one wall is deep red. Then it opens to the bar, which is in a wide open space with a huge, raised ceiling that peaks over a wooden dance floor. Here, the walls are red, but one is dominated by huge windows over-looking the river. The opposite wall has a bunch of equipment for live bands, but the weirdest thing is the peaked ceiling over the dance floor is covered with mirrors, like it's a disco. It's like the place can't decide whether it's a Nordic-architecture dance club, seedy dive, or upscale restaurant with a view. The smell, however, is pure seedy dive.

The place is empty except for one older couple at the bar, and the bartender leaning over the bar talking to them.

"Hey, Mo!" Ashley yells to him.

The bartender straightens up and throws a towel over his shoulder.

"Hey sweetie," he says. "Who's this with ya?" He looks at Andy like he's some kind of underage kid trying to sneak into the place, but as soon as he sees Ashley holding his hand he seems to relax.

"It's my boyfriend, Andy. Is it OK if we dance?" Andy hoped the answer was "yes," since she had already dragged him to the middle of the dance floor and was continuing straight over to the juke box.

The couple at the bar turns around. "No, no dancing!" the guy says, and he seems to be only partly joking. "He raises the price of beer when people dance."

Ashley stops and puts one hand on her hip. "Mo!"

"What? House rules. What do you care anyway? You ain't drinkin',"

"Still," she says, then addresses the couple: "Get your orders in now, I guess. It'll take me a few minutes to pick out some songs anyway."

The man looks at Mo and orders two more while Ashley turns to the jukebox.

"Your boyfriend, huh?" Andy says as she looks over the list and immediately starts punching in songs.

"Why, don't you want to be?" He could die every time he hears that sigh in her voice.

"Maybe I do," he says, pointing to a couple songs of his own. The glass of the jukebox is warm. "Maybe I just never got a chance to officially ask you."

"Gimme some money," she says. "Never got a chance? We hang out almost every day. What were you waiting for? A full moon on a Tuesday and angels in the sky?"

He gives her a dollar from his wallet.

"Maybe I was waiting to make sure you were going to say yes."

The music starts thumping out of the jukebox and she drags him out to the dance floor, then switches to her dreamy voice: "Oh Andy, you're so sweet, and kind, and gentlemanly, and stupid."

He puts his arms around her waist as Crowded House starts to sing, and returns the dreamy voice. "And you, Ashley, are so beautiful and sweet and angelic and— and demonic."

She smiles and pulls him closer, her arms wrapped around his neck, until he pulls back slightly, then dips his chin so he can look at her with puppy eyes. Even her earrings match today: Purple stones on gold studs.

"Ashley Marie Hudson? Will you be my girlfriend?"

She plays it up like she's in the high-school production of a classic drama.

"Oh, yes, Andrew Gardner. Oh, yes!"

"To have and to hold? To take to the movies?"

"Oh, yes!"

"To make out with as often as possible?"

"Oh, yes!"

They dissolve into laughter as the song continues, and he can feel her body pressing against him, the occasional brush of her shoes against his as they shuffle on the wood floor, her knees, her thighs and hips warm and that mysterious combination of both strong and soft at the same time, her belly flat until it gets to her chest, where she seems to be pressing even harder into him. "Hey now, heeeeeeeeey now," he whispers to her along with the song. "Don't dream it's over…" and all of it, the dance floor, the couple at the bar, Mo's, the summer that's going by way too fast already, all of it just fades away until there is nothing left but him and Ashley, pressing close, swaying to the music and wanting it to last forever.

"You know," he says into her ear. "You don't have to be scared of me. I'm not going anywhere."

She doesn't say anything for a while, just holds him tight, but seems unhappy that he's broken the moment by bringing that up again.

"It's not you I'm scared of Andy," she says. "I'm just scared of what's going to happen to us."

"What's going to happen to us? What could happen? We've got all summer, and when school starts, we'll be in school together. And once we graduate, we can do whatever we want. We can go to the same college, whatever," he says. "Don't you get it? It's like we finally found each other, after waiting all our lives, and you're already worried about how it ends? This is where it all starts!"

They let the music talk for them while they sway to the hypnotic organ in the song.

"It's not that," she says finally. "It's just, you know, what if we move again? My mom has a habit of, well, losing her job. And we have to eat. So we move to where there's another job, you know? What if that happens?" She stops dancing, and just looks at him, her arms still around his neck. "I can't lose you now, Andy."

Andy starts them dancing again and kisses her cheek.

"You're not losing me," he says. "Don't even think like that. Besides—" Now he stops and looks at her. "Besides. Worst case scenario here. And I mean worst-case, right? Worst case is you move away and we finish our senior years at separate high schools. As soon as we graduate, bam! We're back together again. You can move here, stay with us until college starts, or I'll move there, get a job and an apartment. Then we go to school. And we're together. You can go to New Jersey, too. Or I'll go wherever you go."

By now, the song has ended and another one has started, but they don't even seem to notice what Whitney Houston is belting out.

"I don't know," she says. "I mean, that sounds great, but—"

"But nothing," he says. "You think a little thing like distance can separate us? Besides," he says as they start moving to the music again. "You of all people, worrying about the future? You're like some sort of, I don't know, like those Zen guys that only live in the moment, or a female Holden Caulfield or something. You never worry about stuff, and you're worried about what might happen to us in a year?"

"Did you know I love that book?"

"Everyone loves that book," he says. "It's just not cool to admit it because the book's too perfect. Everyone identifies with it, so no one wants to be caught identifying with it. Liking it is too cliché. Which makes no sense if you think about it – a book about being alone in the universe and feeling that no one understands you is universally accepted by everyone who ever reads it, so everyone continues to be alone so they don't look like everyone else."

She's laughing out loud at him now.

"You're like, that, have you ever seen that Woody Allen movie, 'Love and Death'? Where they go on and on about philosophy and stuff and end up in un-winnable arguments with themselves?" she says. "You're just like that."

"Now I'm Woody Allen?" he says. "If you thought I had a complex before…"

"Buy me a Coke?"

"Maybe in a minute," he says. Hell, you're her boyfriend. Go for it. "When the song's over. I like the way you feel pressed up against me."

78

There's that devil smile again. "Yeah?"

"Yeah."

"Well then, how's this?" and she scrunches even closer so that he's laughing.

"Almost good enough," he says. "Come on, you thirsty little chicken."

"Lemme drive," she says as they stumble out into the bright sun of the parking lot. It's stopped raining, and the sun is out, sparkling off the dripping trees and the mud puddles and Andy's mom's car.

"OK. You've got a license, right?"

"I know how to drive," she says, and gets behind the wheel of the maroon Dodge Omni while Andy gets in the passenger side.

She starts the car, and then cranks the radio. She usually reaches over from the passenger seat and turns it loud, but now she's really cranking it. They both buckle up and she tosses her hair before putting the car in reverse.

And then she guns it.

The car lurches backward so violently Andy's seatbelt locks up, but she's on the brake quickly, mashing it to the floor almost has hard has she had hit the gas.

"Whoa!" she says, and shifts it into drive, then mashes the gas down to the floor again.

This time the car leaps forward toward the traffic on four-lane Bluffton Road, and Andy's stomach is in his throat. "Oh, God," he says involuntarily, but before they reach the street, she's stomping on the brake again, this time with both feet.

They both sit silently for a second, the car's little engine still winding down from its sudden ass-kicking. Is she crazy? Drunk? Just a really bad— no maybe the worst driver ever?

"Maybe you should drive," she says, looking at him sweetly.

"Uh, and I'm going to swear here, just so you know, but what the fuck was that?" It's taken a while, but he's finally sweating.

She laughs like she did the first day she met him, when she offered him lemonade she didn't actually have.

"Well, I've watched a lot of people drive and it looked really easy, so I figured, I'd just, you know, do it, and it would work out," she says. Then gives him her sheepish look. "Maybe you'll teach me?"

"Oh my God," he says. "Oh my God. You know my life passed before my eyes? You're in there worrying about next year, and I'm out here thinking I'm going to die in the next 5 seconds. You don't know how to drive? At all?"

"Well…"

"Well, I guess that was a pretty stupid question, given that you just turned Mo's parking lot into the Indy 500," he says. "Give me the keys."

They could just change seats without shutting off the car and taking the keys out, but Andy is still trying to catch his breath and frankly wants nothing more than to see the keys safely out of the ignition. So she puts the car in park, turns it off, takes out the keys and gets out of the driver's seat, while he gets out of the passenger seat. They meet near the hood ornament, and as the sun slants toward evening, she's the most beautiful girl he's ever seen.

She holds out the keys.

"Thank you," he says, reaching for them, but she snatches them back and drops them down the front of her shirt.

"Oops," she says. "Where'd they go?"

Nearly kissing on the couch in his living room with his mother 10 feet away was one thing. Now they're in the middle of a parking lot on Bluffton Road and she's got his keys down her shirt. He's either going to have to kill her or marry her; there's just no in-between.

He steps toward her and raises one eyebrow, then deftly reaches with his left hand for the bottom of her shirt, pulling it out from where it's tucked into her pants, then grabs the keys as they fall out the bottom with his right hand.

He holds them up and winks. "Now," he says, "let me show you how to drive."

In his dream, Ashley is lying next to him and they're not even kissing, she's just there in the way being there in dreams means so much more than it does in real life. He can feel the warmth of her skin near his, feel her breathing and—

"Andy!"

He opens eyes he hadn't realized were closed and becomes aware that Ashley is lying next to him, in the grass, on the blanket they had spread out in a sunny spot on a hill at Shoaff Park, overlooking the road and the trees and the river, and the sky had seemed to stretch out before them as they ate and talked.

"I can't believe you fell asleep," she says, and she's laughing again and as he sits up and yawns it occurs to him that this moment, this feeling, this everything is not just like a movie, but just the opposite. Movies are an attempt to be just like this. People go to movies so they can have this, even if it's only pretend, even if it's only for a while, even if they have to pay for it and leave the theater wishing it would never end.

"I can't believe you fell for me," he says, and he's staring into her eyes and he means it. Her eyes aren't just blue, they're a hundred shades of blue, like a thousand different blue shards arranged in a perfect pattern around her pupils.

"You know," she says, "if you stare into someone's eyes, you can see their heart."

"Yeah?" He looks again, stares as deeply as he can into the blackness at the center of her eyes, but all he can see, floating on the surface, is his reflection.

"All I see is me," he says before he understands.

"Exactly."

EIGHT

It is high summer, when the trees soar and the breeze is slow, the grass deep, and the world is exploding with life. Every square inch seems to be crawling with something, and the inches themselves are alive – tree bark and plant root and soil. Even the inanimate feels the flow of energy, as vinyl siding expands with the heat of the day and contracts in the cool, asphalt fills its own cracks, and ice cream seems bent on escape from the confines of a cone. Children explode across the landscape, and tired adults find new life, discovering both vast reserves of energy and a deeper lust for rest.

Quiet in the middle of this teeming, swarming world lies the egg, small and white, nestled carefully into an incision made into a twig on a tree branch, high above the ground. There is nothing to distinguish it from any of the nearly 600 identical eggs nearby, or the thousands within the locust tree that branch stretches from, or the millions in the branches on the trees lining this city block, or the billions in this neighborhood or the trillions that make up this brood, a community scientists have decided to call Brood X despite names meaning nothing to the brood itself.

The locust tree stands 50 feet tall, its feet hemmed in on one side by street, on the other by sidewalk, with only a narrow strip of grass to itself. Still, it reaches high, its branches arching upward and outward, its leaves a cluster of tiny green flakes on a stem reminiscent of a palm frond. It reaches over the dense, deep foliage of a maple in the boulevard, but seems willing to share its airspace with a similar locust in front of the same house. The two were planted at the same time, after disease killed the elms that had grown there, and seem almost to be a matched pair.

In their upper canopy, the sky seems bluer, the breeze more fragrant, while the noise of the traffic below is clearer but now separated by distance and seems to have less effect.

A closer look at the branches shows curious wounds – slits cut into the bark of the twigs. Like a dugout canoe, the twig seems to wrap around the eggs, its skin sliced open by a female cicada eight weeks earlier.

But today, the relative quiet in the treetops ends for the cicada egg.

The day before, one or two of the eggs began hatching, today there will be hundreds. Tomorrow, a few stragglers, and the sliced open twigs of the tree will begin to heal.

There are two dozen eggs in this two-inch long slit, and all of them will hatch today. The third one from the end opens in late morning, just as the sun rays burst through an opening in the canopy above and warm the branch. Coming out of the egg is a yellowish-white nymph, just one sixteenth-of-an inch long, looking a bit like a tiny, white lobster that has grown straggly hair. It stretches its newly released legs for the first time, pausing for a moment in the sun, as if it is catching its breath before heading out into the world. The pause does not last long: After just a few seconds, the nymph begins running wildly up and down the branch, where upon it almost immediately falls to Earth.

The fall – about thirty feet – would be disastrous to the human body. To an insect of this size, the distance is equivalent to falling a mile, straight down. But the cicada nymph is so small and so light, its fall is cushioned by the air itself. It descends like a feather to the grass below.

Immediately, the nymph begins searching the ground for any opening or crevice, but it can make its own if needed. This one finds a crack in the dirt where the grass meets the sidewalk. It has no idea what a sidewalk is and no reason to care either way, it just knows it needs to get underground and immediately burrows down into the crack in the dirt, digging a tunnel down, down, down almost two feet, tearing away the earth in its way using those lobster-claw-like front legs as shovels. Its journey downward is the human equivalent of digging a hole thirty-eight stories deep, but finally, it finds what it is looking for: a tree root.

Not just any root, of course, but a rootlet – the tree root equivalent of a twig. When it finds the rootlet, it stabs the rootlet with its sharp, sucking mouthparts and begins to draw out sap.

It will feed on this rootlet for the next seventeen years.

On this day, it feeds on the sap until its strength has returned from its tunneling and then returns to work. Only this time, instead of digging out the tunnel, it is closing it up, sealing itself into a tiny chamber, empty except for itself and the rootlet. Unless the chamber floods or is damaged somehow or the rootlet dies, this will be home for almost two decades. It is smooth and nearly round, it will not change except to get bigger as the cicada does.

The cicada nymph feeds the rest of that warm summer and into the fall. Even as fall turns to winter and the sap stops running, the nymph continues to draw sustenance from the rootlet: Its needs are so small and the amount it takes is so minute as its metabolism slows with the cold that whatever sap remains in the rootlet during the winter months is more than enough to sustain it until spring.

In that first spring, however, a change begins: Within his hard, outer shell, his body underneath is beginning to transform. Slowly, away from light and air and everything except the rootlet, the nymph has become something different. Finally, his body seems to withdraw entirely from his exoskeleton until it becomes a suit he can simply remove instead of an integral skin. When he emerges from it, he is slightly changed – larger, and less worm like, but not much.

Once his new exoskeleton dries, he returns to the rootlet and begins feeding again, drawing out life from the tiny tree branch and waiting for the next change. That will come in two years, and another one will come two years after that. There will be a fourth change three years later, and yet another nine years after that.

With each shedding of the skin, a transformed insect emerges from beneath, the way a born-again Christian emerges from his old shell of sinfulness in a baptismal river. Five times he will change, dramatic leaps as he evolves into something far larger, and far different than the tiny worm-like creature that emerged from the egg.

And while he waits for each change, the world revolves around his tiny chamber. Presidents come and go. Loves are lost. Children are born and die too young. Old people live on long after they wish they could stop. Careers change, and change again. Entire industries disappear and new ones form. Corporate titans rise to power and are thrown down. Millions become billions; dollars become pennies. Niagara Falls moves closer toward Lake Erie. The Grand Canyon gets deeper in some places, filled in in others.

And still the cicada waits.

The rootlet he sucks on is attached to a root, attached to a trunk that pushes out of the earth and rises nearly five stories into the air. By the time his waiting is done, the tree will have grown another ten feet, produced and lost more than three million leaves and added seventeen rings to its girth. The sidewalk it grows next to, where the nymph found a crack in the dirt and began its burrow, will be heaved upward another two inches by the tree's growth as it pushes its way through the soil.

For seventeen years, he will wait.

The Civil Rights movement needed only twelve years to go from a local bus boycott in Montgomery, Alabama, to a national movement, to see a Nobel Prize for Peace, enactment of the Civil Rights Act, the Voting Rights Act, and the martyrdom of Martin Luther King Jr. The cicada will wait in its underground chamber through all of that upheaval and half a decade more before his time comes.

Seasons come, seasons go. Seventeen summers he waits. Seventeen winters. Sixteen springs.

Finally, in the seventeenth spring, something awakens in him and his uncounted brethren spread across fifteen states, from New Jersey to Illinois and from Michigan to Georgia. What the call is, how they just seem to know, is a mystery that has evaded humans since the creature was discovered more than three hundred years ago.

Whatever the trigger, the cicada breaks out of his chamber and begins digging toward the surface. Once there, he digs an opening but does not emerge. If the ground is wet, he will even construct a small mud cone around the opening to keep the water out of his tunnel. But still he waits just below ground, seeming to anticipate yet another signal.

Finally, on one night in May or early June, they emerge all at once. Billions of cicadas come out of the earth and begin to climb on whatever they can find, seemingly driven to get as far away from the soil as possible. No other creature on the planet is so synchronized.

But the insect that emerges from the ground is a far cry from the tiny bug that entered it seventeen years before. This one is nearly two inches long, and looks much like a brown, wingless beetle with huge eyes and legs meant for climbing. At least for now.

This one happens to find the same locust tree he hatched in and fell out of seventeen years ago and begins crawling up the trunk. After climbing about a foot, he stops and his final transformation begins.

He sets his climbing claws deep into the bark so they cannot let go and his skin – a brown, translucent shell now – cracks down his spine as he arches his back. He arches farther and farther, until his head begins to pull out of the shell, followed by his front legs. Soon, he is halfway out of his old exoskeleton; a soft, white cicada emerging from a now dusty, useless brown husk. He is milky white except for his shocking red eyes.

In about an hour, he is free and again transformed. No longer a juvenile nymph, he is now a fully-formed adult complete with something he never needed in his long years underground: Wings.

He again begins climbing, searching for a place to take cover amongst the leaves while his new skin hardens and his wings dry. Once there, he waits again, for up to six days while his new shell forms into a built-in armor. He will feed occasionally – sticking his sharp mouth into twigs to draw sap – but mostly he just waits.

Finally, on the sixth day, he knows his moment is close. For the first time, he spreads his wings, and flies a little – clumsy, erratic flight where he knocks into branches and the tree trunk and even a person on the sidewalk below, but after nearly two decades in a two-inch mud chamber, it is more glorious than any soaring eagle has ever felt. After a little while, he returns to the tree, eats a little and waits for dusk.

For today, even as he leaped into the air and felt himself carried upon the arms of the wind, he felt yet a new stirring inside him: Something much more powerful than the need to molt and break out of his old skin, more intense than the summons to come up from underground. It was a need that has brought down the powerful and lifted the humble, a call from across the millennia he could not ignore.

He needed to mate.

In his tiny insect brain, he has no idea what mating is. He does not feel a longing for love. He has no knowledge of romance, intimacy or even just raw, animal sex.

But he is filled, consumed with the need to find a female cicada.

For seventeen years he waited underground. Sixty-eight seasons came and went while he waited. He has transformed and left his old casing behind six times. He has grown twenty-four times larger than the nymph that left the egg. The sun has traveled more than 300 million miles in its orbit around the center of the Milky Way while he waited and grew.

But this moment, this time, this identity was what he was waiting for and working toward all those years, this moment, when he would find a female and continue the cycle.

Just behind his head and shoulders sit what appear to be ribbed plates. They are like corrugated drums, attached to muscles, and when those muscles flex, it creates a sound like the one made when you flex a dent in an old metal pan. Beneath these drums in his thorax are huge sound chambers, like that of a guitar, for amplifying the noise created. There is one on each side of him, for each drum, plus a third that serves both. Within these sound chambers, amplifying the resonance even further, are disks he can move to modify the notes.

The cicada lifts his head into the night air, and smells the clover mixed in with the grass, the last of the tulips as their once-gorgeous blooms now droop and begin to rot, the heavy, heady scent of hyacinths that line the driveway nearby. He can sense there are hundreds of his brethren nearby, each of them feeling the same yearning, each with the same understanding of what it means to wait, wait day after day, year after year for one moment, one perfect, gorgeous summer moment as the sun sets and the trees change from shade to shadow to near black in the warmth of the night.

He looks out into the darkened heavens, reaches into the ache of waiting and longing, and sings, his cry rising out from the leaves where he sits, across the yard, and around windows lit from within. It rises up toward the fading sky, where Venus is taking over for the sun, and echoes through the trees.

For a moment, he sings alone, his shrieks seeming to reverberate across the centuries his species has existed, but he is quickly joined by others, their chorus rising and falling in great, crashing waves of desire – calling, pleading, howling for a soulmate to ease a pain they carried for seventeen years without ever knowing it was there.

NINE

"I'll tell you why not," Scarlett said. "In fact, I can give you about seventeen reasons why not."

This isn't going well, he thought. They were at her place, and she had just come back downstairs from putting Abigail to bed.

They had had a great meal – turns out she really knew her way around the grill, and he spent as much time flirting with Abigail as he did with Scarlett while she cooked – and afterward they talked as Abigail played on the floor. Scarlett had planned for them to eat out in the back yard, but the weather had turned cool and it seemed like it was going to rain, so they stayed in. Her house had homey touches, like curtains instead of blinds, and a few house plants, but mostly it was Abby's things that made it look like a home; the toys in the living room, the booster seat attached to one of the kitchen chairs, the sippy cups on the counter.

The walls mostly seemed to be different shades of beige, but at least they were decorated by some cool black-and-whites of jazz musicians, and one big Georgia O'Keefe that seemed even more colorful and amazing thanks to the contrast. The first time he had been in her house, he had paused in front of the print of "Jack in the Pulpit No. IV" and as Scarlett passed by she said, "Nice vulva, eh?"

There had been none of that tonight. Though her place was always clean, it had been spotless this time. She was trying. And she wasn't afraid to let him know she was trying. Not that he wasn't. He was shaving every day now, and even wearing cologne. He hadn't worn cologne in years.

"So Abby, what do you think of this guy?" she had asked the little girl at dinner.

"Mmmm," she pondered. "He's tall."

"I've been called worse," Andy said then, and laughed, but felt bad about what he was about to do. Not because it's wrong, he thought, but because it will hurt her. And while that's not fair, it has to be done. I've got to go. I've got to do this.

After she put Abigail to bed, he told her of his plans to find Ashley.

Now, he was doing damage control.

"You know, it's not just the fact that it's been seventeen years, either, Andy, it's that it's crazy, and just a little bit stalker-like," she said after her initial disbelief. "Can you imagine if someone you dated in high school – *in high school* — suddenly showed up at your door after seventeen years? Not just, you know, bumped into you at the grocery store by chance, but showed up at your house because they were looking for you?"

"Yeah, I know, and I know you're right," he said. "And I know I'm not really explaining it well."

"And here's the other thing, Andy," she said, sitting down in the chair across from him instead of next to him on the couch. "I know you think this will like solve all your problems or something, but I really don't think it's healthy. Indulging this fantasy really cannot be a good thing."

He picked up his wine glass, then set it down. She had really gone all out tonight – grilled cedar-plank salmon, herbed potatoes, some sort of Spanish red wine. And then he does this.

"The thing is – and seriously, I'm not trying to put anything on you or try to say there's something with us or whatever – but you know this is also for you, you know," he said. That got her attention, but he wasn't sure it was in a good way, because then she really looked at him like he was crazy.

"Look, whatever there is between us, it's not fair to you to have this ghost just like, floating out there. I mean, look at it this way: Right, I haven't seen her in seventeen years. So think about that. The last time I saw her, she was seventeen and like, perfect, right? Well, in my stupid head, she is still seventeen and still perfect. And as wonderful as you are – and you really are wonderful, Scarlett – it's not fair for you to have to compete with that. Not that you're not perfect, but, you know what I mean. No one could compete with a memory like that."

She picked up her wine glass, then set it down again when she realized it was empty.

"And look, I'm not going there to sweep her off her feet or whatever. I'm not going to ride up on a shining white steed, right? It's just that I have – well, it's like thinking she died and then finding out she didn't. She's still alive out there somewhere, and I just want to know what happened. Where'd she go? And why?"

She sighed and started rolling them both cigarettes.

"And listen. Listen," he said. "It's like this. You are in my head. You are in my head all the time. But so is she and there's not room for the both of you. I want to get her out. I only have room for you."

She stopped with the cigarettes and stared at him. Her mouth was frowning, but her eyes were not. That had done it, he thought.

"You know, she's probably married, has a bunch of kids," he said. "You know what's really going to happen, don't you? I'm going to find her and just look like a complete, stupid idiot. Which I probably am, but still."

"Yes, you are," she said, and sighed. "Here, let's go outside so we can smoke these. If Abby starts yelling or whatever I'll be able to hear her if we're just on the back porch."

They stepped outside into the darkness and the buzz of the cicadas. She pulled out her lighter but he already had his out and lit before she could, and he lit hers first, her eyes glowing with the flame for a second.

He lit his, then slipped his arm around her waist and felt her stiffen and then growl – growl – at him, before relaxing into his arm.

"So what's your big plan? Do you know what you're going to say? When you find her, I mean?" she said at last. "What do you wear to something like this?"

"You're asking me?" he said. "I have no freaking idea."

Up high, between the branches of the trees, there were stars.

"Well," she said, taking another drag. "You better think of something."

Back inside, they refilled their wine glasses silently, then sat on the sofa and just looked at each other for a minute. She had really looked dolled up when he got there, but now she seemed disheveled somehow, like she had been knocked off balance. Her lipstick looked rough, and her hair had given up the fight.

"I'm sorry— " she started.

"No, you— "

"No, I am. I have no right to be telling you not to go. I'm not— I'm just— "

"No, Scarlett," he said. "Scarlett," and she was crying then.

"It's just that you, and everything, and it's been, and … "

"Scarlett."

And then she was straddling him there on the couch, taking his hands and pressing them against her body.

"Just say you'll come back," she said, and willed herself not to cry, but there were still tears at the corners of her mouth. "I can't— just say you'll come back."

He took his hands off her and moved them to her waist, stopping her hips, then put his hands on her shoulders and pulled her face down to his.

"I'll come back," he said, then wiped the tears from her face. "I'll come back."

"You promise?"

"I promise," he said, with no earthly idea whether it was one he could keep or not. "I'll come back."

She leaned over and grabbed her wine glass then, and chugged it down, the red wine spilling down one side of her mouth a little, and when he kissed her, he could taste the wine and the tears mixing together and later he would wonder whether that was a good thing or a bad thing, or whether it was something that just was, like the way she took him to her room after that, and locked the door and then stood before him and undressed, her eyes locked on him, piece by piece she undressed while he sat, staring at him as if she was daring him to look away, daring him not to love her. And only then, after she stood there before him with nothing on, the way the sea is both beautiful and terrifying, and he reached out for her, reached out and grabbed her hand and whispered, "I'll come back" – only then did she turn off the light and come to him.

Despite staying up too late packing the night before, Andy had again woken up feeling refreshed and with a new sense of purpose. Finally, everything was ready, and he looked around the little house: back door bolted, windows locked, toaster unplugged, air conditioner off, car loaded. He had clothes, toiletries, camping gear, cans of Pepsi, beers and music. The oil was changed, the tires rotated and a new air freshener installed.

The newspaper and mail were on hold, and he had three entire weeks off of work – two had not been a problem, but negotiating for that third one in a row had not been easy. He had credit cards, cash, an atlas, and a small notebook like the one he had seen a reporter using when the river had flooded last summer.

As he did a final walk around, he had to fight the urge to close all the blinds. He knew in his head that every police officer in the country will tell you visibility is the key to avoiding break-ins. He also knew that closed blinds and curtains not only hide thieves inside your house – which is what they want – but broadcast a message to anyone passing by: "I'M NOT HOME." But that was all in his head; his heart screamed for him to close the blinds and curtains, and not leave any lights on.

He went with his head, opening the views of his empty house to the world. After a final pause, he locked and dead-bolted the front door and got in the car, cranking up Tom Petty, then rolled slowly down Vesey Avenue, out of his little neighborhood and out onto Bluffton Road. Past the Hall's restaurant, the really great little Mexican place, the Chinese buffet and the bakery outlet, then the road curved along the St. Mary's River, neighborhoods to his right, the river and Foster Park to his left. He and Ashley used to ride their bikes to Foster Park all the time, just to hang out.

Around the curve of the river, Engle Road ended at a T intersection, and straight across from Engle is Mo's, where Ashley took him dancing and tried to drive his mom's car. As he turned right onto Engle, he stood on the gas for a second and let the tires screech loudly in a kind of burning rubber shout-out to her memory.

As he drove down Engle, he tried to figure out whether he was driving away from his past or toward it. There was Kekionga Middle School, where he had learned to play ball as a kid in the city parks department's summer programs. There was Ardmore Avenue, where they used to go when they went over to his dad's friend's place by Junk Ditch.

There was The Dome, a giant inflated, well, dome, that had indoor soccer and a driving range and stuff. When he and Sally were kids growing up they thought it was about the coolest place in the world.

At the end of Engle, he turned on to Jefferson, and passed Casa's, or as everyone he knew called this one, "Casa with an exclamation point." There were a bunch of Casa Italian restaurants in town, and each one had a slightly different name. Supposedly they each had their own theme, but to him they were pretty much interchangeable. Still, it was always a big debate over which one to go to. Growing up, Casa Mare usually won out, just because it was the closest to Kensington and had more seafood on the menu. This one was Casa Restorante!, but these days, as long as they had their sausage and peppers dish on the menu – and they all did – he really didn't care which one he went to.

As he looked at all these places with what seemed to be new eyes, he realized he was saying goodbye. Not that he wasn't coming back, but he knew somehow he wouldn't be coming back the same. How he would be different, he didn't know, but he knew this trip was more open-ended than just where he'd be going on the map.

As he turned on the interstate and accelerated up the ramp, he ran down a sort of mental checklist in his mind. What if she's married? So what? You're not going there to win her back. You're going there to settle this. Besides, there's a good chance she is married, probably has kids and a happy life. Be prepared for the fact that she's happy without you. What if she's in California? No problem. Three weeks off work and I can drive there in like three days. Even at six days there and back you've got two weeks to find her. What if she gets angry and says she hates you? She might. We'll deal with it. What if she loves you? Then what? Then you deal with it. What about Scarlett? What about her? You're going there to settle things. Relax.

His mind rolled with the miles, until he got close to Michigan. As many times as he had been there, he was always amazed by the trees, and even more amazed by the way they seemed to start at the border. Did Indiana have some policy against trees? Or did they draw the border back in the 1800s based on where the trees stopped growing?

Regardless, as his Grand Am rolled past signs for Satek Winery ("Rhymes with Attic" the billboard said) and an outlet mall, the trees started in earnest – mature, serious trees as far as the eye could see, not like the patches of scrub you see here and there in most of Indiana. Sure enough, within a half-mile was the state line, and if he remembered right, he would be pretty much driving through trees all the way to Marshall.

It turned out he remembered more trees than there actually were, but still, the stands of mature hardwood – even going past at 75 they looked to be mostly oaks – were impressive, and there were areas where the highway cut through forest that extended for what seemed like miles. The effect was so complete it was a little like the interstate was a river with steep banks, where the tree tops were level ground and he was flowing along with the current below.

Flowing along with the current was a good description, he thought. He hadn't even really known how to pack, since he didn't know how long he would be gone, or for that matter, even where he was going, beyond Kalamazoo. He figured he would mostly stay in hotels, but brought camping gear in case the mood struck. It seemed like this was one of those times when sitting by a campfire thinking things out underneath the stars would probably be necessary at some point. Of course, he had lots of memories of camping from childhood, too. He remembered the smell of the tent and the campfire and the way the mornings felt when the day was new and his mom was making bacon on the camp stove.

As the trees alternated with fields, the fact that his memory had enhanced things since childhood only reinforced what he was doing: His mind had played havoc on him over the years, now it was time for a dose of reality. Of course, it was also a journey back to his childhood, he thought, if your teenage years can be called childhood. He hadn't been up here in a long time, but the memory of those family vacations were all coming back to him now. Thanks to those trips and scattered relatives, he had a passing familiarity with most of Michigan's Lower Peninsula and most of the highlights of the Upper Peninsula, as well.

He was not, however, familiar with Marshall, but it seemed to be a good place to stop for lunch. True, it was less than two hours out of Fort Wayne, but he hadn't gotten on the road as soon as he had planned and now, well, it was time to eat. Besides, he wanted to check the place out. Ashley had lived here almost a year that he knew of, and he wanted to see what it was like.

Off the interstate, it looked like every other town in the Midwest with highway ramps – a four-lane road lined with franchises. But he had heard Marshall had an amazing downtown, so he kept driving east. Soon, the Applebees and fast-food places gave way to homes, then more stately homes, and then truly gorgeous old homes, and finally, a Yield sign at a huge traffic circle, crowned in the center with a white columned fountain. Under huge shade trees, the scene was straight out of a Normal Rockwell painting as mothers pushed strollers around the fountain and children romped on the grass.

He drove around the circle a few times just to take it all in – a Bed & Breakfast in a house that was at least 150 years old, the town hall, and what looked to be a gorgeous Hawaiian manor house. Finally, he exited east, and found himself in a little downtown lined with antique stores, restaurants and even a hardware store.

He took the first parking spot he saw and got out, only to have the Normal Rockwell experience continue – everyone seemed to know each other and seemed genuinely glad to see them. Ashley lived here for a year? She either fit right in, or it was sheer hell.

He walked past a few antique stores, and across the street was what appeared to be an actual full-serve gas station. He checked his watch – what year was it? Finally, he ducked into a little restaurant called the Dugout. By the time he sat down, the waitress had already filled his coffee cup.

"Let me get you a menu, hon."

Hon? Had she really called him "hon"? Wow.

The menu looked like the one at his mom's house, only way less healthy. Meatloaf, lots of stuff that included potatoes and gravy. Two kinds of onion rings. Wait – two? There were regular onion rings and what the menu called their famous hand-dipped onion rings.

Before Andy realized it, he had received an ice water and the waitress had her order pad poised.

"Give me the bacon cheeseburger with the, uh, hand-dipped onion rings," he said.

"You want anything to drink?"

"No, coffee's good," he said. "Can I get some more sugar, though?"

"Sure, hon."

"Oh, and, this probably sounds weird, but where can I find a map of town?" That got her attention.

"A map of Marshall? Hold on."

She walked two tables over and grabbed a professional-looking lady with short hair and stylish glasses.

"Sandy, you got any town maps with you?"

The woman dug in her brief case. "There you go."

Like that, the waitress was back with the map.

"There you go, hon. Sandy's the Chamber of Commerce, eats here almost every day."

"She runs the Chamber?" Andy asked.

"No, she *is* the Chamber, hon," she laughed. "Welcome to Marshall."

He looked over the map as he waited for his food. Turns out he had driven right past what he was looking for: South Mulberry Street was two blocks before the Circle. He pulled out the little notebook and checked the address written there, though he had it memorized, had had it memorized since the day he found it at the library.

His cartography was broken by the arrival of his food and the awe-inspiring onion rings. They were colossal and each one covered with amazing amounts of fried batter. He used about a half a bottle of ketchup, and halfway through realized he could have lived without the burger entirely if only he had ordered enough of these things. Screw college, he thought while reaching for his third napkin. If I had grown up here, with these onion rings, I'd have never left.

"Can I help you find anything?" It was Sandy Chamber of Commerce, now standing at his table.

"No, I was just looking for an address." Though she clearly wanted to sell him the town, it struck him as the most genuine sales pitch he'd ever gotten. This woman truly loved this place. "I think I found it."

"Oh good. Someone's house? If I know them I can help you find them if you like."

It should have been creepy, but here, it was just, well, nice. He realized that though she had her briefcase with her like she was leaving, she also had her coffee mug with her.

"You can sit if you'd like," he said. "I'm Andy."

"Hi, Andy, I'm Sandy. What can I tell you about Marshall?"

"Well, I was actually just looking for the house where someone lived a long time ago. But I don't think she's lived here since she was in high school. You probably don't know her, Ashley Hudson?"

"Ashley Hudson?" Up close, Sandy was clearly older than she had looked across the busy restaurant. "Well, I do run the Youth Advisory Council for high school seniors over at the community foundation. How many years ago was this?"

Andy laughed and threw his napkin on his plate.

"Seventeen." I can't believe I'm telling her this.

"Wait, so it was like 1987? That was my first year – I'll never forget that," she said, and that warm smile was back. "Ashley? Did she have long blonde hair, real pretty? Lived with just her mom, right?"

Holy crap.

"Yeah, that's right." Wow, this really was a small town. And this lady is good. She could sell manure in a shit storm.

"I only knew her that one year, before she went off to school, but I remember she was smart as a whip. Really impressive, especially with everything else going on in her life," she said. "And you're looking for her?"

"Well, I knew her before she came here," he said. "So I just thought I'd see where she had spent some time."

Either she sensed that was all he was going to say or she really had to go, but she suddenly looked at her watch and stood. Or, I completely sound like some kind of stalker, he thought.

"Well, best of luck to you, and if there's anything you need, don't hesitate to ask."

And with that she was gone. Still, it was kind of scary to find evidence that Ashley had really been here, that she wasn't just a shadow. It was also a little cutting – she had done well here. She had moved on after him. She got on with her life. Even when he didn't.

Still. There was a long road ahead before there were any final verdicts to be made, and he wasn't going to turn back now. His stomach full of onion rings, he paid his bill and walked back to the car.

Driving back toward the Circle, he wished he had thought to bring a camera. He didn't know why he suddenly felt the need to document things, but he had the urge to capture this place, to see it on paper, to have a piece of something concrete he could point to. Whatever. This isn't about making a scrapbook, it's about finding her – the real, live, Ashley.

Past the Circle, he found Mulberry Street, and turned left, watching the house numbers climb until he reached the cul-de-sac at the railroad tracks. There: 396 S. Mulberry St. The last-known abode of one Ashley Hudson.

It looked like any other house on the block, though it was set back a little further because of the circle of pavement out front. It looked like no one was home, so he got out and leaned against his car, just looking at the place.

He could imagine her sitting on that front porch. He could see her silhouetted in the upstairs window. He could see her mom's giant, junky car parked out front.

But his reverie came to a crashing halt with the blast of a freight train's horn. The train had somehow surprised him, and now it was shockingly close and amazingly loud as it roared and rumbled about 15 feet away. No wonder Ashley's mom had been able to rent this place, he thought, the trains would bounce you right out of bed. He couldn't imagine what they must sound like at 4 a.m.

Just as he started to turn to look at the train, something in the sound caught his ear – an undertone in the rumble or the roar of the engine, but suddenly he heard the roar in his ears as he stood over the sink that night, nine months after she left, the porcelain so dry and he knew, knew what his warm, wet blood would look like against that dry surface, how his wrists would look giving up his life the way she had once given herself to him, the roar of the screams he heard in his sleep, and the way the Song of One had changed into Silence and then something worse than silence, a sound only he could hear, a sound so low, so deep, like the very foundations of the Earth were groaning with the weight of their burden. That sound was what he heard now, and then as the rumble turned to the rattle of freight cars he remembered the nightmares, the dream where Ashley was on a cross, crucified, but forgiving all his sins, her blood washing down on him the way he imagined his own blood pouring out into the sink with all his pain. He remembered the other dreams, the ones where he was locked away, where he didn't have to pretend any more, where he could at last be safe with his pain, he could hold it, cling to it the way she had once clung to him, only to wake up and realize he was not locked away at all, and his pain was a sharp thing, a thing that cut him no matter how he backed away from it.

Finally, the last freight car passed and the world became silent, as if he had gone deaf. In the quiet, he realized he wasn't seventeen anymore and he wasn't in pain anymore. The cuts had become scars, the pounding, thunderous train had become nothing but steel tracks in the sun. How could something so big, so loud, so massive, just be gone, as if it had never even been there at all?

He watched the train disappear down the tracks, its rumble now inaudible, lit a cigarette and smoked it hard, finishing it in just a few drags, then got into his car and headed toward Kalamazoo.

Finding campus had been easy. Finding the student newspaper office on the campus, not so much. But when he did, he was greeted by a head full of dark curls cut short with bright eyes underneath. She wore a huge, grey sweatshirt with "WMU" in navy lettering on it, and jean shorts.

Were her eyes sparkling because they always sparkled or sparkling because she looked like she had been bored half to death before he walked in?

The campus newspaper was in the basement of the student services center, but for a basement it was well lit and seemed cleaner than he imagined a newspaper would look. And quieter.

"Where is everybody? Are you closed?"

"No," the girl laughed. "It's summer. We only publish once a week in the summer so there's hardly anyone around. There's hardly anyone on campus, for that matter. What can I do for you?"

Thanks to Emma at the library, he knew what to ask for.

"Yeah, do you have a name file?" he said. "I'm trying to find someone who was a student like 15 years ago."

The girl thought for a minute.

"Name file? No, but we have an electronic archive. We can look up names in there easily," she said. "Would that work?"

Man, this might be a short trip. "Yeah, perfect."

The girl moved the mouse on her computer and the screen lit up. In just a couple of clicks she had a search window up.

"All right," she said. "Who are we looking for?"

"Ashley Hudson. A-S-H-L-E-Y and Hudson is, you know, just what you'd think."

She talked while she typed.

"And you said fifteen years ago?"

"Well she would have been here from fall of '88 to spring of '92, or later if, you know, it took five years or whatever."

"Uh-oh," she said even before she hit the "search" button on the screen. "Yeah, this archive didn't start until like 1996."

Sure enough, the search came back with nothing.

"Did you have a name file or anything before that?"

"You know, I've only been here like two years so I don't know. But we can ask the advisor. He's been here forever. Just a minute and I'll go ask. You can look around if you want while I go find him."

There wasn't much to see, just a few cubicles and desks. Lots of computers. But near the front desk was a rack with what appeared to be every college newspaper in the state, and even one from Ball State University, just down the road from Fort Wayne. He was about to pick it up when the girl returned.

"He said they had lots of paper files, but they were all kept by subject, so unless she did something important enough to have her own file you would never find her," she said. "We have all the papers from that time in the morgue, but again, you'd have to look through every single one."

"For four years," he said.

She tilted her head. "Yeah, sorry."

He got lost trying to find the library, so what should have been a five minute walk turned into a half-hour tour of campus, and when he finally arrived at the library it was from the opposite direction he intended.

Still, he found it, but when he did he wondered how he could have possibly missed it – not only was it huge, but it was unmistakable: Its walls were as flat as a glass-covered skyscraper, but appeared to be made of brilliant white and black stripes that ran horizontally from the ends of the building toward the center, until they neared a huge, central clock tower, where they abruptly turned 90 degrees and dove toward the ground. It was as if a striped skyscraper had been split in half, then bent and folded down, revealing the clock tower the way a peeled banana reveals its fruit.

If he was reading the map right – and that couldn't be taken for granted – he needed to go through the clock tower and enter the library on the other side.

The entrance looked even stranger – with its curved façade, white rectangular columns and black windows above, it looked like a stylized skull. With the white buildings and white concrete courtyard, he had to squint in the bright sun, and the temperature was rising quickly.

Welcome to the Library of Death, he thought, then immediately took it back when he stepped inside. The air was cool and the dark-tinted doors had led him into a three-story tall rotunda, filled with light and marked by a round information desk at the center.

While the courtyard had been empty and desolate, inside was a hub of cool activity. The girl at the information desk sent him to Periodicals downstairs.

"Turn right at the bottom of the steps and you can't miss it," she said.

As he descended the stairs he couldn't help but think how young all the students looked. After all, they couldn't be that much younger than— Oh crap, he thought. They're almost 20 years younger than I am. They're not that young – I'm just that old.

The girl at the Periodicals desk didn't help him feel any younger. She probably thinks I'm some old professor, he thought, as she led him over to a computer station.

"For the time period you're looking for, you'll look the name up on here and then write down the dates and page numbers you want," she said. "Then you look up that paper on the microfilm over there. For later stuff, it's all on the computer, so if you need something for about 1998 or later just let me know, otherwise you have to do it this way."

This time he got a hit, but only one, and it didn't look promising:

HUDSON, ASHLEY: Sept. 26, 1990
"Siedschlag hosts homecoming bonfire, marshmallow roast"

Sure enough, the article was a story about a marshmallow roast, and Ashley was quoted talking about how the event had raised $300 toward a local charity. Not only did that not tell him anything about where to find her, but it was just more proof that she had gotten along just fine without him.

He was getting ready to go when the Periodicals girl walked by.

"So did you find what you were looking for?"

"No, I kinda struck out."

She stopped and came back.

"Oh, no. Well, what are you trying to find again? Maybe I can help."

God I love libraries, he thought.

"A student from back in the late '80s and early '90s. I looked her up like you said, but I only got one hit, and that was for a story about a marshmallow roast."

"And you looked her up in the Western Herald, right?"

"Yeah."

"Well, let's go back to the computer and try the Kalamazoo Gazette, just for fun. It's the city paper, but you never know," she said, walking briskly. "I'm assuming you Google'd her already?"

"Yeah."

This time, she took the controls of the computer, and immediately got two hits. Jackpot, he thought, until he saw the headlines.

HUDSON, ASHLEY: April 18, 1992
"Engagements: Hudson-Stibitz" Page 2F.

HUDSON, ASHLEY: Aug. 28, 1993
"Weddings: Hudson-Stibitz" Page 3F.

Suddenly, he just wanted to get out of there, like his clothes were hot and sticky on prickly skin and he needed air. He realized he was bending over awkwardly toward the computer screen and stood up quickly, making the room tilt a little.

"Here, I wrote these down for you," the girl said, but it was coming through a tunnel.

"Great, thanks so much," he said. Damn. Double damn.

"Can I help you with anything else?"

He crammed the paper into his pocket and just stood there, feeling the paralysis climb from his feet and ankles into his knees, up his legs toward his chest. Any second now it would get hard to breathe.

"No, I'm good. Thanks again." She started to walk away, and he felt his chest seize up.

"Wait— wait a second," he got out, fighting it off. She turned around. "Where can I take you to dinner tonight? I mean, where— where's...

I'm just visiting and need to eat somewhere. Is there anyplace good? Nearby, I mean?"

She blushed a little. "Well, if you like pizza, there's always Bilbo's. They've got great sandwiches, too. It's right on the edge of campus, up that way."

Talking seemed to push the paralysis back down, so he went with it.

"Yeah, sorry, I wasn't trying to ask you out, I don't know why it came out that way. I mean, not that, you know, I wouldn't but just that I wasn't. Asking, I mean."

She seemed conscious of how she was standing. "It's OK. I go there all the time anyway. Maybe I'll see you there."

"Yeah, I'll be, like in the Old People section or something. You can look for me."

"All right," she said. "I gotta, you know, work and stuff."

"Yeah," he said. "And I gotta, you know, look up these newspapers."

As she walked away, he finished his own thought, "so what's left of my pathetic life can be hammered on some more." You idiot.

Then she was there again. "And um, make sure you get the cheesy bread and dill dip. My freshman 15 was like all from cheesy bread." She looked down at her hips. If she had put 15 pounds on there, Andy had no idea where it was hidden.

"Tell you what," he heard himself saying. "If I see you I'll buy you some. Whatever it does to you it seems to be working just fine." Why was he saying that?

She was blushing again, then pointing with her thumb over he shoulder and mouthing the word "work" as she backed away. He felt himself smiling. Idiot.

As soon as she was gone, the paralysis returned, but it was changing form. His legs were still numb, but he forced them over toward the microfilm area, while the feeling in his chest changed to an emptiness, like his body had somehow opened to the heavens. There were stars inside him, vast galaxies of solar systems, and at the center of it all, a giant, black hole drawing everything to it. He could feel time and space curving into the hole in his chest as he walked toward the files, eons of time bending into his emptiness, every memory of Ashley being pulled into its darkness, stretched out as the forces drew them in even as he clutched at them trying to keep them out. The way it felt holding her hand in Mass, at the school registering for the classes she would never attend. Sitting with her on the porch, laying on her bed, feeling the brush of her skin against his – all of it was rushing into an un-fillable vacuum at the center of everything he was.

The engagement notice said she was a WMU senior in library science, and that she would be marrying James Stibitz of Kalamazoo in the summer of 1993. He was also a WMU senior, majoring in business administration. The wedding announcement said they had married June 26 in Kalamazoo and honeymooned in Mexico – about the last thing he needed to read, really – and that they planned to reside in Traverse City, where he would be working for Melton Corp.

But it was the photos that haunted him.

Even in the poor quality reproduction of microfilm, she was beautiful. In the engagement photo, she seemed only slightly older than when he knew her. The same, only more mature somehow. She was smiling, and it seemed sincere, but it wasn't the smile he imagined she'd have if she was head-over-heels in love with the guy. It wasn't the smile she used to give to him.

In both of them, she had her hair pulled up, but it was different now. Now it seemed darker underneath, and the blonde was more like highlights on top. And there were parts that were not pulled back, long bangs that curved gracefully around her face.

The wedding photo, however, was different, and harder to look at. Because in that picture, he could see nothing but love in her eyes. Damn, what a beauty, he thought. I can't believe I lost her.

But he had. That much was clear now. Not entirely clear – there was nothing to say they hadn't divorced just the way he and Susan had. All he really knew was that she had gotten married and moved to Traverse City. Still, seeing her photo – even from eleven years ago – was strange. It was like he knew her, and yet, he didn't. Instantly recognizable, yet completely impossible.

He printed out both articles, and pulled out his little notebook and wrote: "June 26, 1993, becomes Ashley Stibitz. Traverse City, Mich."

He packed up his gear and headed for the exit. He would need to find this Bilbo's place, some place to stay, and a nice bar stool to keep warm for the evening. He hated to say it, but he hoped the Periodicals girl didn't show up. It just seemed like too much effort and effort was about the last thing he could manage right now.

And besides, he would need to call his old buddy Myers to see if he could deal with a visitor on short notice at his place up in Traverse.

TEN

"In view of the damage often occasioned by unusual insect outbreaks, such fears are not unreasonable, when, without warning this Cicada suddenly emerges over greater or smaller areas, filling the ground from which it issues with innumerable exit holes, swarming over trees and shrubs, and making the air vibrate with its shrill, discordant notes."

—"The Periodical Cicada"

"So what's your class like, Sally?" Ashley's turned half-way around in the front seat, talking to Sally in the back. In return for taking Sally to her summer dance class, Andy gets to use his mom's car. At first he was aggravated, but after a while, it's almost like he and Ashley are pretending to be parents and Sally's their daughter. If nothing else, thanks to Ashley he's had more fun with Sally this summer than he has in years. They were best friends when they were little, now – at least until he met Ashley – they were like worst enemies. He hated to admit it, but it was kind of nice having a kid sister again.

"It's all right," Sally says. "In some ways it's a lot better in the summer, because there's hardly anyone in the class and so it's like having your very own private dance teacher, but you also sweat a lot more and it's grosser. And if you're not doing good that day you can't really hide behind other dancers because it's like, just you and a couple other girls."

Most of the time, he thinks of Sally as a little kid, and most of the time she seems to act like one. But when she's dancing, it's like she becomes someone else, someone older. Maybe she uses up all her effort then and just has nothing else to give, he thinks. He'll have to ask her about it some time when they can talk.

"Hey look at that!" Ashley says, and she's pointing at an orange Toyota.

"What?"

"The license plate. Look – it's AMH. My initials."

"So what's the 576 stand for? Your weight?" A punch to the shoulder answers for her.

"Don't you do that? I always do that," she says. "If I'm looking, I can usually find plates with AMH at least once a day."

"Hey look for mine," Sally says from the back seat. "Look for S-A-G!"

"You look for SAG," Andy says. "I'm looking for my own."

"What's the A stand for, Sally?"

"Anne," she says. "For my Aunt Anne. She's the best, but we hardly ever see her because she lives in Iowa. OH MY GAWD LOOK!" she screams so loud Andy nearly swerves off the road. "THERE IT IS! S-A-G!"

"Geeze, Sally! You scared the crap out of me!" Andy says. "I'm trying to drive here. For crying out loud, it's just your initials."

"That is sooo cool!" Sally says, still excited. "What a cool game, Ashley. You rock."

Andy can only roll his eyes as he pulls the car into the dance studio's parking lot, but Ashley's clearly loving being like a big sister.

"What time are you done?" he says as Sally gets all her crap together. Taking her to dance is like moving a circus.

"Five-thirty," she says. "Bye! Love ya, Ash!"

As the door slams, Andy shakes his head, but Ashley laughs. "You're lucky," she says. "She's really a great kid."

"Yeah?" he says, and pulls her toward him. "So are you."

Her kisses are long and passionate and he would be perfectly content to spend the next hour or so doing nothing but this while Sally dances inside.

"Thanks for doing this," Ashley says as he parks the car in the nearly empty parking lot of North Side High School. The building is big – three stories of red brick rising up next to the St. Joseph River – and part of it is round, with a low, domed roof and classical columns on the front steps that make it look like the Parthenon in Rome.

"What are you talking about?" Andy says as they get out of the air-conditioned car into the afternoon heat. "You act like I'm doing you this huge favor, when you know I would do anything to spend time with you. You need a ride to Texas? Let's go."

She laughs. "Not Texas. Take me to … Malibu!"

"Malibu it is," he says, holding the glass school door open for her. "But first, college. And that starts with your senior year. Seriously, you're going to love Mr. McFrederick."

"I hope so," she says as they walk into the school lobby. "I haven't really had good luck with counselors so far. They take one look at my record and see all the transfers and they immediately put me in shop class or home-ec, and it takes like a month to find a teacher who will fight to get me into trigonometry. By then I'm a month behind so I have to work twice as hard as anyone else."

The school looks just the same as it does when it's filled with students, but feels so different. Maybe it's the way their voices echo or just the silence in general.

"That's what's so great about Mr. McFrederick," Andy says. "He seems to have a way of seeing past what's on paper."

Mr. McFrederick's door is open, but Andy knocks anyway.

"Mr. McFrederick?"

A big-boned black man in a green army jacket turns around. His skin is coppery, his wavy hair cut close and his eyebrows almost as thick as his mustache. He also has gold, wire frame glasses, making him look like some kind of cross between a black revolutionary and a kindly professor.

"Oh, hey Andy!" he says. "How's your summer going?"

"Good," he says, leading Ashley into the small office that looks more like a library than anything, with books everywhere. "This is Ashley Hudson, she needs to register."

"Great, nice to meet you Ashley," Mr. McFrederick says, standing and shaking her hand, then motioning for them to sit. "Did you bring transcripts and all that crap or did you have them sent here or are we just starting the process?"

"They should have already been sent here," she says. "Andy's been very goal-oriented."

"Ideally," Andy says, leaning forward conspiratorially, "we'll have every single class together, sir." Then smiles.

Mr. McFrederick only stares back at him. He likes to play tough.

"*Riiiiiiiiiiiiiiiiiiiiiiiiight.*" Then he turns to Ashley. "Let me go see if your paperwork's here. You said Hudson?"

"Yeah."

"All right, I'll be right back."

As they wait, Andy looks at Ashley's legs. Good lord they're beautif—

"All right, here we go," Mr. McFrederick says as he strides back into the room. "Holy crap, girl, this is impressive as heck."

Ashley blushes. "Usually counselors say what a mess it is."

"Yeah, well, usually counselors are— well, never mind," he says. "Listen, it's federal law that I can't violate your privacy, so I have to ask if it's OK for Andy to be here. Because if you're the slightest bit uncomfortable, he's got to leave, OK? It's the law."

"No, it's cool," Ashley says. "He takes good care of me."

"You've been taking good care of your grades, Ashley. Considering how much it looks like you've moved, and how many classes – what do they do, put you in home-ec every time you move, assuming you're way behind?"

"That's exactly what they do."

"But then you obviously got moved into the classes you belong in at some point, and you still managed to kick butt and take names in them," he says, his eyes barely looking up from the sheath of papers.

"Thanks."

"All right, test scores. Where are they? Ah, here. ACT – nice!" he says. "Well, I don't know why you're here, because you obviously don't need me. You're set."

"But look at where her scores were sent," Andy says. "Nowhere."

"Well, I was gonna get to that. What's your plans for college, Ashley?"

"Well," she says, and shifts in her seat. "I hadn't really gotten that far."

"You don't think you can do the work? Or you think you can't afford it? Or you've just never known anyone in your life who's done it so it seems impossible?" Mr. McFrederick asks, leaning back in his chair and fixing his eyes on her like he cannot wait to hear her answer. "Because you can clearly do the work. You get in a stable situation and you can work rings around most anyone out there. So which is it?"

"Uh, the second two, I guess." She looks down. Mr. McFrederick sits up, then leans in like he's about to share a conspiracy.

"Look, with these grades, these test scores and what I'm assuming is a single mom's income? You can write your own ticket. Almost any state school you can name would offer you merit scholarships – probably full ride – and financial aid will easily make up anything they don't cover," he said. "With a little work and some creativity, even private schools would not be a problem, especially if you target your choices. What I say next may sound like I'm stereotyping or putting you in a box, but in this case it works to your advantage, so listen – some of these private schools would like nothing better than to take a hard-luck case with potential and make a diamond out of her, you understand? They look for diamonds in the rough. And when I say private schools, I'm talking about Ivy League schools on the East Coast, the kind that when you graduate you don't just leave with a diploma, you leave with connections and doors that open for you like magic. I'm going to go out on a limb and guess there haven't been a lot of doors opening like magic in your life so far."

"No, not so much," she says. "You're being serious?"

"Seriously, worst case scenario – and I mean worst case, unless you like get arrested for marijuana or blow off your senior year – is you might have to take out some student loans," he says, and leans back in his chair. "But I don't see that happening, and even if it does, these are loans through – and guaranteed by – the federal government. You don't pay them back until you're out of school, the interest rates are low, and the payments can be based on how much you make with that bright, shiny degree. It's a can't-miss. But you won't need any loans, Ashley. With a good essay, and there's people that can help you with that, they'll practically pay you to go. You could even follow show-off Andy over here to some crappy school like Princeton instead of a quality institution like Purdue." Under his army jacket is a Purdue sweatshirt.

Even Ashley was laughing now.

"All right, what do I have to do?"

"First, take these books home with you and start picking out colleges that sound like they'd match your style. And – listen now – when I say match your style, I don't mean the way you are now, however you think about yourself. I mean the ones that make your heart race because you think they might make you the way you want to be, the secret way you never tell anyone about, the You in your best daydreams. You know what I mean?"

"Yeah."

"Then pick about eight or ten of those and we'll send them your scores. The ones that bite we hit with your application, transcripts and an essay that will have them drooling."

"What kind of timeline are we talking about?"

"Well, it's mid-July now, if you bring me your list in a week, I'll help you get your scores sent so you don't have to pay for them. By the time school starts we'll have your essay done and should be filling out applications," he says. "By Christmas all you have left to do is see who's giving you the best deal and choose your school. Graduate and it's off to the races."

"You make it sound so easy," she says, crossing her arms.

"In some ways it is," he says. "None of it's difficult, it's just unfamiliar. You've done the hard part – that's these grades and test scores. Don't confuse unfamiliar with difficult."

Andy's still listening, but his eyes are wandering over the rows and rows of books crammed into the tiny office. Or they are until Mr. McFrederick's voice gets all serious.

"Ashley, you have a really great future ahead of you," he says. "I don't know why you've had to move so much, but the only thing that can stop you is if you don't believe in yourself. Go out there and grab this, because it's all yours."

She's staring at Mr. McFrederick like a true believer.

"And also stop dating chumps like Gardner over there," he says. "He's nothing but trouble."

Andy parks his mom's car on the street near Ashley's house, but everything's wrong. The lights are on, and not only is Ashley's Mom's car there – taking up half the street – but so is some blue pickup truck Andy doesn't recognize. What's she doing home?

The fact that Andy parks there at all is silly, since he only lives four houses away, but part of the plan: If he parks at home after a date and walks Ashley to her house, his parents know when he pulled up and exactly how long it takes to get her home. But if he parks at *her* house – or better yet, on the street near, but not directly in front of her house – then even if Barbara does happen to be home and hears him pull up, it could be any neighbor parking on the street. Then they can spend all the time they want – until curfew anyway – making out in the car and neither Barbara or his parents are any the wiser.

But not this time. They had gone out to see "La Bamba," and then got desserts, and since it was Friday night, Andy expected they'd have the house to themselves, as usual. And he had a feeling that tonight she was going to let him go further than just under her shirt like last time.

"That's Les's truck," Ashley says. "What's he doing here?"

"You think something's up?" he says.

"That's her guy from work. He might be her boss, too, or one of the bosses or something, I'm not sure. Whatever. It's probably nothing," she says. "You wanna kiss me?"

"Mmmmmmm, maybe," he says, reaching for her. "You wanna kiss me?"

"No," she says giggling, between kisses.

"Yeah, right."

But they're clearly both distracted, and other cars keep driving by and finally they both – at the same time – say "You wanna go in?"

They get out, and as they walk to the door it seems the cicadas are noticeably quieter. Maybe it's the weather, Andy thinks.

"Hey, Mom," Ashley says as she opens the screen door. Barbara and some guy with huge muscles and a mustache are sitting at the kitchen table. They both still have their blue Kelly work shirts on, his says "Leslie."

"Hey, Ash," Barbara says, lighting up a Capri. Smoke already hangs in the kitchen light. "You know Les. Andy, this is Les."

Andy crosses the room to shake his hand, but Les doesn't move. He's short, but built like a tank.

"Howdy," he says. His thinning hair is black and shiny like he's sweating. Andy guesses that *no one* calls him Leslie.

"Uh, nice to meet you," Andy says. He's seen guys with both beer guts and muscles before, but it's still hard for him not to stare at the combination.

"We're goin' upstairs," Ashley says, and grabs Andy's arm. "Come'on."

As they tromp up the steps, Andy can hear Les saying something about "well if it happens" and "seniority" and "you know I'll try but" and "it could be me, too, you know."

When they get to Ashley's room, she closes the door.

"You hear that?" he says.

"Yeah," she says. "Sounds like layoffs."

Andy's stomach drops at the word he had been thinking but didn't dare say, even to himself.

"Might just be rumors," he says, as she lays down on the bed. He just stands there.

"No, not in a factory," she says to the wall. "There's no such thing as a rumor in a factory. I've learned that."

Andy is silent, even as his mind is racing.

"You know, there's lots of places here," he says. "I mean, Fort Wayne is actually a big city, not like Muncie. There's a lot of shops she could get into. Heck, maybe even GM."

"Yeah," Ashley says, but she seems distant, like she's withdrawing.

"Hey, listen," he says. "It's gonna be all right. Whatever happens, nothing changes us, right?"

She's quiet for a minute, then looks at the clock.

"You probably better get home," she says.

Oh please, don't do this. Don't pull back, don't withdraw before anything even happens. Don't, don't, don't—

"Come here," he says, lying down next to her and pulling her tight. "Us. Youandme. No matter what. You think that just, just goes away?"

Finally, she looks in his eyes, and then she comes back from wherever she had gone to.

"No, it never goes away," she says. Then the temptress look suddenly appears. "Listen," she says. "They're here now, but I bet you anything they leave. They'll probably go out, and she'll probably be out all night. So I was thinking you could come back."

"Back?"

"Yeah. If she's going to be out all night, she always leaves me a note, so I'll know not to expect her or be freaked out when I get up in the morning and she's not there. When she leaves, she'll leave the front porch light on. But after she leaves, I'll go down and check for a note. If she's not coming back, I'll turn the light off. Then you'll know."

"I'll know?" The drop in his stomach had been replaced by an entirely new drop in his stomach.

"You'll know to come see me."

"Like, sneak out?"

She smiles.

"What time?"

"Whenever. You'll have to wait for your parents to be asleep, right?"

"Yeah." Hell yeah. Oh man, would his parents kill him if he got caught. Oh man, would it be worth it.

"So, whenever you get here and they're gone," she says, "I'll unlock the front door for you."

The living room lights are on and the TV's going, but his parents are out in the kitchen, finishing their wine. The 11 o'clock news is just starting as he walks in – right on time. Usually, they're full of questions for him and he worried it would look weird when he just wanted to go straight to bed, but there was no way he could talk with them tonight. Luckily, they don't seem to be in the mood for a Q&A either.

"You wanna get the back door, son?" his Dad asks.

"Yeah, I got it," Andy says. "Good night."

"Good night, Andy," his Mom says.

"Good night."

As he turns off the kitchen lights and locks the back door, he can hear his Dad locking the front door. As he opens the basement door and starts down the steps, he can hear his parents going up the steps directly over his head. With the privacy of the basement, he can do pretty much whatever he wants down there, but the one thing he'll have to be careful of is going out – the basement door and the back door are right under where their bed is on the second floor. If they're going to hear anything, that's going to be it.

Downstairs in his room, he tries to plan it out calmly, but he's too excited to think straight. It's just after 11 now, Barbara and Less will probably leave by 12, he thinks. The bars are open till 3, so leaving at 12's not crazy or anything. Speaking of crazy, he thinks, you're going to sneak out and go see Ashley. Holy crap.

So should I leave at 12? What if they're still there? I can always come back and wait for a while. No, I'm most vulnerable when I'm leaving and coming back – there's no way I'm risking that twice. Plus, you want to give them some time after they leave to make sure they're good and gone, he thinks. If they forgot her purse or something and they're only a block away, they'll come back. If they've been gone for a half hour, they're gone for good.

So go there at 1 then? What do I do until then?

He carefully sets his alarm for 1 a.m., then moves it off the night stand right onto his bed so he can turn it off the instant it goes off to make sure no one hears it. With my luck, he thinks, Sally will be getting up right about then to take a leak or something and then come down here and start asking all sorts of questions, like, I don't know, why are you dressed and going out?

He debates putting pajamas on, then figures changing clothes is just one more hassle he doesn't need at A-Hour. Still, his mind races as he lies in bed, staring at the ceiling, waiting for time to pass, waiting to fall asleep, thinking about the way, when she's really tired, a bit of an accent creeps in from when she lived in southern Indiana. Heck, he thinks, it doesn't have to be southern to get an accent – anyone from outside Fort Wayne can have a little bit of an accent. Ashley works hard to hide hers, and does it well, but he likes it when he hears her slip into it, like he's a comfortable old shirt she can be herself in.

Sleep finally, mercifully comes – just minutes before 1 a.m. and the alarm is not only jarring, but seems shockingly loud and it takes what seems like forever to get it turned off. His heart racing, he lies still listening – anything? He decides to wait until the clock clicks over to 1:01 to make sure before he makes a move. Nothing.

He stands up carefully so the bed makes hardly any noise, then starts creeping toward the stairs. You know, if I was getting up to use the bathroom I wouldn't be all quiet like this, and no one wakes up then. And that involves closing and opening doors, toilets flushing and running water. What are you so scared of? Right, just because you're fully dressed and have a breath mint in your mouth, why would anyone think you're doing anything but going to use the bathroom?

Top of the stairs now, and he works the door silently. Man, I could be like a Navy Seal or something, he thinks. Now the test: The back door. The deadbolt is silent as it slides in, then thunks as it clicks fully open. Pause… silence. Now do the door handle just like the stairway door, then the storm door, now close it … carefully. As he reaches into his pocket for his key, he breathes the outside air and already he's breathing Freedom. Don't get ahead of yourself. Key in, turn slowly … and thunk. Pause… silence. Close the storm door and – and you're out! Holy crap!

Working the gate silently between the backyard and the driveway seems like child's play after the deadbolt and storm door, and his tennis shoes are completely silent on the driveway as he strides toward the street. His parents' bedroom looks out over the backyard, so there's no chance of being seen except by Sally, and she's been asleep for hours.

At the end of the driveway, he takes a left onto the sidewalk in front of the house and starts north toward Vermont Street and the heaven that waits there. He thought it would be darker, but his eyes are adjusted and the streetlights down the boulevard make the neighborhood seem like it's lit up like Paris. Almost all the houses are dark, only the front porch lights at the Jeffries' burn bright.

He looks around as he walks: With the light from the antique-style streetlights in the boulevard, the trees arching over the street are lit from below, making them look like the columns and arches of a darkened cathedral, and the few cicadas still singing echo among the branches the way a single cantor's voice resonates through a great hall.

Condoms. Damn. He should have brought a condom. No, he had thought about it before and decided not to. Well, mostly. He had thought about buying some just in case, but couldn't bring himself to do it – partly because he was afraid to walk into a store and buy condoms, but mainly because he didn't want to give Ashley the wrong impression, like he had planned on having sex. What if she was offended? Besides, he told himself, he had always planned on being a virgin until he got married. True, he wanted to do everything a girl would let him right up to that line, but he had always pictured himself as a wait-till-your-wedding-night kind of guy for the Real Thing. Save himself for the night he got married. At least, that's what he told himself until he met Ashley. Now, he was thinking he had saved himself for the girl he was going to marry, which was close enough.

That stops him.

Yeah, he thinks, this is it. Me and Ashley. She is the one. There is no question. I mean, how could there be? So if she wants to, yeah, I will. At least, I will sometime. Not tonight, since, you know, I was too stupid to buy a condom. On the other hand, they could talk about it. He could tell her. Tell her he had been saving himself, which is why he wasn't prepared, but now he knows – he doesn't have to save himself any longer. Because she is the one he had been saving himself for all along.

Of course, you're assuming she's going to want to go all the way, he thinks. No, I'm just preparing for every possibility. Planning is good. Planning will get you through most any—

There's her house. There are no cars in front. The porch light is out. Holy crap.

He doesn't remember the steps from the corner to her porch, just the feel of the aluminum door handle on his palm and fingers as he presses the plastic button and feels the latch click. Then the door is open and he's trying the handle on the wooden door and it's open and the door swings wide and even though the front curtains are closed the room seems bathed in silver light that caresses the sleeping form on the couch, crowned by a mass of tangled blonde.

He hadn't noticed the chill in the air outside or even that there had been a breeze, but the air in the living room is warm and still and even from across the wood floor he can feel her breathe, feel his heart beat with hers, and he sees – even under the light blanket – the way her arm drapes from the couch to the floor, only her bare fingers showing. She's so beautiful he considers not waking her. He'll just close the door and sit in the moonlight and listen to her breathe and watch her sleep and know, know, know in his heart that they are One and will always be One and were always One years – centuries – before they ever met.

Finally, he closes the door, and she stirs, but the spell is still cast as she opens her eyes to see him, standing in the light of the moon.

"Hey," she whispers.

"Hey."

"I thought you'd never get here."

"Me too."

She pulls back the blanket.

"Come'ere."

He takes off his shoes and lies down next to her under the blanket.

"How long were you here?"

"Just a few minutes. I was watching you sleep a little. You were so beautiful I wasn't even going to wake you up." She smiles. "I could have watched you till dawn."

"You can't stay till dawn, though."

"I know. My parents will be up by seven."

"We should go up stairs so we can set my alarm clock."

"Yeah. If we oversleep, I'm dead."

Another smile.

"Ashley?"

"Yeah?"

"I just— this just feels so nice, being here with you. Like, you know, like we don't have to worry about, I don't know. Everything."

"Yeah, I know. But, there is one thing, though," she says, and he realizes they're still whispering. "Did you bring something?"

"Bring something?"

She blushes. "You know – protection?"

Protection? Like pepper spr— oh.

"Oh, um, not really."

"Not really?"

"Well, see, I had always thought that— "

"It's OK, I bought some for us."

"You did?" His heart was already racing, but now it picked up speed.

"Yeah, Emma told me you would never buy any yourself so I better be prepared."

Freakin' Emma Dunne. He should have known. "Emma knows?"

"No, she just knows you, and knows we're in love, and warned me that if I left if up to you, you'd be a virgin forever."

"Well, I was planning on waiting until, you know, I got married or whatever, but then I met you and everything kind of went out the window."

"I'm the same way, you know," she says. "This is my first time, too."

"Yeah?"

"Yeah."

"Are you nervous?"

"Yeah, a little."

"Good, because so am I."

"Let's go upstairs," she says, and pulls back the blanket. She's wearing a sleep shirt, and her long legs are bare under the moon.

They lock the front door, and Andy grabs his shoes to take upstairs, just in case there needs to be a speedy exit at some point. Upstairs, she closes her door and sets her alarm for 5 a.m. From her underwear drawer, she pulls out a box and sets it on the nightstand.

"I um, I had like this whole speech planned about how, I was going to wait, but that now that I found the person I was waiting for and, you know, just in case you wanted to, you know…"

"I just can't believe we finally found each other," she says. Outside, a lone cicada, muted by the walls and the drafty windows, sends out its call to the night air, a piercing cry out into the silence that echoes up the alley and off the backs of houses.

"So what do we do?"

Devil smile. "I don't know," she says. "Maybe this."

As her arms envelop him, he pauses on the edge for a moment, wondering whether to leap or crawl back. Even the waiting is exquisite, but at last, he jumps – falling into her kisses, feeling his heart dive headlong into the air, knowing there is no danger of hitting the ground, that if he just gives himself to flight that gravity will never hold him again and they will soar, free from all that had once held them down.

Outside, the lone cicada's call suddenly falls completely silent, and the night, so warm and lazy, continues her quiet crawl toward dawn, less that one single, solitary sound.

ELEVEN

"The earliest mention of this insect is in a work entitled 'New England's Memoriall,' by Nathaniel Moreton, printed at Cambridge, in 1669. The following transcription of this account, the original of which I have not seen, is taken from an editorial note to an article on the 'Locust of North America' in the Barton Medical and Physical Journal of 1804:

'Speaking of a sickness which, in 1633 carried off many of the whites and Indians, in and near to Plimouth [Plymouth], in Massachusetts, he says, "It is to be observed, that the Spring before this Sickness, there was a numerous companie of Flies, which, were like unto Wasps or Bumble-Bees, they came out of little holes in the ground, and did eat up the green things, and made such a constant yelling noise as made all the woods ring of them, and ready to deaf the hearers; they were not any of them heard or seen by the English in the Country before this time: But the Indians told them that sickness would follow, and so it did. He says, "Toward Winter, the sickness ceased;" and that it was "a kinde of pestilent Feaver."'

—"The Periodical Cicada"

The car was again headed north, this time out of Kalamazoo toward Traverse City. There would be plenty of time to think, as it was almost 200 miles up there, with only the first two-thirds of it on four-lane expressways.

He pulled out of the Starbucks drive-thru and onto the highway headed north, remembering the night before. He had gone to Bilbo's after all, despite deciding not to several times, and the girl from the library was there with her friends, just as he feared.

Amy, her name turned out to be, and rather than being the awkward, stupid scene he imagined, it had actually been a nice time and the cheesy bread with dill dip was, in fact, awesome. Still, as the girls laughed and told stories about dorms and people he had never heard of, all he could think of was Ashley sitting there, in that booth, with girls just like these, living the life they were living, living it without him, moving on, doing something with her life, and he wondered if the girls here had liked her, if she had had friends, friends like these, classes and dorms and stories about profs and football games and getting drunk.

Somewhere north of Grand Rapids, the play-by-play rehash was interrupted by his cell phone ringing. It was Scarlett.

"Hey."

"Hey you, how's it going?"

"It's good," he said. "I'm driving from Kalamazoo up to Traverse City."

"Traverse, huh?"

"Yeah, I found something that said she got married and moved to Traverse."

"Married, yeah," she said. "Well, you know, that happens. Now what?"

"You know, the same thing. It's not about that," he said, trying to believe it. "It's about, you know, closure. Find her, get things between us straight, get my head straight and then go back home and get on with my life."

The other end of the phone was silent.

"And, you know, maybe when I get back I might even ask you out," he said.

"Hmmm. Well, maybe I'll say yes," she said.

"Good."

"Listen, Andy, I just feel like I need to tell you I don't need you."

Wait, what?

"Just, you know, that I'm fine without you. I mean, I like you and everything, it's just, I had a life before you and I'll have a life after you."

Damn. Now this?

"Are you breaking up with me? Scarlett?"

"No, oh no. No, I wasn't saying that," she said. "I just, I'm sorry, I guess that came out wrong. Well, not wrong, just not in context. I'm just trying to say that, you know, don't base your decisions on me. That, well—"

He started to see where this was going.

"Wait a minute. Do I sense some regret?"

"No, not regret, really. Just—" she paused. "It's just that, even though I came on to you, I'm not desperate. Lonely, maybe, but not desperate. Anyway, I didn't want you to, I don't know, not pursue something because you think that I'll be devastated or whatever."

He laughed a little.

"So I'm just chopped liver? Your life is just as good without me?"

"No, it's much better with you," she said, and he could hear her smile even through the cell phone. "I guess I just didn't want you to think that because I was tired of using a vibrator that I can't live without you or something. That because I had sex with you that, you know, I'm pathetic."

He liked this girl.

"So I am just a piece of meat," he teased. "You only want me for my incredible body and smooth sexuality."

"Don't forget your cool sports car," she said. "And your knowledge of insects. That's a real turn-on, too."

"Well, Ashley appears to be married, or at least she was 11 years ago, so you're probably the only woman in the world willing to hear my incredible insect stories anyway."

"Wow, that's a relief. Listen, Andy, I'm sorry if what I said came out wrong, I was just trying to—"

"Oh I know what you were trying to do," he teased again. "You took me into your bedroom and took all your clothes off and now you want me to think it didn't mean anything, that it was, you know, purely casual. I bet you probably would have left at first light again if it hadn't been your own house."

"OK, now you're just trying to push my buttons."

"Sounds like you have a vibrator for that."

"I'm hanging up now."

"No you're not," he said. "Because you haven't let me say that I care about you. And I do. I know this trip is a real pain in your ass, I totally get that. But it doesn't mean I don't care about you, because I do. And I'll be back soon, and part of why I'll be back – even if I'm just your, I don't know, your concubine or something, is to be with you."

"You're sweet," she said. "For a pain in the ass."

He was always surprised at how hot it seemed on top of a sand dune. But as he came out of the woods into the bright sunshine at the top of the hill, the temperature seemed to jump about ten degrees. The sand got whiter, the wind blew harder and none of it seemed to matter at all as he saw the earth fall away from him in a jaw-dropping view.

He was standing on Pyramid Point, a peninsula that juts north out into Lake Michigan nearly two miles, giving him what seemed like about a 300-degree view of the lake. Pyramid Point got its name from the pyramid-shaped dune rising 320 feet above the beach. The trail from the parking lot climbed about 200 feet to the top of the wooded dune, where it suddenly ended with what seemed like a view of the whole world, save for the 45-degree drop of sheer dune to the water. It was one of the most incredible views in the state.

Andy sat down in the sand and pulled his shoes and socks off, then buried his feet to find the cool sand underneath the surface. It took a minute for his eyes to adjust to the harsh sunlight, but when he could really look around he could see the only thing bluer than the sky was the blue of the water following the curve of the earth as it pulled the inland sea to it like a cerulean blanket. Eight miles out from the beach was North Manitou Island, almost due north; eight miles northwest was South Manitou – the little islands that to Native American eyes eons ago looked like bear cubs out to sea, while the worried back of their mother bear was formed by the great Sleeping Bear dune near Glen Arbor.

It was a great story, but the fact is the mother bear shape had long since eroded away, so now it was just a sand dune and two cubs helpless offshore with no mother left waiting for them.

From where Andy sat, the islands didn't look like bear cubs or anything besides tree covered islands – deep green forests atop blue, blue waters. And his trip didn't look like anything but, well that was the thing, wasn't it? He didn't know what this trip was anymore.

He thought he knew, but when he had tried to explain it to Myers last night over many, many beers, it kept coming out wrong. Or sounding wrong. Or maybe the whole thing *was* wrong and so there was no good way to explain it.

Even with a four-hour drive up from Kalamazoo to Traverse City he hadn't been able to figure out how to explain it.

"Wait a minute, I'm obviously waaaaay too sober to understand what you're saying," Myers had said after he had settled in and they had gotten down to some serious drinking. It was out on the deck, which looked out over Grand Traverse Bay. Myers was in real estate, and real estate in the area had been going gangbusters, so when someone wanted to sell a little cottage with a lot of potential and killer views, he just never listed it and instead bought it himself. Everybody won.

They had sat on the deck, the Sunday afternoon sun setting over the bay, and Myers had dragged a cooler full of Sam Adams and ice out between their chairs.

"OK, you're here in Traverse, we each have a beer in our hand, we're sitting down, the sun is setting, and I have a grill with a chicken on it, so let's start over," Myers said. "You dated this girl in high school, and now, all these years later you can't get her out of your mind, so you try to find her, and so far you've found out that she's married and moved to Traverse, so you came up here to find her?"

Andy had taken a long pull on his beer himself then.

"You make it sound, so … what's the word? Stalker-like?"

"But, she's married?"

"Well, I know she got married. I don't know that she still is."

And on and on like that it had gone, in between catching up and emptying the cooler.

The good thing was, while Myers was asking serious questions, it was as much to razz him as anything. He was happy to have Andy up for a few days – even on one day's notice – and if it happened to be because he was on some crazy quest for some girl who couldn't possibly want to see him, well there were certainly worse things in the world. Like when Mark had married a witch.

"You know Mark's divorced, right?" Myers had asked while they inhaled the chicken and washed it down with more beer.

"From the vegan?"

"Yep."

"God bless her, but you know, she was Wiccan or whatever, and he, well, he wasn't."

"You can say that again. He was a Jesuit for crying out loud," Myers said, and they had laughed like it was the funniest thing they had ever heard.

They had talked and laughed and caught up until late at night. One of the benefits of real estate, Myers said, was you didn't have to work like at a 9-5 kind of office. He needed to show a house at about 11 and handle some paperwork in the afternoon, but being hung-over wouldn't be a problem. So they could both sleep in a little, Andy would have the day to hit the library or whatever, and then they'd hit the town that night.

But first, Andy thought, as he dug his feet a little deeper into the sand, he needed to hit the beach and think some deep thoughts. Like about the fact that Ashley had gotten married, and that he needed to assume she still was married. So that if he found her and knocked on her door, he would be prepared and not just stand there like an idiot.

It had somehow seemed a little easier to picture the scene when he imagined her single. Just play it straight, and assume she doesn't recognize you right off: "Ashley? I'm Andy Gardner from Fort Wayne." And then let the conversation roll from there.

But, well, that just didn't seem to make as much sense when she had a wedding band on her finger. "Hey, I know you're husband's due home at 5, but I'm your old boyfriend. How you been?" Stupid.

Of course, there were the fantasies, where she drops whatever she's doing at the first sight of him and falls into his arms, but those were just fantasies, and he didn't have time for those anymore. He had three weeks and then it was back to reality in Fort Wayne. There were house payments to make, and a million other obligations to take care of.

Of course, all those obligations seemed to be put in their proper place when he was staring out over Lake Michigan. He had somehow felt a kinship to this water since he first saw it on vacation as a kid. Something about its permanence. It had been here for thousands of years before he was, its waves washing the shoreline, and would be for thousands of years after he was long gone, and whatever petty little problems he had paled by comparison to the ages it had seen. When he was a child, those waves were rinsing the sand, when he was in Ashley's arms they were still there, when he married and divorced Susan they continued, and here they were now, still pouring forth in an unending rhythm that somehow comforted him. As if each wave seemed to be proof that there were some things that did not change. Not ever.

He looked out over the waves for a long time – from up here they looked like ripples, but from the white edges and grinding roar, he knew they were rolling in pretty hard – and each one seemed to be whispering something he couldn't quite make out. Was it that the love he and Ashley had was forever, no matter where their separate lives had taken them? Or that things go on, even if their love hadn't? Maybe they were saying he needed to let her go with the waves, that she would always be a part of him, but not something he could take home and hold in his hands, the way you can hold a Sleeping Bear snow globe souvenir, but the waves mean so much more.

Or maybe they're just saying you're an idiot, Andy, he thought. It was time for lunch anyway, and he still had to walk a half-mile back to the car, plus a 20-minute drive to the closest restaurant, down in Glen Arbor. Still, he thought, what a view. Even if she screams at me and throws me out, this view alone was worth the trip up here.

The Traverse Area District Library was bigger than he expected. Way bigger. It was only two stories, but the huge peaked roof and bell tower made it look even bigger than it actually was, and it was actually huge inside. The effect was even more dramatic because the style of the building seemed to be a cross between Modern Yacht Club and Frank Lloyd Wright – that peaked roof had huge overhangs shading lots of horizontal lines and other Prairie stylings, while the bell-tower and commanding-view windows screamed out for lake views, though its views were of Boardman Lake, a small inland lake where a river paused on its way to Grand Traverse Bay near downtown. There were no yachts to be found here.

"Can I help you?"

"Yeah, I'm looking – this sounds stupid, but where are your phone books?"

The librarian paused for a minute, as if thinking, "yeah, that is stupid" before realizing he meant the ones in the collection, not the one on her desk. "Right this way."

Emma Dunne had taught him yet another great thing about libraries – they stock every phone book in the surrounding area, and usually several years' worth, so you can often find people who have unlisted numbers.

"Usually, people don't start out unlisted," Emma had said when giving him advice for his trip. "But then something happens, like their old boyfriend in high school shows up on their front porch, and then they get unlisted. Just kidding. But if you have the old book, you can still find them. Oh, another thing. A lot of people will get unlisted in the book, but then they won't pay the monthly fee to be unlisted in the directory thing you call. So if she's not in the book, call Information anyway."

"Wow, you're really good at stalking people," he had said.

"I have my moments."

She certainly did, but now the Traverse Area District Library staffer was having hers. She was one of those older ladies that you just can't tell how old she is – does she look younger than she really is, and things like the wrinkles are giving it away, or is she actually younger than she looks, and suffers from things that make her look older, like sagging ear lobes?

"Here you go," she said, striding across the green, no-nonsense carpet. "Anything else?"

"Yeah, do have an archive for the local newspaper?"

She paused again. Maybe she hadn't thought he was stupid before, she just pauses before speaking.

"The Record-Eagle? No, I'm sorry. Well, we do up until the late '80s, but then it was stopped for budget cuts," she said. "If you need something very old, we may have it, but otherwise we have only the current editions."

The 1980s qualify as "very old" now? Oh man.

"Not even a name-file?"

"No, but the Record-Eagle's office is right downtown. I'm sure they can help you there."

Of course, he thought, that may not even be necessary if Ashley's listed in the phone book.

She wasn't. No Stibitz listed at all, not in the Greater Traverse City Area book, the Antrim County book or a half dozen others. No Ashley Hudsons, either, just in case she got divorced and changed her name back. Nothing.

He walked over to the public computer area and Googled her again, just in case. Nothing.

As he walked out, he passed the librarian that had helped him earlier.

"Which way did you say the newspaper office was?" he asked.

121

Pause.

"Right up the street this way," she pointed. "You know how to get back downtown, right? It's right downtown, a big red building with a turret – you'll see it."

"Thanks."

He turned to go, but then was interrupted by the lady who had seemed so distant before.

"Did you find what you were looking for?"

"No, I guess I'll have to try the newspaper."

She set down some books she had been holding.

"Perhaps I can help."

Andy explained what he was looking for as they walked back toward the stacks.

A pause. "You're looking for a person, not a phone number. Let's try something over here," she said and led him back to the public computers. "Try Whitepages.com. It's an online phonebook, and you can leave out the city and just put in the state. I'd hate for her to live one city over from the phonebook you were looking at and not find her."

Sure enough, a James Stibitz showed up in North Muskegon, a few hours south. He would still check the newspaper to see if there were any other clues, but it looked like she had moved, or at least her husband had.

Andy stood up and turned to the librarian. "Wow, is there anything you can't find?"

She paused. "That's what I do. I help people find things."

"Can you find the lost idyll of my youth?"

He laughed, but not really.

She began walking him toward the front desk.

"A lot of people don't know what they're really searching for. They *think* they know, but what they're really after is something else entirely," she said. Then she paused again. "In the worst cases, they never find it because they can't see anything but what they think they're after."

Mackinaw Brewing Company was right downtown in Traverse City and looked exactly like it should inside: lots of exposed brick, cool things on the walls, great food and great beer.

"Give me the Beadles Best Bitter," Myers told the girl.

"Bitter?" Andy asked.

"Trust me. It's amazing," Myers said, then turned back to the waitress. "Oh, and give us a dozen wings for an appetizer."

"I don't trust you. Give me the Belgian Whitecap."

After the girl left with their beer orders, Andy looked over the menu, figuring he'd probably get the Walleye. The Walleye up here was supposed to be amazing.

"So how'd it go today?" Myers asked. "Did you find her?"

"Actually, I did," Andy said as the girl returned with their pints. "She's down in Muskegon."

"Muskegon? You're getting the grand tour of the Lower Peninsula, aren't you?"

"Yeah," Andy said, setting down the beer he had been looking forward to all day. He probably had a beer mustache, he had drunk so deeply, and he didn't care a bit. "The librarian actually found her with this online phonebook thing. Then I went down to the Record-Eagle and some reporter looked her up in their archives. They ran a one-paragraph item a few years ago about her husband getting a promotion and a transfer down there."

"Here's your wings, gentlemen," the girl said at their elbows. "Enjoy."

"You're really getting into this, aren't you?"

"The search you mean?" Andy said between bites. "Yeah, just the search itself is pretty interesting. I've certainly learned a lot in the last couple of weeks. Like if you need me to hunt down someone for you, I could make a pretty good run at it."

"The question is, though, what you're going to do when you actually find her," Myers said, waving the waitress back to warn her they would soon need new beers. "I mean, when you're at her front door and she's inside, what then?"

"I'll try the Peninsula Pale Ale," Andy told the girl.

"Gimme The Bridge this time," Myers said. "I feel like a nut brown all the sudden."

"Yeah, that's kind of the question," Andy said as the waitress left. "I'm not really sure. I mean, the whole thing is about, I don't know, 'closure' or whatever, but I still don't know what the hell I'm going to say. I don't really even know what closure is at this point."

"I guess I'm just still confused about your motives. I mean, are you trying to win her back or something? Didn't you say she's married?"

"Yeah, she's married, but it's not about that," Andy said. "I'm not trying to get her back, I'm trying to put her in the past, I guess. Remember, we were deeply in love and she just disappeared without a word. It was like she died, but no funeral, no grave, nothing. And until I find her…"

The girl was back with their beers and Myers said they would probably be ready to order their meals about the time these ones were gone.

"We're planning on closing the place out, so don't be all in a rush to

123

bring us our food," he said to her. "We don't want to get all bloated on food and not be able to drink the beer properly."

She smiled like it was the funniest thing ever and the 1,000th time she'd heard that, both at the same time.

"It's just— " Myers started, then rubbed his forehead. "I still don't get it. It's like, it's like, like you're feeling guilty about something. That's it!" he said and took a drink. "I'm Catholic – if there's one thing I know, it's guilt. What are you feeling so guilty about? Did you knock her up or something?"

"No, I did not knock her up," Andy said. "And I'm a cradle Catholic, too, remember? But no," he said, and looked out the windows onto Front Street, where tourists were walking by. "No, it's just – what happened? How did she just leave like that?"

"Huh," Myers said. "How old were you guys? Was she younger than you? Was she legal? Let me guess, you deflowered some poor little girl and now all these years later you're coming clean about it."

"No, it wasn't anything like that," he said. "We were both the same age. We were both seventeen. If anything, we deflowered each other."

This was not the conversation he wanted to be having.

"Even if you had deflowered this poor innocent thing, there's nothing to feel guilty about *now*," Myers said. "It was like twenty years ago. She probably won't even remember you, let alone that you exploited her six different ways."

"It was not six different ways," he said. "It was only five. And seriously, it's not about that. It's just that everything was right, everything was great, and then they moved away, literally overnight. She was just gone. And I don't know, I just feel like if I could see her again, see that she's alive and hear her say that she thought about me at least once afterward, that I could move on."

Myers thought about that for a while.

"What you need, my friend, is cheap, meaningless sex," he said, picking up the last of the wings.

"There's meaningless sex, but in my experience there is no such thing as cheap sex, regardless of the meaning."

Myers wiped barbecue sauce from his chin.

"That's true, but with some meaningless sex you don't care about the price. Take her for example." He was nodding at a brunette walking in the door. Her black hair was long and her skin was fair and she carried a tiny black handbag and looked like she might have stepped off the page of a magazine. The guy behind her might have been mistaken for someone who just happened to walk in at the same time as her until she slipped her arm around his waist while they looked around the room for

124

a table.

"No, Myers, that is a price I absolutely could not afford," Andy said slowly, staring openly at her, and as he said it, the woman caught his eye and stared back at him for a moment. Oh shit.

"What? Why not?" Myers asked, and as he did, the woman said something to the man with her, then started walking directly toward them.

"Because," Andy said, "that is my ex-wife."

TWELVE

Awake. Even before his eyes opened, he had been aware of a sound – tones that blended into harmonies, the lower and upper notes in the chord vibrating so perfectly in tune that other notes seemed to appear out of the ether as the very molecules of the air pulsated in sympathy with the beauty of notes so perfectly aligned. That sound continues even after he opens his eyes, and he lies still, not just hearing it, but feeling the very sound waves ringing through the air. Soon, he can hear the waves echoing back across the room, as they are sent out and back like ripples on the surface of the water, and as they arrive back at his body, his heart takes up the sound and begins beating in time with the waves of the chord ringing through every fiber of his being.

This music is new, but he instantly recognizes it, too, as if he heard it in the womb or even before that. It is the Song he once sung in the heavens, he thinks, before all this, and now, at last, he is singing it again, without having to move his lips, without having to think about it, without doing anything at all except embracing its hymn.

A new noise comes, this one not fitting with the song at all. It comes in great crashes of electronic buzzing until he realizes it is the alarm clock, gone off just three hours after he set it after sneaking back in at 5 a.m.

He sits up, fully awake now, but the music continues. It's softer now, but still there, like a soundtrack in his head as he gets up, until it soars back into full volume, his spine electrified and his heart now syncopating across the sound waves as he realizes he can still smell Ashley and their night together, and it all washes over him, the music swelling and filling his head, then the room, the house, the block, the city and reaching out across the land in waves and currents he has never known before.

This is our eternal Song, he thinks. The one we sang together before we were even conceived, the music we sang to each other across the centuries, and now we're singing it to each other again, two voices in such perfect harmony the whole universe is taking up our tune.

He dresses slowly, feeling each movement of his arms swirling the notes, each brush of the clothing against his skin a reminder of her skin against his. He will barely see her today, but it doesn't matter now, because Forever has started, and distractions like jobs and school shopping are nothing compared to the Song, the song that is in the very air he breathes now, the Song he thought he had forgotten after being plucked out of heaven and down to Earth to live and breathe and die, but he remembered – he remembered it the instant she sang it to him, sang it to him with her sighs, and even the way she held him and cooed him to sleep in her arms, their bodies pressed close, the music building with the memory of the eternity they had started before and were rebuilding again.

Upstairs. "Oh. My. God, Andy," come the words. "You look like complete crap."

He looks at his sister, but it takes a moment for the words, muffled by the music in his head, to register and make sense. He just smiles back at her.

"Andy, you're working at 9, right?" That was his mother talking. He nods. "And Ashley's coming over about then, right?"

He thinks hard. Words. You can do it.

"Yeah, I think so." He had done it. Still, the music plays in the background, the foreground, vibrating through the kitchen countertops.

"Good, I want to get to the mall before it gets too crowded," she says. "I think we're going to have a lot of fun."

So many words. And all of them distracting from the music. Why do they have to talk so— Coffee. He had been vaguely aware of the sound of the gurgling at the end of the brew cycle, but it took a minute to connect the sound with its meaning: There's coffee, thank God. He walks in time to the music over to the coffee pot, and pours himself a cup, feeling his sister and mother's eyes on him, but he doesn't care. A little cream, a lot of sugar, and ohhhhhhhh yeah, that is going to work.

He plops in a couple of ice cubes, stirs, then chugs the entire cup and pours himself another. Still Sally and Mom stare, but say nothing.

As he sits down with the second cup, the room comes into better focus. The music is still there, but it's in the background now, like department-store music. He looks at Sally.

"What is wrong with you?" she says. "You don't drink coffee."

"What?" he says, feeling his voice in tune to the notes playing. "I'm just waking up."

"Well, you may be hung over, or way tired, or just retarded or whatever, but I'm excited," she says. "I can't believe Ashley and I are going school shopping together."

Even through the fog that statement creases Andy's brow. I guess it's technically true, he thinks, but Mom offering to take Ashley along as she takes Sally shopping somehow is not the same thing. Whatever. If Ashley makes Sally happy, all the better.

Sally points to the clock. "Good thing I was up early," she says. "You better get moving if you're going to shower before work."

"Yeah," he says. "Just another minute."

In the bathroom, he undresses and turns on the water, but doesn't get in. Instead, he just looks down at himself, marveling at the strange reality that two bodies, so shockingly different, could be so amazing when together. That hers could want anything to do with his. That one could find a mystery he would be content to spend a lifetime exploring. Finally, the steam from the shower brings him back to reality and he looks in the mirror.

His face is the same, same jaw line, same lips, same stupid nose. Same eyebrows, same zits that just refuse to go away.

But his eyes. His eyes that had always been greenish brown. Sometimes browner, sometimes greener, depending on the light, but always green-brown.

Today they are blue. Ashley blue. Ashley shards of a thousand blues blue. All the colors of the sky blue. The music swells again, and he hears her sighs, sees her voice in the irises that have replaced his old ones. Feels himself looking out through her eyes now as the Music expands, becomes deeper and more focused, even as the blue in his eyes sparkle in the bathroom light.

We are One Forever, he thinks. She is me and I am her. One. One song. Two notes forming one chord. One set of eyes, looking out from one heart.

One.

Front porch swing. The weather has cooled a little, and she's wearing the new jeans she bought a week ago shopping with Mom and Sally. She calls them capris, he teases her and calls them floods. All week long, he had been pushing the Music down in his head as best he could, but now, with her near, he can hardly hear anything else. He watches the way her fingers curl around the swing's chain, the way a ligament in her neck moves as she rocks her feet to keep the swing moving in the thick August air.

He sits on the wood of the front porch, feels the grain of the planks as the center of the universe floats like a pendulum a few feet away, all creation humming with the Song.

"I bought you something," he says, not moving, just watching.

Her only reaction is the slightest of smiles. She's been quiet.

"What?" she sighs.

He pulls out the plastic dome-shaped clear plastic egg and hands it to her. He wanted it to be meaningful, but he knew that it couldn't be meaningful in a material sense, because what he really wanted to give her was a diamond. But even through the fog of the music constantly in his head he knew how bad an idea that would be. Besides, even though he had thought about that once in a while before, he could wait now. Now there was no rush, no need to hurry because they are already One.

So instead of a diamond, he had spent what seemed like an hour after work at the convenience store across from Atz's, trying to get the clear plastic egg out of one of the gumball machines. The seven rabbits feet he got before the break-apart pendant finally appeared in the chute had not only made Sally very happy, but also helped enlist her as an ally in convincing his parents of his grand plan to keep Ashley close no matter what.

On the egg, he had written in blue marker, "Tiffany's."

She laughs at the inscription, and the swing slows as she twists the two halves of the egg apart and pulls out the two gold-colored necklaces, each with half a pendant. She takes the two halves and holds them together. "I love you," she reads out loud, then looks at him, the Music seeming to vibrate even the ground and the trees stuck like tuning forks into the soil. "I love you, Andy."

"Which half do you want?" he says.

"Hmmm," she says, then clutches one to her chest and holds the other out to him.

"Ove ou," he reads to her.

"I L Y," she reads back, only she says it like, "I lie." All he hears is the sigh, and the notes in her voice forming the chord of their Song.

A woman pushing a baby carriage walks by in stretch pants and a sweatshirt with shoulder pads. She smiles at them.

"Listen," he says above the music. "I've been talking to my parents."

Had he ever. It had taken him a week, but he had finally gotten them to consider letting Ashley stay there during her senior year if her mom had to move. They hadn't agreed to it – not by a long shot – but they had agreed to consider it.

It hadn't been easy to be clear and purely logical with the Music playing all the time, but he had managed, mainly by arguing fairness.

"If she wasn't my girlfriend, you wouldn't think twice about it, would you?" he had asked. "If she was just some friend I knew, someone who needed our help, you would help."

"That's not the point, Andy," his father had said.

"Yes, that's exactly the point. You're more willing to help a stranger

129

than someone you know and love," he had said. "That's the point exactly. It's unfair to have a double standard that hurts someone you both admit that you love."

"Andy," his mother had said. "You've got to understand that— "

And that is when he had gone for broke.

"What I understand is that you're willing to enforce a double standard just because you're afraid we'll have sex." There. It was out there. It had been a bold move, but times were desperate.

"Now, Andy," his mother began.

"No, I understand that, but it's true," he had said. "When the fact is we could do that regardless of where she lives. I'm just saying. And that makes it even more unfair that you would not offer to help her."

"She could sleep in my room," Sally offered. She had been sitting at the kitchen table the whole time, nearly forgotten, while they stood around the island debating. "Andy is NOT having sex with anybody in there, I'll guarantee it."

"OK, enough of this," his father had said.

"I'm just saying," Sally said. "He's not."

He had had a lot more points to argue, but something told him to stop just then.

"We'll think about it," his mother suddenly said. His father shot her a look, but she returned it. As they left the room, Andy had walked over to his kid sister and given her the last two rabbits feet – both green, her favorite color.

"Nice work, kid," he said.

"Do NOT have sex in my room," Sally had said, eyes like daggers. "I mean it."

"Yeah, right," he said. "You don't even know what sex is."

"Hah, hah. I'm on my period, moron."

"Ooo," he had said, picking up one of the rabbits' feet. "Too bad for these guys."

"Oh my God. You are the grossest person ever. I can't believe someone as cool as Ashley even likes you at all."

He pushes the scene from the day before out of his head as Ashley looks up from her half of the pendent.

"Yeah, so I've been talking to them," he says. "And they're thinking about— "

"Andy, they're going to announce the layoffs Monday," she says. "There's no way my Mom's not getting cut."

"Oh," he says. But wait.

"This is. This. I," she says. "You know I never had a real boyfriend before. This is why not."

130

But all he hears is the song, and thinks that in the end, it might even be better, because now she could actually live here with him.

"But I'm more than just some boyfriend, aren't I? This is, this is what we always said – it's not the end. It's just the beginning," he says. "Nothing changes, right?"

She looks at him, her eyes a thousand shards that he knows because he sees them in his own eyes now. Feels the music in every cell in his body.

She clutches the pendent. "Nothing changes," she says.

"And besides, it hasn't even happened yet," he says, standing up. "We can't worry about something that hasn't happened, right? So let's go do something and forget about this for a while. What do you want to do?"

She thinks for a moment, then brightens.

"Oh my gosh, I almost forgot. Krik Whistler is playing at Tony's tonight."

"Who?" Oh great – they were going to sneak into another bar. One of these days he was going to go to jail because of her, and while he rotted in a cell, she'd be out chatting up the vice cops that put him there. Worth it, but still.

"Krik Whistler," she says. "They're some band from Michigan, I don't know. Emma told me about them – they're supposed to be great."

Emma loves them? Why didn't she say so in the first place?

"All right, what time's the show?"

Andy parks on a side street like four blocks away because everywhere he turns the street is lined with cars. The place must be packed out. They might not be able to get in even if they can get in.

They walk, holding hands, toward the bar, the branches on the trees hanging low in the still August air. The day was cooler than it had been, but the temperature has not dropped like usual, so it's still warm even though the sun is about to set. If it wasn't for the Song, he would notice the air is quiet, the cicadas gone.

As they walk, he feels taller somehow, and thinks about what it will be like to still hold hands when they're an old married couple. She's talking about something, but all he really hears is the sound of One.

When they get to the bar, it's packed to the doorway, where a huge bouncer-type in sunglasses is checking IDs and taking cover charges. We're totally screwed, Andy thinks. There is no way he is letting us in there.

"Hey there, Sunshine!" the bouncer says to Ashley. "You're not trying to get in here, are you?" Even on the sidewalk Andy can hear music pounding from inside.

Ashley smiles. "Oh come on, Mike! We just want to see the band."

"Well," Mike says, looking around. "I got good news and bad news."

She puts one hand on her hip, the other is around Andy's waist. He should have known.

"The bad news is, we're sold out. I can't sell even one more admission tonight," he says. "So the good news, I guess, is that I can't charge you for coming in, can I?"

"Thanks, Mike."

"Listen, though, and I mean it – do not try to drink. I'm risking my butt letting you in here at all, so don't abuse it, all right?"

"Thanks again, Mike," she says, then grabs Andy by the arm and drags him into the sweaty crowd inside.

The music that had been playing – a jarring mash over the top of the Song of One – stops awkwardly, and the crowd roars as they squeeze between bodies toward an open space near the wall opposite the bar. All they can see of the little stage at the far end is the speaker tower on each side and the tops of the microphones, but the crowd roars as the band appears one by one and starts messing with their instruments. When they get to the break in the crowd it's like an oasis – a bit of air in the midst of a hot, sweaty mass of people chanting and cheering as they start in to the song.

This time, the music actually melds with the Song in his head, the electric guitars bending the notes he had been hearing into a repeating, hypnotic rhythm, then the drums begin pounding on top of it. Now it's not just in his head – Andy can put his hand on the wall and feel it vibrating with the music as the guy at the microphone sings over the top of the whole thing. The crowd can feel it, too, and all of them – there must be 200 crammed into the tiny space – are jumping in time to the beat, mesmerizing him even further as the whole world seems to roar to the song of One.

They walk back to the car, sweaty and exhausted, but buoyant. He tries again.

"So I was talking to my parents, right?"

"Yeah. Listen, Andy, let's just not talk about it, OK?" she says. "Don't worry about it."

"No, listen. I know, but they were saying that, if your mom does lose her job, if there's layoffs or whatever, that maybe you could stay here to finish your senior year."

"Stay here?" she says. "What do you mean?" One.

"Yeah, like, if your mom had to move or something, instead of moving, you could just stay here and go to North Side," he says. "With me."

She's confused. "Stay here? In our house by myself?"

"No," he laughs. "With us. Like, you would just live at our house so you could go to North Side until you graduated. So you, you know, wouldn't have to move." Away from Us, he thinks. Us together. Us. Forever. One.

She's quiet. She's realizing how great it will be, he thinks. "Sally even offered to let you share her room."

"Andy, the thing is, my Mom and me, I mean, I know she's not the greatest parent in the world. I know that, believe me," she says. "But the thing is, she did all this for me. And we did it together. We're a team."

We're a team, he thinks. You and Me. One.

"I can't just leave that now," she says. "If she has to move, it's so she can support me. Or like when we had to move here because her boyfriend was hitting on me, she did that to protect me. Yes, he was a complete asshole, but she never thought twice about leaving him, leaving town, leaving her job, leaving everything, for me."

I would leave everything for you, he thinks. We are One.

"I can't just— I mean, I totally appreciate it, but it would be like walking out on her. I can't just leave like that," she says. "Especially now that I've got just one more year of school and then she'll have made it. Everything that she's given up over the years, all the jobs she's had to do and extra shifts she's taken, she'll have made it."

She's right, he thinks, just one more year and we'll have made it. We'll be adults, and there'll be nothing to keep us apart. One.

"I just, I have to stick with this."

She's going to stick with this, he thinks. Us. She's going to stick it out to make sure we're together. She'll miss her Mom after all she's done for her, but she's going to stay here and stick it out. Because we're One.

She stops and looks at him, her eyes catching the streetlight near his Mom's car. They're glistening.

"We're a team," she says.

A team, he thinks. One. You and me. Forever. "I know," he says. Two people, one team.

One chord. One Song, forever.

One.

THIRTEEN

"Hello, Andy," Susan says, her words measured. She's been practicing saying that, he thinks instantly. She said it like she's heard herself saying it. And if she's been practicing it, even in her head, then she's been planning on talking to me. Even eight years later – with this weird kind of wall between us – I can still see right through her. Crazy.

"Hi, Susan," he says, wondering if she can hear the caution in his words. He hasn't been practicing, but figures this could be a chess game of the highest order. Especially since she looks way more beautiful than he remembered. "I was not expecting to see you."

Her hair used to be long and wavy, and it suited her the way it curved around her face and then flared out again toward her shoulders. It seemed natural and gorgeous. But now, now it is straight and cut off right at shoulder level and is stunning in the way that expensive, beautiful things can be simple and perfect at the same time. Now, her brown eyes seem even larger, and the eyebrows that once seemed to frame them are now part of the integrated whole, part of the picture itself. Her lips – had he ever noticed her lips before? – are full and perfectly lined with lipstick.

"I was not expecting to see you here, either," Susan says. "But I've actually been meaning to talk to you for a while." She sets her little black purse on the edge of the table, but still clutches it. "How are you, Myers?"

Now it's Myers' turn to squirm. "Ah, you know, I'm great, Susan. Who's this with you?" The Geek has followed her to their table and is standing there looking uncomfortable. It's a big club.

"Yeah, this is Brian, everyone," she says, picking up the purse a little and then setting it down again. "Brian, this is Myers, and this is Andy, my ex-husband."

Brian immediately reaches out to shake Andy's hand, but his grip is noncommittal. It doesn't matter. All Andy can think is that he just heard his ex-wife introducing him to some guy as her ex-husband. He's way too sober for this.

They're all just standing there stupidly for a moment, when –

thankfully – Myers takes charge.

"Listen, yeah, Susan and Andy, look, you kids probably have a lot of catching up to do, and I'm sure, uh Brian here, would just love to tell me all about the rec-league sports he's no-doubt involved in when he's not doing accounting or whatever, so why don't you two go upstairs to the deck where you can talk? Me and Brian will keep your seats warm. You like wings, Brian?"

Andy looks at Susan and realizes she's looking back at him and that all the sudden she's not so much his ex-wife as she is someone he spent three years married to. He's not sure exactly what the difference is, but there is one, and for now that's enough.

"Perfect. You said upstairs?" he says.

"Yeah, and listen, we'll send a couple of drinks up, too," Myers says, and then sticks two fingers into his mouth and whistles loudly to the waitress. "Hey! We're dying over here!" he calls.

As they walk toward the stairs, Andy can hear Myers talking to Brian.

"Listen, you like Scotch? They have great beer here, but I feel a powerful need for Scotch all the sudden. And beer to wash it down of course, but Scotch…"

They get to the stairs and Andy lets her go first, just trying to be polite, but is rewarded with a stunning view of her navy pencil skirt and legs that seem to extend all the way to the second floor. He didn't remember her legs being that long or that, well, perfect. Hell, he thought, he didn't remember her being anywhere near this hot. If she wasn't his ex-wife, he might try to pick her up.

The upstairs is a miniature version of the main floor, but opens out onto a deck that looks toward Grand Traverse Bay. The sun is getting ready to set and already the shadows are getting long as the sky is taking on a blush of color. The breeze is off the bay and, well, if he wasn't standing here with his ex-wife, it would be damn-near perfect.

"How's this?" she asks, grabbing a table near the railing.

"Perfect," he says. "Man, it's gorgeous up here."

"It is. We've been here a week," she says. "How long have you been here? It's amazing we didn't run into each other before."

"Oh I've only been here, what, a day and-a-half, I guess," he says as a waitress appears with fresh beers for them, courtesy of Myers' whistle. "Myers' place is way out on Old Mission, and I've been kind of holed up, so I'm not really running into anybody."

He looks at her in the now-golden sunlight and can't remember all the bad times anymore, the screaming, the cursing, the endless nights of not talking to each other. Now, seeing her eyes, as dark, dark brown as ever, even in the sun, all he can remember is two kids trying to make it work, even though they both secretly knew they were doomed. In the end, even the fighting had been half-hearted, as they had both given up on whatever they had been fighting for, and the worst part was they knew the other one had, too. Still, for a long time it seemed like it was worth it to charge up that hill, even though they knew they wouldn't be coming back. And in retrospect, maybe they were right.

"It's been a long time," she says. "I can't believe it's been eight years already."

"Well the years have certainly been kind to you. You look amazing," he says. "Somehow better than ever, really."

She smiles, and it's only half-way how she would smile when a stranger would compliment her. The other half is the old Susan, the smile you give someone who sees you at your worst and everywhere in between but still thinks you're beautiful. Andy realizes he is neither strange or familiar to her now, really, and pulls out his cigarettes and lights one, then just for fun offers her one. To his surprise, she takes it, and he lights it for her.

"I've been meaning to talk to you," she says, "Andy."

"Yeah, you know, listen, I've been meaning to call, too, it's just, you know…"

"No, I mean I was going to call you when we got back from here," she says. "It's about Brian." There's a pause while she takes a long drag on the cigarette. Even that seems graceful. "We're getting married."

Of course they are. Of course. For shit's sake.

But you know, honestly, maybe it's the best, he thinks, taking a drag himself. Hell, if it makes her happy, what do I care after eight years? She should be happy. Why not?

"Hey, that's great," he says. "Congratulations. I didn't even notice the ring."

She starts to lift her hand, and then puts it down again.

"I'm, ah, not wearing it," she says, and then looks out at the bay for a minute, then back at him.

"Is everything OK?"

"Listen, Andy, the thing is, you need to understand something. And this is what I wanted to talk to you about," she says. "I'm not wearing it because he gave it to me a long time ago, and it was only this week, up here in Traverse, that I finally said yes. And when I did, well, the ring was at home."

He drains his beer and realizes the cigarette is almost gone already, too.

"Just this week? How long has it been?"

She just looks at her own beer, and then drains it, and holds it up for the nearest waitress to see, and motions for two more.

"It's been six years, Andy." She puts her hand on the little black purse, then takes it off again.

"Oh."

The beers gone, there's nothing to do but look at each other or the sunset, but he can't stop looking at her. What is she saying? Six years?

"We dated for about a year, and then he asked me, and I didn't say no, but I didn't say yes, either," she says. "I just wasn't ready, you know? Part of it was, you know, I still needed to move on from everything with us, and part of it was that I needed to know that this time wasn't— well, that it was— "

Andy pulls out the cigarettes again. "I know what you mean. It's OK, because it's true. You needed to make sure that this really was the fairy tale, because we weren't," he says, and looks up from lighting the smoke to see her looking straight at him. "That was the problem, and we both know it. We had everything – everything, Susan – except that one thing. Lord knows we tried, but we didn't have it, did we? It wasn't your fault, and it wasn't mine, either. It just was. The only fault was that we both tried anyway, and you know, at this point, eight years down the road, I really can't blame us – anyone – for trying."

Now she closes her eyes, and he can see her lashes are long and, again, somehow perfect. How much money is she making these days?

"No, we didn't have it. And you tried harder than I ever had a right to expect," she says. "Which is why there was another part to it. The waiting six years, I mean."

As she says this, the waitress appears with the new beers, wordlessly sets them down and leaves.

"I didn't want to say yes to Brian or anyone else, for that matter, while things between us were the way we left them," she says. "I don't know if this makes any sense or not, but I just, it was like I needed to move on and I couldn't as long as I was still mad at you."

"What do you mean? We're divorced – it's OK to be mad at me," he says. "Heck, no one in the world would blame you for hating my guts. Everyone does it. It's required or something in a divorce. It means you're doing it right, probably."

"I don't know, really," she says, and takes a cigarette from the pack he has left out on the table. The sky is turning orange now. "The only way I can explain it is something that sounds completely stupid. It's that, well, I didn't want to get married again until I was comfortable asking you to come to the wedding. I know that sounds crazy, and obviously I'm not saying you have to go or anything like that, but I needed to be in a place where I could feel good about you being there, for all the right reasons, I

137

guess. It doesn't make any sense, I know."

"Maybe a little," he says, picturing it. Could he be there and be there for her at the same time?

"It's just that, and I know I'm babbling, but we had, what five, six years together, all told? You were an important part of my life. And the vast majority of those years were good times. And I don't want to lose that. I don't want that to be just, buried by all the crap, you know? And I needed to be in a place where I could appreciate what we had and maybe even what we tried to have, before I was ready to try again."

She taps an ash into the ashtray, her ring finger betraying no tan lines. "I'm sorry I'm not making any sense."

"No, it actually does make a lot of sense," Andy says. "I think I know what you mean. I've been trying to put some things to rest myself lately, and this, this makes a lot of sense."

"I'm sorry to spring this on you like this at a restaurant and all. Like I said, I was going to call you when we got back, but when we walked in and you were there, well—"

Things were clicking faster than he could keep up with them, but he could understand that she was right about things, even if he would have to sit down and figure out what they all were.

"You're sure – and I'm not trying to say anything here, other than, in a pure sense of are you sure because you're going to want to be sure – are you sure it's not that there's a lack of something with Brian and that by reconnecting with someone from the past that—" he says, then shakes his head. The beer or something was getting to him. "No, just that, I'm not saying we had something you don't, but just—"

She actually laughs a little at his stumbling. It's been a long time since he's heard her laugh.

"No," she says. "Well, he may lack your rapier wit, or your obvious command of the language, but, no. It really was just that, and again this sounds so dumb, but, I wanted to be able to look back on my wedding day and remember seeing you there, happy for me. I know that's impossible, and I don't think I wanted even that so much as I wanted to be able to want that, if that makes sense."

The sun was gone now, and the cloudless sky had turned all manner of orange and gold and the water of the bay went from slate to purple to slate again. He thought about the wedding again, imagined himself sitting there watching. Could he be happy for her? He thought maybe he could. Then he thought about Ashley, and tried to imagine her sitting in a pew smiling while he said his vows to someone else, maybe Scarlett for lack of any other faces to complete the picture. Could he ask Ashley to his wedding? Could he really say those vows and mean them if she was in the pew watching?

"Hey you kids," Myers' voice cut through the thought. "We were afraid we were going to either find you killing each other or making out. Looks like I owe you some money, Brian."

The four of them had closed the place out, leaving Andy thinking that had to be the latest he had been out on a Monday in years, if not decades. There were toasts and laughs, and stories and jokes and the longer it went on the better he felt about the whole thing. Heck, he would probably even go to the wedding. He might even bring a gift.

"So what's your plan?" Myers asks as he pours another round of coffee. They're both holding their heads and popping ibuprofens as they sit on the deck in the morning sun trying to wake up.

"Well, I figured I'd pack up and drive south," Andy says. "It's what, three, four hours to Muskegon? Stop for lunch somewhere, and I'm there at like one, two at the latest."

"So two o'clock today, you could be knocking on her door."

He takes a deep breath. "Yeah, I guess so," he says. "Kinda hard to believe it."

"Well there's no rush, you know," Myers says. "You're welcome to stay here as long as you want."

"Yeah, no, listen I appreciate it. I just feel like, I'm this close now, I gotta close it out," he says.

"All right, well if you change your mind, just give me a call. Or even if you want to come back up afterward, you've got more vacation, right? Just say the word," Myers says, standing up. "I gotta get ready for work, but you know how to lock up and everything."

Andy stands, too. "Yeah, listen, thanks for everything. Especially thanks for being my wing-man last night with Susan."

"Your wing-man, I wish. Although Brian turned out to be a pretty cool guy, which is more proof you shouldn't judge by looks, but still," Myers says.

"Thanks, Myers."

"No problem."

An hour later, Myers is gone and Andy's out of the shower and packing up. He puts the dishes in the dishwasher, and heads out.

On the road, the day shapes up the way he always thinks of Traverse City – the perfect temperature without a cloud in the sky. The winding road down Old Mission Peninsula occasionally has breaks in the heavy trees to reveal sailboats out on the sparkling bay, while downtown is clogged with tourists, even on a weekday morning. Outside of town, the road becomes a wide, two-lane highway rolling up and down hills lined with tall white pines, and it looks exactly like it did when he was a boy, up here with his parents: Cold, deep lakes of crystal blue water among the hills, the everlasting shimmer of Lake Michigan as the road winds down the coast between hamlets. He could just follow U.S. 31 south, but instead heads west on 72 towards Empire. It's a little out of his way, but it will let him take Route 22 down the coast all the way to Manistee, and there's some things he wants to see.

At Empire, Route 22 turns south until it gets to Little Platte Lake, where it turns west again and heads between Little Platte Lake, Platte Lake, Crystal Lake and Lake Michigan. At each one, the houses go from spare outposts alone in the woods surrounded by cars and motorcycles or four-wheelers to lake houses – little houses on little lots, scrunched close together, but something many people are willing to pay many dollars for: Lake frontage. There's always the bar and grill nearby, which becomes the village's social center, and it's always a place where kids in flip-flops are as welcome as the adults in bikinis and polo shirts.

Near Platte Lake, Route 22 crosses the Platte River, and Andy pulls into a canoe rental at the bridge and stops, then walks out onto the bridge itself and looks around.

It's like seeing a ghost town, but one you used to live in, because this is familiar territory, but it's all changed: There used to be a little tourist village here, with a general store and a campground the Gardners used to camp at. All but the canoe rental is gone, now, eaten up by the National Forest, but he can still remember the yellow bug lights outside the general store, and canoeing down the river to Lake Michigan, where the white-sand beach was wide, and if the water was too cold, you could swim in the warm river instead. He can still remember standing at the mouth, where the waters mixed, one leg on the sandbar in cold lake water, one leg in the warm river water, the sun warm on his face as he felt the river flow past into the chilly embrace of the lake.

Once, when they were canoeing here, he and Sally had tipped over, and his life jacket had gotten hung up on something, holding him underwater. It was Sally that had saved him that day, and the closeness they had shared as children but lost as teens had somehow come back to them after that. There was something else, too. He stares at the water flowing under him, forever toward Lake Michigan and thinks about getting in his car, but instead of heading down Route 22, he'll turn down a side road, the road that follows the Platte River out to the beach. He won't think, he'll just drive through the forest that had once been a campground but was now just trees, with odd grove-like places that had once held tents and campers.

At the beach, he thinks, he will park and follow the river as it cuts through the sand and then finally empties itself into the arms of the Big Lake, an inland sea that will eventually take it to the ocean and oblivion.

Oblivion, he wonders? Or just peace, finally? Maybe, after all its twisting, flowing and moving, there it was finally at rest. Instead of being lost, the water is at last… home.

Maybe he could be at rest, too, there in the arms of the inland sea. Maybe this was where his journey ends — all the crap, all the twisting, all of it just becomes peace as the Lake takes you in. Standing on the bridge, he can almost feel the sand, and wonders how it would feel under the water if he just walked out there. Just walked out and never stopped.

He knows now there is no way his journey ends well. He's going to knock on Ashley's door and the pieces will just fall further apart. He had known it all along, hadn't he? There is nothing he hasn't screwed up. Nothing. He had screwed up with Ashley by loving her so much she disappeared. He screwed up with Scarlett. He had screwed up with Susan. With his parents, with his life. Even with God. Even God didn't seem to want to stop punishing him, and he couldn't figure out why.

That isn't true. He knows exactly why. He knows why the Word hasn't been said and why he hasn't been healed. He had gotten a divorce. He had made a promise to Susan and to God and he had broken that promise to the both of them. His parents acted like they forgave him, but he knew. He had always known, had known it that first time he ever really contemplated the end of his marriage to Susan. He knew it every time he took Communion and knew he was unworthy. Even worse than the divorce, he had married her in the first place. Had made the promise he knew he couldn't keep. Oh, he had known he'd try. That was part of the penance, wasn't it? He had to make the promise, had to try, had to make the sacrifice of marrying Susan to pay for —

To pay for Ashley. That was it, wasn't it? He had loved her too much, more than he loved God or himself even, and he had to pay for that. He would pay for it in years, pay for it in giving himself to Susan when he had never really wanted to.

Well he was done paying. He had no more left to pay. Nothing left to give. I've traveled across this state looking for something I'm never going to find, and I'm done, he thinks. I'm just done. I'm going to drive to that beach and walk into that water and never come out.

Is this suicide? No. Suicide was what he thought about – dreamed about – after Ashley left. That was roaring, screaming, buried in the pits of Hell, and the act of opening up his wrists was just going to be the final chapter in that book. This wasn't that. And he hadn't done it then, anyway. He didn't remember why, now, but he hadn't. This, though, this would just be… an end. Just a quiet, peaceful conclusion. This was collapsing into someone's arms, having given your all, having them tell you it was all going to be OK now. This was solace. He pictures his mother, holding him as a boy, comforting him. Calming his sobs. Stroking his hair.

Where is she now? Where is anyone now?

He is alone, alone with the little waves just a mile away, breaking along the sand in a rhythm like a comforting mother, calling him to her endless arms, and solace.

Where is Sally? She had been here for him when he almost drowned in this river, she had been there for him again after Ashley was gone. Where is she now? She had saved him once, right here in this very river, saved his life. At the time he had been confused about it, thought it was supposed to be Ashley that saved him, but maybe it didn't matter who did the saving, only that he was saved. Maybe some day, he'd figure out why.

Where is Emma? She had been there for him, too, through all that mess. Where is she?

Where is Scarlett? Why did she ever let him go on this trip, anyway?

Where is God? Where is God with all that forgiveness everyone says he's passing out because he sure hasn't seemed to have any for me. Of course, that's the real crux of it, isn't it? Because the truth of it all is that at some point, there is nothing – nothing – worse than forgiveness. The only thing worse than all of this, he thinks, would be actually being forgiven for all he had done. So where is God, then?

At least he knows where Ashley is.

That's right. He knows exactly where she is. He had found her, after all, hadn't he? Maybe she won't have the answers, either – hell, he doesn't know what the question even is anymore – but maybe just seeing her face would tell him something. Tell him he hadn't been wrong to love her. Hadn't been wrong to miss her. Hadn't been wrong that all of this was worth it. Maybe this was the reason he hadn't drowned in the river that day – because after seventeen years, he was going to find Ashley again.

No, maybe seeing her again wouldn't solve everything, but by God it would put some things to rest, wouldn't it? If it all went to hell after that, fine, he'd deal with it. But he wasn't going to go out without looking into her eyes one more time. Maybe at some point he would just walk into that water and never stop walking. But not until he knew why she left him, and the answer to that was just a couple of hours down the road.

He stares out over the river for a minute more, feeling the resolve building. He's going to go see Ashley. See her today.

Farther down Route 22, near Crystal Lake, is the Point Betsie Light House, one of his favorites on Lake Michigan. His mother, who grew up just down the road in Frankfort, always talked about babysitting there as a teenager, watching the light keeper's children while he and his wife were out. He always asked to hear the story, hoping that one day she'd talk about a storm hitting and the light guiding the ships around the point that jutted nearly five miles out into the lake, or what it was like to be so isolated, out on the coast in the fortress of a lighthouse, miles from town. But all she ever talked about was how nice the children were, and how the light is automated now.

Next was Arcadia, with a scenic overlook that offered a stunning view of the coastline to the south. Then came Onekama, another sleepy town on another stunning lake, and then finally meeting up with U.S. 31 again just north of Manistee, which passed for a big city in these parts.

Of course, Manistee had taken on a new life with the addition of a nearby Indian casino, and was itself now a tourist spot that was growing suburban sprawl to its south like unstoppable tumors.

After that, 31 moves away from the shore, and at Ludington it becomes an actual freeway, which makes clear sailing all the way to Muskegon. There are still hills, but they are much more gradual now, and the freeway seems to smooth them out even further, cutting through the tops and filling in the valleys. There's more farms – the land is more productive here, where there isn't as much sand – and the few houses are more like suburban homes that happened to be in the middle of nowhere than the lonely sentries up north.

Finally, at Whitehall, he leaves the freeway and takes the side roads back to the coast so he can follow the shoreline the last leg to Muskegon and Ashley's house. Ashley's house, he thinks. I'm actually going to Ashley's house.

But first, lunch. Myers had told him about a place near Ashley's house called Bear Lake Tavern, said it was great and he had to go there, but as he rolls under the deep summer canopy of Scenic Drive he spots the Red Rooster, which looks like it will fit the bill just fine.

"I'll get that order in for you, hon. Enjoy your beer," the waitress says, when his cell phone rings. It's Scarlett.

"Hey, you," she says.

"Hey, yourself. How you doing?"

"I'm good. I'm having lunch so I thought I'd check on you. Where are you now?"

"I'm either in North Muskegon or practically in it," he says. "I'm like three miles from her house."

"What? Really?"

143

"Yeah, I actually found her, and I'm on my way there now. Well, I was on my way until I stopped for lunch."

"Holy cow, I can't believe you actually found her," she says. "Well, I believe it, it's just, wow."

"Yeah, it's kind of crazy, isn't it?"

"So have you figured out what you're going to do, what you're going to say?"

"No, that's the thing. I haven't really figured it out yet."

Silence.

"Yeah, you're going to want to do that, Andy."

"Yeah, I was thinking I would stop at the beach, get my head straight, get a plan together, and then go see her, you know? Like, keep it casual, but, you know, kind of figure things out," he says.

"Well, that is something to think about," Scarlett says. "I mean, you gotta remember, Andy, you're not seventeen any more and neither is she. She's not just married, she's like 35 years old. She could have a bunch of kids, I mean, she's lived for almost two decades since you last saw her."

"Yeah."

"I'm not trying to be a downer here or anything, I'm really not, but you just have to be prepared, you know? I mean, think about the things that can happen in two decades. Parents can die. You get married, have kids, divorce, heck anything could have happened. She could have a 16-year-old kid in high school by now. And, I'm just sayin' here, but, you know, she was from kind of a sketchy background from what you've told me, so…"

"Yeah, I know," he says. "And I've had a couple of days to think about it, since I found out she got married, and you know, I mean it was never that I was going to come in on a white horse and sweep her off her feet, anyway. It was never about that."

"Well, not consciously, anyway."

Damn, she had a point.

"That's probably true," he says. "But I know what the deal is, and like I said, it was never really about that. So it's just about putting it all to rest."

"Yeah, that's a good attitude," she says. "Get some closure. You know, you just wanted to get things settled, find out what happened, right?"

"Right."

"All right, well listen, I gotta get back to work, so, be careful and all, and good luck."

"Hey listen, Scarlett," he says.

"Yeah?"

"Thanks, for everything," he says. "For understanding and just, you know– "

"It's all right," she says. "Just do what you gotta do."

"I will."

"Oh, and one other thing," she says. "She's probably fat now, so, just be prepared for that." He laughs and beer almost shoots out his nose.

"All right," he says. "I'll see you soon."

FOURTEEN

The cicada sits on the branch in the early morning light, tired from a night of singing to the countless females he could sense nearby but that never seemed to come to him. He had started singing at dusk, and he had screeched his song to the darkened skies with all his might, just one part of a mighty chorus of need sung by thousands of his brethren, hoping against hope that she would hear him. She, too, must understand the pain of seventeen years of solitary existence, he thought, and she too, had transformed for just this moment.

He had begun his song a few weeks ago in a locust tree, the same one he had hatched from an egg in, but eventually, in his lazy search for food and desperate search for a female, he had flown a few houses away. His flight, always erratic, now was barely controlled, and he clumsily bounced off tree branches, a fence and even a planter before finding the shade of an oak tree to roost in.

Flight, though it thrilled him, was also taxing, and was getting harder by the day. For seventeen years time had been nothing to him, but now, in just a matter of a few weeks, he was dying of old age. His life's purpose had almost been met; soon, he hoped, the journey would be over and he could simply wait for the end to come. Already he could tell it would be soon.

He would still sing after she found him, to be sure, but it would be a new song then, one that told both of the yearning, but also of its balm, and of the glorious coming sunset. When that ultimate dusk finally came, he knew it would be in a burst of colors more magnificent even than that of the sun slipping below the horizon and, at last, after nearly two decades, he would know peace.

The Cicada Killer Wasp, *Sphecius speciosus*, leaves the burrow she has dug into the sandy soil of the yard at the corner of Kensington Boulevard and Vermont Avenue and begins searching for food. Not food for her, but for the eggs she's carrying in her belly.

By chance, she flies due south from her burrow, which takes her first to the maple tree in front of the Stanciu's house on the corner. She sees the trunk and begins circling it, terrifying any humans around, though she would not sting them even if she ran smack into them, which is unlikely, because at nearly two inches long, with black and yellow markings, most humans immediately run the other way at the first sight of her. She circles the trunk in an upward spiral, searching each branch for a cicada.

But the tree is small – not much more than a sapling – and though there are thousands of cicadas nearby, none of them happen to be on the little maple at this moment.

She moves on, farther south, finding an oak. Again she circles, slowly working her way up, up, up until the first branches, which are almost 20 feet off the ground. She takes her time now, searching each branch, until she sees him.

Then she pauses.

Her instincts – hundreds of thousands of years' worth of training hard-wired into her DNA – tell her this is a cicada and it is prey, but something isn't quite right. It's much smaller than the cicadas she is used to, and darker in color. She does not know that her normal prey is the annual cicada, which live two or three years, versus the seventeen of the periodical cicada. She only knows that her normal prey is grey or green and is up to twice her size. This one is mostly black, and about the same size as she is.

She does not know that compared to him, she is just a toddler – only a year old, and only two weeks since she's hatched from her pupal cocoon. But it's been a busy two weeks. When she emerged, thanks to the pheromone she was emitting, she was nearly instantly discovered by the males that had hatched a week or two before. Even without the pheromone, the males were hanging out outside the burrow she was hatched in, waiting for whatever virgin females might emerge. She mated quickly, and stored her partner's sperm in a chamber in her thorax. When she eventually lays an egg, she will have to decide what gender the egg will be: male eggs will be laid as is, female eggs will be fertilized with material from her spermatheca.

But that is in the future, and the future does not matter to a cicada killer wasp, perhaps because there is so little of it – her entire life span after emerging from the cocoon will last about four weeks. In this, she and the cicada have something in common. His entire life span above ground is a similar period of time. Of course, his life span is usually over by July, when hers – timed to the emergence of the annual cicadas – is just beginning, and it is only by chance that their paths have crossed.

Confused by the size and coloring of this one, she circles again. She's getting conflicting signals – there's the insect that doesn't look quite right in front of her, but there's also the call of her burrow. After mating, she spent most of the last two weeks finding a spot to make her own burrow and digging it deep into the earth. She had hatched and mated a few blocks away, then flew off looking for a new place to set down roots. This yard had everything she was looking for: well drained, dry sandy soil, good southern exposure, and even a southeast-facing slope. For the owners of the yard, freaked out by the giant wasps that seemed to take over their yard every year, the combination of conditions was not as fortunate. They had tried insecticides a few times and various other means, but none were effective. The one thing they didn't try would have worked best of all – a sprinkler. But they had not, and so the soil remained dry and sandy, allowing her and dozens of other females to dig burrows up to three feet long and up to two feet deep.

Now, she has a new imperative: Fill that burrow with eggs – and cicadas for the hatched eggs to feed on. Finally, that instinct is more powerful than the problem of a cicada that is small and oddly colored, and she moves in for the attack.

Even if he had seen her coming, which she took care to land on him from above and behind, so he did not, there would have been little he could do. Even flying away would have been fruitless against her speed and agility in the air.

She drops down out of the sky, lands on top of him and buries her stinger into his back, her poison instantly spreading through his body.

But her poison doesn't kill, or even hurt. It paralyzes.

It's her, he thinks. He doesn't know what intercourse is or how it is supposed to feel, only that he needs to find a female and mount her, but now, for some reason, it seems that the female has mounted him instead. It doesn't matter – he can't move at all, but his head swims with ecstasy as he is lifted into the air, thinking the female is carrying him off somewhere for their ultimate liaison. It's worked, he thinks. She's heard my song and has come for me.

They're flying now, over the sidewalk, and though he can't move to look around, he can see they're heading north and that the flight – unlike the bumbling flight he had known – is steady and sure.

They cross a street, and then they dip down toward the grass. Is she tired? he wonders. Or perhaps our heaven will be in the grass there.

She sets him down on a little pile of sand next to a hole in the grass, then pushes his deadweight inside. This must be her nest. It's dark here, he knows, but soon we will together know a great light.

He still has not seen the female, but can feel her pushing him from behind, deeper and deeper into the burrow, until at last it opens into a little chamber not unlike the one he spent seventeen years in a few lawns away. There, in the dark, underground, he comes face to face with her, but cannot see her for the lack of light. He should be frightened, he thinks, but all he can feel is love. Love for this female cicada he knows will be one with him soon, and love for creation as she presses herself against him and deposits something on his back leg, right on what happens to be a chink in his otherwise well-armored body.

Soon I will understand, he thinks. Soon.

Then the female leaves, and he waits in the darkness. Many thoughts run through his mind – Where has she gone? Why am I still here in the dark? Why can't I move? – but a few days later, when the egg hatches into a wasp larva, those thoughts are still on the female and how he wishes she would come back so they could die together and see paradise. Still, he feels the love for her, and if he could move, he would sing for her, sing her back to their nest, sing her back to be One, sing her a song of love and the end of their days. Because of the paralysis, none of his thoughts are on the wasp larva, now slowly, but painlessly, eating him alive. The larva may look like a small worm now, but inside she is a baby Cicada Killer Wasp that will winter in this chamber, just as he spent so many years in his, then emerge to find her own Cicada prey. His thoughts remain on the song until the larva has eaten him from the inside out and, at last, all consciousness ends.

FIFTEEN

Andy sat down on the aluminum-framed lawn chair and pulled it close to the fire, feeling the fabric straps stretch under his legs. Sally and his parents were already sitting there, his parents both starting beers and Sally cracking open a Grape Crush. The sky was still light in the treetops, but the campsite was being overtaken by shadows and already faces were glowing in the light of the fire. Already stars seemed to be stabbing through the gray veil of sky overhead.

He had tried hard to be angry, had nursed the hurt and bitterness all the way up here – a torturous drive from Fort Wayne to the Platte River – but it was no use. There was something about staring into a campfire that just mellowed him, and he felt the cooling night air and the dancing orange light melt away the sullen mood the way waves on a lake lap at the shoreline.

He had begged all week for his parents to let Ashley come along on their annual Labor Day weekend camp out, to no avail. School was starting Tuesday and the girl had enough going on in her life right now with her mom getting laid off from Kelly's, they said. The last thing she needed was to go camping clear up to Traverse City.

Andy had argued that the opposite was true. With all that going on, what she needed most was a nice weekend of camping, he said.

Logic, however, did not prevail and so instead of hanging out with Ashley, sitting around the campfire and going canoeing with her, it would be nothing but him and Sally all weekend. Great.

But now, as a full moon rose through the trees, he thought that maybe it wouldn't be so bad after all. Since he and Ashley had gotten serious, Sally had been a lot more fun to be around, anyway. She looked up to Ashley and had begun acting her age for a change. Maybe she would turn out to be all right, despite the last few years.

Heck, he and Sally had been best friends when they were kids. Maybe they could get some of that back. And though Ashley wasn't around, there was still the Song of One, humming always in the background, the way you can feel a tuning fork continue its tone even after you can't hear it anymore. He could feel the Song in the trees, in the sweet smell of the campfires burning all around them and in the crackling of the pine logs on their own fire.

"Are we gonna have s'mores?" Sally asked.

"Only if someone's willing to get up and get all the stuff out," his mom said. "I'm beat."

Andy looked around. After the long drive, they had set up camp and now, the summer over, no one was moving.

"Don't look at me," his dad said. "They sound good, but not good enough to get up and make."

Sally looked crushed. Normally Andy would say something to her like, "What, are your legs busted? If you want them, make them," but what came out was, "I'll get 'em for you." He was as surprised as she was.

"Chocolate's in the cooler," his mom said. "The other stuff's in the food box."

A few campsites away, he could hear someone strumming a guitar and singing. He wished he could play guitar. He wished Ashley were here.

"Here you go, kid," he said, handing her the marshmallows and a stick. The graham crackers and chocolate he put on the picnic table.

Soon, Sally had volunteered herself into roasting marshmallows for everyone, and she had four of them on one stick, with four different degrees of doneness ordered, as well.

"This is impossible!" she laughed. "How can I burn one for Mom and have Andy's almost raw?"

"Easy," Dad said. "Just try to get them all perfectly done – you can almost guarantee one will be burned and one will be raw."

They all laughed then – almost like a real family again, Andy thought, and then wondered why he had thought it. They were a real family. They hadn't ever stopped. Maybe he just forgot to notice these last few months.

His mouth full of s'more, he looked up at the stars and just as he wondered if Ashley was looking at them right then, too, a breeze blew, a cold breeze that smelled of autumn. Summer was over.

"Mom and Dad are acting weird today," Sally said. They were walking through the KOA toward where the entrance met the highway, which was right near the bridge over the river. There was a general store and the canoe rental place there. "It's like they couldn't wait for us to leave."

It was true, Andy thought. They had been a little anxious to get rid of us.

"They probably want to get in the tent and get naked," he said.

She punched him – hard – on the arm. "Oh my Gawd, Andy, I can't believe you said that." She shuddered. "Oh. Geeze."

He laughed, and pretended he was going to punch her back.

"No, I think they want to talk about whether Ashley can stay with us or not," he said as they reached the road. "Mom said they'd think about it, and they really haven't talked since then, at least that I've seen."

After waiting for traffic, they crossed the highway to the little general store to buy gummy bears. Andy carried a backpack with their lunch in it, but Sally wasn't going anywhere without gummy bears. The store was the kind of place that sold groceries, fishing gear, souvenirs, candy and camping supplies.

"Well, if her Mom does move, I hope they let her stay with us," Sally said. "It would be nice to have a big sister for a change."

When they had walked up here last night for some pops, there was an old guy running the place. Now it was a teenager in sunglasses.

"What, am I really that bad?" Andy asked.

"No, just, you know, it would be nice to have a big sister to talk to," she said. "One thing I do worry about though, Andy, is what if she moves in and then you break up? What are you going to do if she lives with us and you break up?"

Andy paid for the gummy bears. "That's not going to happen."

"I know, I'm not saying that," she said, then stopped and looked at him as they walked outside and the screen door slammed behind them, jingling the bell tied to the wooden frame. "I'm just saying, what if it does? What would you do?"

"That's not going to happen," he said, and let himself hear the Song for a moment. "Why would we ever break up?"

They crossed the bridge over the river, then crossed the highway again to the canoe rental place.

"All right guys, be careful out there and see you in a couple of hours," the guy said after outfitting them with lifejackets, oars and a canoe.

Sally jumped in the front seat, stowing the backpack behind her, and Andy shoved the boat into the water, then jumped in himself.

"All right, where we going?" he asked. "Left to Platte Lake or right to Lake Michigan?"

"Lake Michigan!" Sally cried, digging her oar into the water.

The morning was perfect for canoeing – plenty of sunshine, but a nice breeze so you weren't sweating. The water was higher than usual, so tree branches that normally hung low over the water now dipped down into it, hiding the banks.

And the water! Rivers in Indiana are muddy affairs, with water the color of a teenager's cream-laden coffee. They are wide and flat, slow and opaque.

But the Platte River is a trout stream, its water perfectly clear, showing off its sandy bottom with the occasional rock or old tree. Most of the river would reach only to Andy's knees, or waist at the deepest, and only the really deep pools – where the stream bends back on itself, usually in shadows – keep secrets.

Soon, Andy knew, this river would be thick with salmon heading upstream, at the end of their lives, fighting to get to the spawning grounds before they died.

"Come on, paddle!" he yelled, and playfully splashed water at Sally's back.

"I'm paddling," she cried.

Their banter was continued as they went under the bridge and into the woods west of the highway. The river here was pedestrian, running mostly straight along the Lake Michigan Road, until it abruptly turned south, around Mud Lake before emptying into Loon Lake. Suddenly, they were in the middle of nowhere. Kingfishers swooped low over the water, then back up into tree branches where they sat like lords. An otter slid down the bank as they approached, moving like black mercury down the sand and into the water before disappearing from sight. Trees rose up on each side of them, even as the underbrush seemed to reach down toward them. Andy half expected to see a moose on the bank.

Soon the forest gave way to Loon Lake, a calm, hidden expanse with barely a ripple as it spread out amid the trees before the river continued on toward Lake Michigan. As they cruised across Loon, he remembered the endless hours he and Sally had spent together as children. "Nothing could separate us," he thought. "Best friends and worst enemies." His parents had dozens of pictures of them snuggled up together at night in their footie pajamas, his red, hers yellow. "I missed her," he thought, "and didn't even realize I was missing her."

After the lake, the river continued on much as it had, mostly straight, through deep, lush forest, until about the last mile before Lake Michigan. That last mile bowed around sand dunes, and the river suddenly became a zig-zag of curves as it bent back around itself and flowed through tiny cutoffs that created islands, like it was doing everything it could to avoid flowing out into non-existence.

By now, they were canoeing like experts, able to spin the vessel at will, stop and turn as needed.

"Where are you going?" Sally asked as Andy steered them out of the current on a particularly sharp bend.

"Over there into the pool, where it's calm," he said, aiming the boat for the southern bank where the waters darkened in the shade and not a ripple rose. "I thought we could take a little break there and maybe see some more otters or something."

The boat slid silently toward the bank as they coasted, until Andy slid his paddle back into the water like a rudder and suddenly turned the boat to put Sally right into the tree branches that reached all the way down to the surface. He had intended to go through the branches, into the dark, silent waters behind them next to the bank, but Sally thought he was goofing around and grabbed hold of one of them, stopping the boat, and tipping it precariously.

Andy leaned hard the other way to keep from going over, then dug in with his paddle, thinking some forward momentum might right the craft. At the same time, Sally let go of the branch she had been holding, and the bow shot forward, upon onto a log, covered by the high water. Sally felt the canoe slide up onto the solid surface and stood up, but the log was far from level, and the boat seemed to flip with a force Andy never knew it could have, pushing him hard under the shadowed water, where a branch from the same log hooked on his life preserver.

There had been no time to gasp before he went under, and he fought from involuntarily doing so now, but realized that even in the shade, he could see the sunlight shafting down to him through the water. He kicked, he struggled, but the branch was snagged on the back of the life jacket and held fast, right where he couldn't reach it.

Was he going to die? He was, wasn't he? Now, just as he had discovered Ashley and the Song, it was all going to end, and over a stupid canoe. The light came down through the water like a prism, like the thousand shards of blue in Ashley's eyes, only now clearer, more crystalline. He could see the trees on the shore, arching up over him, while the light reached down to him through their branches, like lifelines. He was going to be part of that light now, the very light in her eyes, and at that thought, he stopped struggling. He felt a peace come over him, even as his lungs burned and his eyes bulged. He and Ashley would be together in the Light, he thought; One for real, One forever.

Hands, splashing, screaming and a rush of air as the water seemed to pull away from him and then Sally, still screaming, was holding, yanking him out of the water while he coughed and gasped for the air that now seemed to roar in his ears, so different from the calm of the water before.

"Oh my God, Andy, are you OK?" she shrieked, and he realized she was crying, hot tears amidst the cool water they were standing in up over their waists. "Breathe Andy, breathe!"

He did. But with each breath, the fear of dying and the pounding of adrenaline was replaced by a different fear. Why had he stopped fighting to live? Why had he been so sure that if he died, he wouldn't be leaving

Ashley, but joining her?

"Oh my God I'm so sorry, Andy!" It was Sally talking, still holding him and crying as he stared dumbly at her.

"You saved me," he said at last, wondering where this new thought had come from: It wasn't supposed to be you that did it. "You saved me."

She cried harder now. "Oh my God, Andy."

He realized she was still holding him, and now he lifted his arms and held her back, telling her it was all right. He was fine. "You saved me," he said. He felt a new, cold detachment to everything that had just happened, and realized it wasn't that he had stopped fighting to live that scared him. It was the thinking that he was going to be with Ashley that truly frightened him. The first one made perfect sense in his mind, given the second. But where had the second come from? And why had he thought – not just a thought, but knowing – that it wasn't supposed to have been Sally that saved him? It was like listening to a record and only later realizing all the songs had been played out of order.

Finally, they began to right the canoe, pulling it up on to the bank to dump the water out of it, and Sally's tears were replaced by a torrent of words, explaining over and over about how she fell in, too, but when she came up she couldn't see him and at first thought he might be goofing around, but soon saw him under the water with a look on his face she had never seen before and never wanted to see again, and she was sorry for standing up, so very, very sorry.

"It's OK," he said. "You saved me." But all he could think was that something had happened under the water, something had come to him, some realization, but he was having trouble figuring out exactly what it was now. And if Ashley was gone somehow, if something had happened to her, then why was he alive?

"I guess we should go back now, huh?" she said.

"Why? We've got our swimsuits on. We've got all day. By the time we leave the beach our clothes will be mostly dry," he said. "Besides, if we go back now, all we'll do is freak out Mom and Dad and then we'll have to sit in camp all day."

Sally stared at him.

"You almost died, though," she said, slowly now. "It's like you don't even care."

"But I didn't die," he said. "You were there. I'm fine."

And she *had* been there. He wasn't sure why, but she was. It wasn't supposed to be Sally, but it had been. He wasn't supposed to be alive, but he was. There was no changing it.

They sat on the bank then, quiet, looking down at the water now so still it was like a mirror.

"I know we haven't gotten along the past few years, but I'm glad you're my sister. I really am."

She didn't say anything, but took his hand and held it, the way she had when they were little and they were inseparable.

Finally, they threw everything back in the canoe and shoved off again, and as they glided downstream, he heard the Kingfishers, the breeze and in the distance, the waves on Lake Michigan. But he did not hear the Song.

Like realizing the furnace or some other sound that runs in the background is suddenly gone, Andy realized the Song of One had stopped. No more humming. No more vibrations. No harmony. No Song. A new dread began to fill him.

At the beach, where the river turns and runs parallel to the shore for almost 200 yards, they pulled the canoe all the way up onto the sand, as if to get it as far away from the water as possible, and stripped out of their wet clothing to the swimsuits they wore beneath.

Their lunch was dry inside a Ziploc bag in the backpack, but neither felt like eating. Instead, they spread towels on the sand and lay in the sun, lost in the thoughts of what had happened and what had almost happened.

"Did you think you were dying?" Sally finally asked.

"Yeah."

"Was it scary?" She seemed afraid to ask.

"Yeah."

"Are you mad at me? Even a little?"

"No, not even a little," he said. "You saved me, remember?"

"Did— did your life flash before your eyes?"

"A little," he lied. "I suddenly remembered the day Mom and Dad brought you home from the hospital, this little tiny baby. And then you pulled me up."

She was quiet then, until much later, when he stood up and looked around, as if he was ready to move on.

"Do you want to build a sand castle with me?" she asked.

"Yeah, that would be great."

Sally started to walk toward the lake shore, but he stopped her. "No, let's cheat and build it here by the river, instead."

"Cheat?"

"You know, if we build it over there, the waves from the lake will wreck it. If we build it over here, by the river, it will never get wrecked until someone walks on it."

"That's cheating?"

"I don't know," he said. "It just seems too easy if you don't have to worry about the waves. But I want it to be easy right now."

They built. There were moats and towers and outbuildings and walls, and bridges made from driftwood. In the middle was a courtyard.

"Here's where Prince Andy and Princess Ashley get married," Sally laughed.

Andy laughed, too, because there was nothing else he could do. Silence, where there had once been the Song, hung in the air. He could feel the sand digging into his knees.

Without looking up, Sally asked, "Do you think you guys will get married some day?"

Part of him wanted to say yes. But there was another part of him, now, too.

"If you do, can I be a bridesmaid?"

"Of course," he said. "You saved …my life."

The trip back to Fort Wayne had been a wild one. With Sally's Walkman on and her face buried in Teen People, he had hoped to be alone with his thoughts, but it was hard to figure anything out when he couldn't stop staring at the sky and its churning cloudscape and weird, greenish light that seemed to be coming not from the sky but from the ground. And of course, there was the silence, the loss of the Song, made worse by the fact that the radio stations his parents were listening to were constantly interrupted by tornado warnings. His dad drove with even more concentration than usual, but somehow, they skirted between the storms and arrived back in Fort Wayne alive and unharmed. Once they crossed the Indiana border, it seemed, the air calmed and the clouds returned to form and it was hard to even remember how frightening things had looked just a few miles before.

Tomorrow was the big day – not just Senior Year, but Senior Year with Ashley. Mr. McFrederick had not come through on getting all their classes together, but there were a few AP classes they had together, and could he really ask much more? They'd share a locker, of course, and they were on the same lunch hour, so aside from a couple hours in the morning and an hour in the afternoon, they'd be together all the time. He couldn't wait to get home and go see her. She was probably still figuring out what to wear.

As they pulled into the driveway, Andy barely waited for the car to stop before he was jumping out and running down the street.

"Hey Andy! You gotta help unload!" his father yelled at him, already two houses away.

"I will," he yelled. "I'll be right back!" Idiot parents.

But as he rounded the corner he was surprised to see Barbara's car was not out front, and there were no lights on. They probably ran out to get something at the last minute he thought, but still—

The disquiet grew as he stepped on to the front porch and the place didn't feel right. Like something was missing.

He knocked, then tried the door. It opened.

Inside was the couch and the loveseat over in the sunroom, and the table and chairs were still in the kitchen, but everything else was gone. The TV Guides and the TV were missing. The blanket on the back of the couch that Ashley cuddled up in. The stuff on the kitchen counters. One of the cupboards was open; there was nothing inside. Ashley's bike was gone. The refrigerator door was open. Its shelves were dark and silent.

What? They couldn't leave without all their furniture, he thought. He pushed away the voice that said the house was a furnished rental. He pushed away the memory that there had been no moving truck when they got here.

He wanted to yell out for her, but was silent, like everything around him.

The clock was missing from the living room wall.

He walked up the stairs, and heard every footstep echo through the house. No. It's not.

At the top, he looked in Barbara's room first. The bed was there, and the dresser. But two of the drawers were half open, and they were empty. The bed was stripped to the bare mattress. The closet door hung open to reveal an empty space.

No.

Then the bathroom. No tooth brushes. No nothing. In the tub, a shard of a bar of soap remained, dry. He thought he would be able to hear his heartbeat as he walked toward Ashley's bedroom, but he did not. He heard nothing but his footsteps and the rustle of his jeans.

The bed was there, stripped. The dresser he had helped fill three months before was empty. The walls were bare. He saw the window, remembered her hand gripping the frame in ecstasy as they returned to One. Saw the thousand shards of blue in her eyes. But there is no more One. There is just — Nothing.

It can't be.

He felt like he should be nauseous. He felt like he should feel stupid, ashamed, humiliated that this had happened. He felt like he should fall down or scream. He felt like he should say something or do something or kick the goddamn door in or put his fist through the wall, or cry like a damn baby.

But he did nothing. He made no noise. He didn't move. Did not disturb the air, the air that She had once breathed. That She had once moved through. That had surrounded her and been warmed by her skin. That had once hummed with their Song.

He did not move his feet on the floor that She had once walked on, had sat on with him. He did not imagine the future without her, because there was no future. He did not contemplate Senior Year without her because there was no Senior Year. There was just Nothing. Like this place. This place of silence. This place that must remain exactly, precisely the way it is this instant, he thinks, like a memorial to something he could not even remember now.

A memorial to ... something. It was hard to think what it was. Because the memories churning in his gut were all somethings, and he could no longer remember what a something was in the middle of all this Nothing. This great, expansive waste of Nothingness that surrounded him and filled him and emptied him and became him, until he was Nothing, too.

Slowly, he backed out of the room, walked down the stairs, across the living room, and out the front door, which he locked. Out, he thought, out, out, out. Just get Out into the Nothing. From Nothing into Nothing. Nothing from Nothing. Empty and gone into Nothing.

He stood there for a moment, his hand still on the door handle. He could feel the words in his head, but could not say them, even to himself, could not imagine them. So he steadied himself on the door, just for a minute more, and then finally let go, dropping away, falling backwards – arms out wide – into the Nothing.

SIXTEEN

"Under normal conditions the periodical Cicada remains in evidence in the woods five or six weeks, occasional individuals occurring later, but as a rule their disappearance is almost as sudden as their appearance and is complete in the first weeks in July. Mr. Butler, writing of the 1885 brood in Indiana, says that twenty-three days after the appearance of the Cicada a perceptible decrease in numbers was observed, chiefly from a disappearance of the males. On July 15, nine days after they had disappeared from the river valley districts, they were still abundant and active in more elevated situations.

Mr. Hopkins found on the hills near Morgantown, W.Va., that the dates of the Cicada appearance were about normal, the first adults appearing on May 20, the first general appearance not coming, however, until the 24th. Oviposition began on the 13th of June, and by the 17th of the month the leaves on the wounded twigs began to wither. All had disappeared by the 4th of July."

—"The Periodical Cicada"

This time it's the roar of the lake that moves him, long before he can see it. The parking lot at the Blockhouse is high up over Lake Michigan, but ringed by trees that block the view. But even here the noise is striking as he walks the short path downhill to where it turns away from the road and into the trees, where the trail heads along a ridge line to the beach. The noise is a constant grinding on the wind. The sound dips somewhat as he enters the forest, but not for long, and soon he sees why.

When they had camped here as kids, the trail from the Blockhouse to the beach was one of his favorites. First of all, there was the Blockhouse itself – a replica of one built by early settlers to protect against natives and whoever else might be a danger – it was set on top of a sand dune, one of the highest in a park filled with them, and the views out its rampart windows were over the tree tops as far as the eye could see, a green canopy of oaks, maples and beeches, studded with white pines that spiked up out of what looked like a solid carpet of leaves. To the west, after just a short carpet of trees, was the endless slate expanse of Lake Michigan.

But the trail through those woods was even better. Here, the trees were massive in the valleys that stretched from either side of the ridge trail, and their canopy so thick that there was almost no undergrowth whatsoever, just a forest of tree trunks rising ten stories in the air, supporting a cathedral-like roof of emerald and jade.

Not anymore. Some time recently, winds had knocked down many of the trees, and the cathedral floor is a tangle of brush and busted limbs, trunks crisscrossing each other under huge openings above that let sunlight down to the ground that hadn't seen any in eons. Already, undergrowth has shot up, greedily eating up the light and creating shocks of green where before there had been none.

Andy stares at the scene for a minute and realizes that what at first looks like wanton destruction is actually the beginnings of new life. Nothing new had grown here for decades, and now there are shrubs and young trees growing. Covering the ground and stuck to tree trunks everywhere are cicada shells, the brown husks left behind after their final transformation, but he can't hear any singing in the trees. What he can hear is the sound of the surf just a couple hundred yards away now, like the roar of the wind. The trail ends on top of a sand dune about twenty feet above the beach, a beach that, thanks to it being accessible only by trail, he has to himself, just like he remembered.

The change from the forest to the beach isn't as dramatic as it was at Pyramid Point, thanks to the fallen trees, but the sound of the waves here is overwhelming – there are so many waves audible at once that it's impossible to make out individual ones crashing and they all mash into a massive, pounding sound as the water beats against the sand.

He sits down near the water and lights a cigarette, which isn't easy in the wind, takes a few drags and thinks about the journey he's had from that day seventeen years ago when Ashley disappeared, to here and now, on the beach just a few miles from where she lives. In some respects, it's a miracle he's even alive. There had been a few close calls in that first year after she left, but every time he thought he had reached the very bottom, he had decided it might be worth it to keep trying. Why? He still doesn't know. If his life has a purpose, it seems there's no telling what it is.

Oh, for a while, he had told himself he was alive because of Susan, that there was someone out there for him after all. But he knew better. Still, maybe Susan was right. Maybe his time with her wasn't such a bad thing after all, even though it had ended badly. That didn't mean the rest of it was garbage, did it? Maybe not. And maybe it wasn't even over. Clearly, the romance was, but maybe they could still have something, something – well, it was hard to call it a friendship, but, in some ways it might even be more than that, given what they had been through together.

For an instant, he thinks that maybe, just maybe, it was better to be thirty-four than it would be to be seventeen again. He hadn't seen that one coming.

He takes a last drag on the smoke and tries to picture himself at Susan's wedding. You know, he thinks, sitting here by the waves, next to a lake that just seems to go on forever, maybe I could. I can see that. I could even be happy for her.

Which leaves only Ashley to figure out. Of course, that one's a little more difficult isn't it? It was like his feet had been poured into concrete that day there on her empty front porch, his arms paralyzed and his heart stopped and everything frozen except his brain, which could only gaze at the emptiness and wonder what had happened, wonder at the vacant silence.

And now, here he is, seventeen years later, wondering what it all means. What was this trip even for? Was it some crazy, stupid hope that maybe somehow he wasn't paralyzed anymore and he could win her back, like Myers – and Scarlett – had said? Was it so she could reject him, once and for all, rather than just disappear into the ether? She had left with no warning, and no word after. Would she be angry when he showed up?

He's just a few minutes from her front door, and he still doesn't know why he wanted to – needed to, had spent weeks trying to – knock on the damn thing.

He had decided he could be happy at Susan's wedding, and now he tries to picture himself at Ashley's wedding. It had been a shock seeing her wedding picture at first, sure, but after a few days he had gotten used to the idea. But what if it was *his* wedding, and Ashley was sitting there – unmarried, unattached? Could he really marry someone else? That was the one question he hadn't dared to ask himself before he married Susan. If Ashley had been sitting there in the pew, unmarried, unattached, could he have married Susan?

No.

No way. And if he had been honest about that then, he never would have, either. But what about now? Could he marry Scarlett – or anyone, for that matter – with an unattached Ashley looking on?

He thinks of the last seventeen years. The depression. The paralysis. The broken relationships. The bad dreams and waking up knowing there's another day to live and no real reason you can think of for living it. The endless waiting for something to change. The things sealed into a box, stacked away in a dark corner in a room he never goes into in a basement he avoids.

He pulls out the pendent and stares at the words, "ove ou." Love You? Yes. Over you? Hardly.

But maybe he should be. Maybe this is about getting over her. Closing the door on it. Without thinking, he takes the pendant and walks across the sand to the edge of the water, where he can feel the concussion of the waves crashing down, then hurls it out over the water. It hangs in the air a second, then disappears the instant it hits the surface.

Maybe he doesn't know the answer to all these damn questions, he thinks, but he sure as hell isn't going to find them sitting here. If it's answers he wants, he's going to have to knock on Ashley's door and learn what's inside. He might not like the answers, but at least he'll have them, and that's something. He might not be over Ashley, but he never will be if he doesn't do something about it.

He thinks about Scarlett, too – he's basically leaving her paralyzed while he figures all this out. Isn't he cheating her out of some resolution if he doesn't knock on that door? Doesn't she deserve an answer, too?

He looks out over the pounding waves for a moment, then stands up. It's time to go see Ashley.

The drive to her house takes him across Bear Lake Channel, lined with boats and sailboats, and as the road rises up the hill and becomes lined with houses, he watches the numbers slowly climb – ten blocks away, then nine, then eight. They are long blocks, and it's amazing how on the left side of the street, they are just normal houses, some with white picket fences, while in most places on the right side, they're lake houses, jammed close together, with only a driveway and garage visible from the street, while the "front" of the house faces the lake.

Finally, he finds it, the little white house with blue trim, on the corner across from a park that sits on a bluff over Muskegon Lake. It, too, has a white picket fence, surrounding what appears to be an English garden.

He parks on the street and kills the engine. The driveway is either on the other side of the house or there isn't one, so he can't tell whether anyone's home or not. He sits behind the wheel a minute, then double checks the address, even though he's double checked it about eighty times. When he looks up, he sees a car driving past and without thinking he reads the license plate: AMH 247.

In that moment, he's seventeen again.

They're driving his mom's car somewhere, laughing and listening to music. He's holding her hand with his right, steering with his left, and they're both looking at license plates, looking for their initials, when he sees it: A plate he had never seen, or at least never noticed, before: AMG.

He points to it, and says, "What about that one?"

She looks confused at first, then catches on: Ashley Marie Gardner.

But she doesn't laugh. She doesn't giggle. She doesn't– she doesn't anything.

There's just silence.

He can hear the car's engine clearly, the sound of the wheels on the pavement, the other cars on the road. His heart, being squeezed like a fist. God, he's so stupid. Why did he say that?

"You know, Andy, just because we both want it to last forever doesn't mean it will," she says. "Don't think I don't want it to, but..."

"Yeah." He tries to concentrate on the road and not think about what's happening. Just block it out, he thinks. But she's still trying to explain. She doesn't have to. He knows. It's too late. Not that he was asking her. She didn't have to say yes, that wasn't the point. The point was that she wasn't supposed to say no. But she was saying no.

Block it out. Pretend it never happened. Just block it out, he thinks. Move on. Just– it didn't. OK? It didn't. Find the Song of One again. It's got to be out there. It's got to be playing. You just can't hear it over what a fucking idiot you are.

"Look, for as long as I can remember, my entire life has been completely upended about every six or eight months," Ashley says, and when her voice sighs on "about," the Song is back. The music is back and he can forget it all because it's OK. They're OK. They are One.

Then he's back in his car again, and he's 34, and he realizes that at the time, he thought he would never remember that moment, that he had pushed it down, out of his head completely, but he hadn't forgotten at all. The Music hadn't drowned out her words. He remembered. He remembered every word like she was sitting here next to him, though he wasn't even listening at the time, only hearing the Song.

"Everything changes except mom and me, and maybe I change too, because all your friends change, your town changes, your bedroom changes," she had said. "The things you look at every day change. Everything. But some things you do take with you. Some things don't change, even when the whole world does. I don't know what's going to happen with us, Andy, but I know that this – you and me and this summer and what we've had so far, that doesn't change, Andy." She had squeezed his hand, and he gets chills feeling her skin on his, even now, because it's so real. "Not ever."

That never changes. Not ever, she had said.

He looks up from the memory. He's trying to change it, isn't he? He's trying to change what happened seventeen years ago, and he's trying to change everything – every single thing – that has happened since then. Every damn thing.

Maybe, he thinks, he's been paralyzed because he's trying to change things that can't be changed.

He thinks about knocking on her door, seeing her open it. That wouldn't change a damn thing either, he thinks. Not a thing. Not the darkness after she left, not Susan, not anything. Not me, not her, not that summer, not now. Nothing would change, and I would be exactly the same mess I am sitting here now.

Not like this, he thinks. If I'm going to see her, if I'm going to get on with my life, if I'm going to – to anything, it's not going to be by crawling back into this hole. Not like this.

He feels like he's at the opening of a dark tunnel – he can either turn around and go back in, or climb out into the light.

He looks at her door. It's just steps away, but it may as well be on the other side of a canyon.

Not like this.

He puts the car in gear, checks his mirrors, then stops. Wait.

He grabs the notebook and the pen off the passenger seat and starts writing:

Ashley,

I was in the neighborhood and thought I'd stop and say hello. Call me sometime, I'd love to catch up with you. 260-461-8444.

Yours,

Andy Gardner

He tears the sheet out of the notebook and turns to open the car door, but there's someone standing at his window. His first thought is it's someone telling him he can't park there, but when he looks up, he is struck by the sensation of seeing someone he instantly recognizes but does not know, a face that is so immediately familiar it is ingrained into his very being, yet different than what he remembered. And he realizes he's remembering details he thought he had forgotten, the beauty mark high on her cheek, the shape of her mouth.

"Hello, Andy."

Ashley – an older version of her, but still Ashley – is leaning in the car window. "Why don't you come inside?" she says, and she's laughing at him, but it's a nervous laugh.

Andy knows he's just staring at her, not saying anything, but it doesn't seem possible to do anything else. Her blonde hair isn't pulled up like it was in her engagement and wedding photos, it's down around her shoulders like when she was a teen. It's coarser now, and the roots are darker, but it still frames a face that somehow combines classic beauty with an innocence Andy had never been able to quite describe, something in the play of her cheekbones and eyes. Her eyes. If he had recognized nothing else, Ashley's eyes – with their thousand shards of blue that caught the sunlight – would have given her away instantly. How many hours had he stared into those eyes that summer? How many more had he stared into their memory after she left? Nearby, he hears a lone cicada begin singing.

"You had that exact same look on your face the day we met," she says, and it's hard to believe her voice is real after only imagining it for so long. "Remember, when you were mowing the lawn?"

Now he laughs, too. "Yeah, I almost drove the mower up a tree or something. How did– ?"

"Emma told me you were looking for me," she says, and opens the car door for him. Though she sounds more relaxed now, she also sounds more serious. "Come inside, I'll make some coffee and tell you all about it. You want some coffee?"

"Sure. And here," he says, handing her the note. "I was going to leave this in your mailbox, but that's kind of pointless now. I guess now you've got my phone number."

"Wait a minute," she says as he gets out of the car. "You weren't going to come to the door?"

"It's ah, kind of complicated," he says.

Her smile fades. "I know," she says, but then he realizes he's standing next to her – close – and he takes her in his arms and their embrace is as easy and natural as he sometimes dared to imagine it would be and for a moment he can forget all that has happened, until she pulls away and the moment ends. "That's my fault it's complicated," she says. "It's actually more complicated than you know. Come inside."

The little kitchen is filled with sunlight, the wood trim painted yellow and there's matching towels. There are pictures of two school-age children on the refrigerator. They're darling, and they have Ashley's eyes. But they also have dark hair, like the guy standing next to Ashley in the picture on the mantle when they walked in. There's music playing, a guitar and a woman's voice, high and longing, and Andy feels as though he could fall into it and float away in its grief and wonder. *"You've saved me,"* the woman sings, *"and you don't even know it."*

Andy can feel the warmth of her from across the room, but it's all moving too fast, like there's a drum beat pounding out a rhythm that drives everything forward.

"That music's great," he says. "Who is it?"

"Her name's Elaina," Ashley says. "She's a girl from here in town. I love it. But first, Andy, I want to tell you I am so sorry about what happened."

"No, listen, first – you look great. It's amazing to see you." And it's true. The feeling is like when he had been surprised by the train in Marshall – the calm, expected, comfortable monotony of his life had been replaced by the undeniable presence of her in the room, breathing, living in the same space as him. But it's also undeniable that at the lake just a few minutes before, he was ready to move on, ready to be over her, ready to accept the fact that while he had found her, she was just as inaccessible as she was when she had disappeared and now, seeing her, talking to her – smelling her when he had held her in his arms in the street – his feelings were just as powerful as they had been that one, perfect summer.

She pauses, and seems both impatient and perplexed at the same time – like she's blushing from the compliment, but also surprised by it, and he wonders if she expected him to be mad at her. The truth is, he expected to be mad at her, too. She had wrecked his life. He should be angry.

"It is, Ashley, I mean it," he says. "It's great. You, I— I never stopped thinking about you, and here you are, still amazing." Even as he hears his own words, he thinks of Scarlett and her green eyes and dark brown curls and he wonders if all this is really just so Ashley can reject him to his face, to make it clear that it's over, so he won't have to doubt himself again. Like he needs to hear this lock click shut before he can open a new one. He tries to be angry, but cannot, not with her here, in front of him, alive.

She takes down two coffee cups out of the wooden cupboard, one yellow, one blue, and pours the coffee. She hands him the blue one, then moves cream and sugar from the counter to the table where he's sitting. *"And I wonder if you feel like I feel,"* the woman on the CD player is singing. *"I'll teach you how to sing and then you can teach me how to love again..."* Through the music, through the table and the walls, through their hearts beating in the same room, Andy can feel the vibrations of the Song. After all these years, it's still there. Does Ashley feel it, too?

"I am sorry, Andy. I'm so sorry I left you like that and never wrote. But there really was a reason. And, I guess I never stopped thinking about you, either."

She opens a drawer, then looks confused, and opens another. Shaking her head, she hands him a spoon with her left hand, a gold wedding band on her ring finger.

"Did you forget where your spoons are?" he jokes.

"No, I, uh— I rearranged the kitchen this morning, Andy," she says, and crosses her arms, then uncrosses them. "I cleaned the house from top to bottom and changed everything around in here when I found out you were coming. I don't— I didn't... I've been dreading this, Andy, because I just knew you had to be mad at me for what I did. You had to be. You deserve to be. And I was scared to face up to that because it would just crush me if you hated me, and I know you should. You should hate me for what I did." She sniffs and wipes at her eye. "But the truth is, I also couldn't wait to see you. Even if I didn't want to admit it to myself. I had to do something sitting here waiting, so I reorganized the kitchen and now everything's mixed up and I can't even figure out where the spoons are."

Andy looks down into his coffee cup, sees his reflection floating there, distorted and translucent. All these years, he had examined every one of his feelings about Ashley, from hatred to longing and everything in between. But he never contemplated how conflicted her feelings might be.

"So Emma told you I was looking for you? She knew where you were?"

Ashley sits down at the table and moves her hair behind her ear. When she does, the gold chain on her neck moves and half of a break-apart pendant slips out from inside her blouse. It says "I L Y."

She's married, but still wearing our pendant? And Emma knew where she was?

"Emma's always known, Andy. We've kept in touch ever since Mom and I moved to Marshall."

Andy tries to concentrate on spooning sugar into his coffee, but he knows it will only distract him for so long because it's far too hot to drink. He doesn't look up, and realizes he almost feels like he can't catch his breath. How…?

"You kept in touch with Emma but not with me? Then why are you still wearing our pendant?"

She takes a drink of her coffee, then sets down the cup. She takes a breath and looks down.

"Andy, I never wrote to you because I was pregnant," she says in a whisper and looks away, then looks at him and looks away again. "I was, I— I found out like the day we got to Marshall." He wants to grab her hand. They should be holding hands, he thinks, but he knows they can't, even though he senses she feels the same way. "We, you and I…" Ashley says. "Well, the pendant, it's really for our baby, more than you, Andy. Not that it's not for you, but I wear it to remember her. I miscarried over Christmas break that year." She wipes her eyes again.

Andy looks around the room, trying to take in what she just said. I was a father. Or I had been. With Ashley. We were a family. One. Or we were.

"I'm so sorry for leaving like that, Andy, but I never wrote to you because I knew that if you knew about the baby, you'd drop everything and try to support me. You'd never go to Princeton, you'd never do all the things you were supposed to do."

He tries to take a drink, but can feel the coffee instantly burn the tip of his tongue when he sips at it. How had she kept this from him? *We should have been together through this.*

"You gave me a life, Andy, a life I never would have had otherwise. I was in all AP classes at Marshall and I got a full-ride scholarship to Western." She looks up from her coffee and directly into his eyes. Even since the street, he had forgotten how blue they were. "That happened because of you, Andy. I figured the least I owed you was to give you your own life back. I figured I'd have the baby, place her for adoption and once it was done I'd write to you."

I could have been there for you. I should have been there for you.

"But you never wrote. Not even after you lost her."

He feels something he can't explain, like she's reaching out to him across the table, something powerful and eternal. She shifts in her seat. *Even after all this,* he thinks, *she feels it, too. She does.*

"I couldn't lie to you, Andy. I knew if I heard your voice I would tell you everything and it would ruin your life. Just like I knew if I ever saw you again, I…"

Andy can feel the texture of the wood table under his fingertips, the way his feet touch the floor. Every cell in his body is pulling him toward Ashley. But he looks at her wedding band and holds back.

"Seventeen— " he begins. *Get a grip. This is madness. She's married. Why are they doing this to each other?*

"I guess your plan didn't work, though," he says.

"Yeah, I wanted to talk to you about that. It turns out I wasn't the only one keeping secrets."

Finally, the coffee has cooled to a tolerable level. The music on the CD player has stopped and a clock shaped like a ladybug over the stove ticks loudly.

"What do you mean?"

"Emma always told me everything was fine with you. That you went to Princeton, that you had a great life. Only when she knew you were coming to see me did she tell me the truth. I didn't even know you were still in Fort Wayne – she made it sound like you were in New York or something."

He sets down his coffee

"I'm so sorry, Andy."

"Did Emma know? About the baby?" As he asks this he realizes that this whole trip has been a lie. That he thought that for once, he was taking action in his life, that for the first time his destiny was going to be based on something he did, instead of something that happened to him. But here he is, sitting at Ashley's kitchen table, and the things she is saying and doing are changing his life for him. Again. Even Emma was doing it from four hours away – Ashley doesn't even have to answer the question: Of course Emma knew. His whole damn life was one where he was an afterthought, an unintended consequence of other people's actions – his entire life story could be told by what women had done to him. He realizes the music on the CD player has started again, but the only words he can pick out are "paper love" over and over.

"Yeah, Emma knew about the baby," Ashley says, and looks out the window. "She knew I was pregnant and I told her I had lost the baby, but something got messed up when I told her and she apparently thought I got an abortion. I never really understood that until we talked the other day, but that's apparently why she never told you anything. She said she thought it would kill you to find out I had aborted our baby. It wasn't just that she was doing what I asked, she thought she was protecting you, too, just like she tried to protect me from knowing how badly I hurt you. We were both protecting you, I guess. Or we tried to."

Andy stares down at the coffee cup, briefly considering throwing it across the room. Still, Ashley was right about one thing: He was the one who hadn't moved on afterward.

"It wasn't your fault," he says. "It was me. I just— "

Now she looks almost angry.

"Andy! What was it you said to me once? We were destined for greatness? And you— you just— "

The Song still played, but it was almost in a mocking tone, and it was fading.

"Look, the life you have is great, and you should be happy. I'm not saying that at all," she says. She sounds older, like a parent. "There's nothing wrong with what you're doing and how you live. But you *settled* for that. You settled without even trying. And the worst part is, Emma says you're not even happy. You could be happy with your life, and instead you're just— I don't even know."

She was right. He worked behind a desk at a cabinet company. Who knows where he'd be if he had followed the plan and gone to Princeton? He might even be happy.

She looks down at her hands and whispers, "And I know it's unfair of me to hold it against you, like you're trying to make me feel bad about what I did, because I know you're not. And I know you should never forgive me for what I did, leaving like that. I know it. But you could have hated me and moved on. You could have been angry and still lived your life. That's all I ever wanted, was for you to be happy."

He can hardly breathe.

"And I missed you," she says. "I still do, I think, because even though you're here, you're not the Andy I knew then."

"I know," he says, looking at her face. God, that face. What would he give to see that face every day? "I guess I thought that you and I were all that mattered, and when I lost you, I somehow lost everything. It just—

"The thing is," he says, and he hopes he can make this clear, "is that I'm trying to change it. I know I kind of got myself in a rut, but I'm ready to get out of it. I am. And I thought if I could just see you once more, if I could somehow settle things between us, or find out what happened or whatever, that maybe I could move on, you know? Start over. It was like I was paralyzed that day and I'm just now breaking out of that shell. But I'm breaking out. I'm going to. I just couldn't when I didn't even know why you left." He looks her in the eye. "And I missed you, too."

She reaches out and grabs his hand and he starts at her touch.

"I know," she says. "Leaving you... it broke me, Andy. It just, it was like tearing a house down to the foundation and starting over. And then when I lost Lilly... Jim wasn't the love of my life, Andy. No one but you ever could be. But he was understanding, and getting married was a way to— I had lost everything, Andy. I lost you and I lost Lilly, and..."

"Lilly? That was her name?"

"Oh yeah," she says, and sighs a little on the "yeah." "Our baby's name was Lilly. Lilian Andrea, because I thought Andrea sounded like Andy."

Almost unconsciously she fingers the pendant. "That's the other reason I wear this. The "I L Y" sort of looks like 'Lilly.'

"Actually, this isn't even the real one," she says, letting go of it. "I had worn it so much all the finish was off it and the chain broke like sixty times, so on the first Mother's Day after we were married, Jim gave me this one, which he had made. He understood. The real one's in my hope chest."

Andy looks around the kitchen. He had thought finding Ashley would be about confronting her – but somehow it had turned into confronting himself.

"I uh, I had the other half of the pendant, you know," he says. "I actually had it until about a half-hour ago."

"What?"

"I'm an idiot," he says. "I thought I was ready to move on, so I threw it into Lake Michigan right before I came here. Now I wish I had it, and moving on is..."

He shakes his head and takes a drink of coffee to keep from saying anything else, his tongue tingling where he burned it before.

"Emma said you're seeing someone, but she didn't know how serious it was," she says, then looks him in the eye. "And I'm really sorry about your marriage not working out, Andy. I really am."

"Well that is one thing that is definitely not your fault," he says. "So, um, you're happy and everything? You've got kids now?"

She smiles and walks over to the cupboard, but doesn't take anything out. "Yeah, Jim's a great father. The kids are in fourth and fifth grades now. That's Mark and Sarah," she says, pointing to the pictures on the fridge. "It's good." But the Song is getting louder, and slower, and he can see that she hears it, too, as she first crosses her arms, then moves her hair behind her ear again.

"Andy, you know I wish things had been different, but... but this is where we are today, and I feel like we just have to be grateful for the time we had together," she says, but she's shifting her weight and seems to be breathing deeper. "I know I'm grateful we got to see each other again."

Andy feels like he's on a mountaintop, swaying between falling off one edge into desire, or off another into an evil, brooding darkness. Where was the right path down?

"Listen, Ashley, I'm sorry – I'm so sorry about the baby. I wish I would have known so I could have, I don't know, I guess there was nothing I could do, but I wish I could have at least been there for you."

He feels the pull even stronger now, and his heart is beating in time with the Song.

"You were," she says. "That was the only thing that got me through, was knowing that you were going to have a great life. And that you had given me a life. Without you, I would have ended up just like my mother. I survived because I felt like I had to live up to what you gave me."

He wants so badly to just stand up and take her in his arms, and he can feel that she wants the same thing, but... There's no way I can ask her to give up her children, her family, for me. At the same time, he has to know.

"And now?"

She seems to sense his urge to reach out to her, and crosses her arms across her chest and stands up straighter. "Don't ask that, Andy. Don't. Because you know. You know and I know, but we also know what can't happen. I have a husband and two children and you have, what's her name?" She's shaking her head, but he knows. "It can't. Because we would both destroy everything for, for a moment that both of us know can't last and neither of us wants that. Not really. Not like that."

"Scarlett. Her name's Scarlett." Even if we were to be together, he thinks, could we ever get back what we once had? Or maybe it's that much more precious because it is gone forever.

"We have to accept our circumstances, we have to," she says. She sets down her coffee cup, then picks it up again. "Even if..."

"I know," he says. "Listen, I'm sorry for everything—" and he pauses because he can't really put into words the rest of the thought, something about all these years being worth it. Not worth it, exactly, but not wasted on an image, a phantom that never existed. "I just – like you said, I've got to move on. And I felt like I really needed to know what happened to be able to do that."

It was time to end this charade. I'm not going to just sit here anymore and wait for whatever happens next. I'll do the right thing and be on my way. It's time for me to start making my own decisions for a change.

He stands up, and wraps his arms around her. "I'm sorry," he whispers, trying not to smell her hair. "I'm sorry about Lilly. I'm sorry for bringing all this up, I'm sorry about— about everything."

She stands stock still, her arms at her side, as if she's afraid to move, afraid that she'll put one hand on his shoulder and they'll both fall off the precipice. He was sure of himself when he stood, but now, as she carefully uncrosses her arms and wraps them around his waist, he feels the same fear on the back of his neck and in his spine and for a moment could forget his resolve, forget about his life being a constant buffeting in the wake of other's movements and let this river of desire carry him into the aching, longing heat still churning between them. The mountain underneath him sways, trying to tip him until he falls into the ageless wanting that seems to cry out to him, until finally, she straightens. "You should go," she says.

It's not until he's in his car, miles down the road and merging onto the freeway that he realizes that his cellphone is ringing, that the phone no one ever calls has six missed calls and is ringing again.

SEVENTEEN

"If we can not satisfactorily explain the reason for the long larval life of the periodical Cicada or the conditions which led to the origin of this peculiarity, assuming it to be abnormal, we can at least see certain advantages coming to the species therefrom. Among these are the protection from attacks of parasitic enemies, since we can hardly conceive of a parasite limited to this Cicada which could possibly extend its existence over an equal number of years. Its occurrence, also, in overwhelming numbers at almost the same moment everywhere within the range of the brood prevents its being very often seriously checked in its aerial existence by the attacks of birds and other vertebrate enemies, which fatten on it in enormous numbers. For this species this is a most important consideration, for it is naturally sluggish and helpless and seems to lack almost completely the instinct of fear common to most other insects."

—"The Periodical Cicada"

Andy grabs the ringing phone and answers.

"Andy, it's me, Scarlett. Thank God you finally answered."

Andy moves into the slow lanes where he can concentrate a little better.

"Sorry – I left the phone in the car. What's happening?"

"We're at the Parkview ER. I just got done talking to the police, answering the exact same questions for like the forty-seventh time."

"The ER? The police?"

"Mike brought Abby home with bruises on her arm, like he grabbed her and shook her. He claims he didn't do anything, but like I'm going to believe that lying sack of shit. So I had to call the cops and now we're at the ER waiting to get her checked out."

"Is she OK? Are you OK?" He had kind of been looking forward to the four-hour drive, thinking it would give him a chance to clear his head, figure out where things stood. No chance of that now.

"I think she's fine, but, you know the whole thing with the cops, and they arrested Mike because she clearly had bruises and of course it was right in front of her, and now we're just sitting here, waiting, so, yeah, physically she's probably fine but, you know…"

"So she's not hurt or anything otherwise, though?" Jesus.

"No, she doesn't seem to be, but obviously I want a doctor to make sure."

"Yeah, yeah, that makes sense. Hey, listen, when you're done there, why don't you just go to my parents' house? It's only a few blocks away, and it'd be a good way to get away from everything, and then I'll meet you there as soon as I get back."

"You sure? That sounds great, but, I don't want to—"

"No, it's cool. I'll call them right now. I'll stop at my place to turn on the air and then be right over."

"Yeah, OK, that sounds great."

"OK, I'll call them right now, so if you don't hear back from me, then it's all good, just head over there when you're done."

"Yeah, OK. And listen, Andy, thanks so much."

"No, as long as you're OK, that's all that matters. I'll be there as soon as I can."

Andy hangs up the phone and realizes Scarlett needs him, and more than that, he likes that she needs him. He wasn't sure yet what to think about Ashley, and maybe he never would, and he still needed to figure out Scarlett. But for now, the fact that she needed him was enough.

Andy pulls up to the little white house in the little neighborhood by the river, puts the car in park and turns it off just as early evening begins to change to dusk.

As Andy gets out of his car, Scarlett's Honda comes down the road and pulls into her driveway. He runs across the street and opens the car door for her.

"Hey, I didn't expect to see you," he says. "Abby's good? Everything's OK?"

"Yeah, listen thanks so much. Your parents are awesome," Scarlett says, walking to her front door. "They're all having a blast together – your dad's down on the floor playing with her – and your mom, of course, is in heaven. We're going to spend the night there, just in case Mike gets released, which I doubt, but you never know, so I came back to get a few things – I hadn't expected to need pajamas and whatnot when we left for the hospital."

As Andy sits in her kitchen, he can see Scarlett going from room to room with a duffel bag, grabbing things. He realizes that, more than anything, he's comfortable with her. Yes, sometimes she frightens him with her directness, and he's entranced by her green eyes, and maybe they don't share that incredible oneness that he and Ashley still have, even after all these years, but it doesn't really matter what he and Ashley have, does it? She's married, and happy, and whatever they had, however powerful it was, it was in the past. And now her knew: She had loved him all these years. She hadn't left because she didn't love him, hadn't disappeared and never wrote because she didn't love him, she hadn't ever really gotten over him. And that – knowing the last seventeen years hadn't been wasted on a stupid teenage fantasy – meant everything, certainly much more than their current circumstances. Yes, they had been deeply in love once, and it had mattered. As for the present, all he really knows is he wants it to be with Scarlett. And at least when he's here, watching her move, it doesn't feel like she's just a fallback position.

"I gotta tell you, Scarlett," he says. "I missed you. I really did, and I can't believe you put up with me running off on a stupid quest like that."

Halfway between rooms, Scarlett stops. "Oh, God, I'm sorry, Andy. I didn't even ask you how your trip was. I'm sorry – this has all just been so, so screwed up. I'm sorry. You didn't fall in love with her did you? You didn't come over to break up with me because you're running off with her?" She holds her poker face for a few seconds before laughing. "I'm ready to go, I think."

"No, if I was going to do that, I would have just called you and done it over the phone," he says as they walk toward the door. On the porch, Scarlett pauses while she retrieves her keys out of her purse.

"You're a putz," she says, digging around for the keys. Before she can pull them out, Andy grabs her by the waist and pulls her to him.

"Listen," he says, moving her curls away from her face so he can see her eyes. "I know I'm an idiot. I know. And I know trying to find my seventeen-year-old crush was stupid, but now I know after all these years that that's done, and I can put it in the past where it belongs. Now I can focus on the present."

He pulls her closer. Dusk has fallen, and though it's been going on for a while, he finally hears the cicadas making their electric maraca sound from the shadows as waves of resonance seem to blanket them. "I don't know what the future holds, but I know I want to spend the present with you."

Their reverie is interrupted by a pickup truck roaring up the street, then screeching into Scarlett's driveway, throwing gravel. The driver slams the truck into park and jumps out.

"Son of a bitch," Scarlett says as a wiry, muscled guy in a dirty t-shirt stomps toward them. "Mike, you have exactly zero seconds to get the hell off my property. You have no right to be here and you are leaving NOW."

Mike doesn't even slow down.

"You listen to me, whore," he says, his words thick. From five feet away they can smell the booze on him.

Andy steps between them. "OK, OK, no one wants any problems here," but Mike is already up in his face.

"Get out of my way punk, or I'll do to you what I'm going to do to her." Mike's got a slight mustache and a tattoo on his neck, but what scares Andy is his eyes. They're angry and bloodshot, but they're also desperate, and that frightens him more than his obvious muscles.

"You're going back to jail, Mike," Scarlett says, opening the door. "I'm calling the cops."

Mike grabs Andy to shove him aside, but Andy stays in the doorway and puts his hands near Mike's shoulders.

"Mike, it's OK, man, listen to me. It's OK." His voice seems to have a calming effect, so he continues. "Listen, this has been rough, I get that, OK, but there's no point in making it any worse, all right? Don't make it any worse. Just relax."

Mike seems to take it down a notch, then looks out towards the road, towards the river.

"She took everything. Everything. And now I'm going to lose my little girl, too."

"It's OK, Mike, it's gonna work out."

Just then, Scarlett comes back. She's holding an aluminum baseball bat, and her eyes are on fire.

"Cops are on their way Mike. You're going back to jail," she says. "First thing in the morning I'm getting an order of protection, and then I'm going to make sure you never see Abby again."

Mike struggles to get past Andy, but Scarlett menaces him with the bat. So much for the calming words. He's never seen her this angry, and it's almost intimate to see her this raw.

"What are you going to do, Mike? Beat me like you beat up Abby?"

"I didn't do it!" he screams. "You can't take her!"

Mike reaches around Andy and grabs a handful of Scarlett's hair, but there's no room for her to swing the bat around Andy's frame, so she kicks Mike hard in the groin, knocking him down the steps. As he lies on the ground, it's as if he curls into himself and something else emerges. When he stands, the drunken, raging Mike has been replaced by something much more sinister. The frenzy is replaced by what looks to Andy to be pure, controlled malice. His words are slow, but no longer slurred.

"If you take her away from me," he says, looking them in the eye, "I will kill every single one of you. I will kill you Scarlett, so help me. I will kill you, I will kill your pansy ass little friend here, and I will do what I have to do."

Andy's world seems to slow down, and he gradually realizes the cicadas are screaming louder than he's ever heard them.

But Scarlett only smiles. Then she hands Andy the baseball bat, and pulls a tape recorder from her shirt pocket, the little wheels on the tape spinning and the red "RECORD" light glowing menacingly.

"Tell it to the judge, Mike," Scarlett says, holding up the recorder. "You're going to jail."

For an instant, Andy sees the desperation in Mike's eyes again, sees the way a man can turn when he is hurt so badly that something in him changes, changes into darkness. He thinks about how he had been in darkness himself, in those first years after Ashley left, and how he turned that darkness on himself, when he could have just as easily done what Mike is doing now, and turned it on others. He wonders how close he was, what it would have taken, where the line is between the visions of a sink red with your own blood and visions of the blood of others. How close are any of us, really?

That's when Andy first sees the gun; when Mike pulls it from behind him. It looks heavy in Mike's hand and Andy can see Mike's slender arm slow with the heft of it. He lifts it toward them, then swings it left, toward Scarlett.

Andy knows there's no talking him down this time, no calming words that will diffuse this situation. He sees his choice in absolute clarity, and makes it without hesitation. He steps toward Mike, not raising the bat but already swinging his wrists and forearms as hard as he can for maximum torque and power. Even though the bat is still low, Mike sees the aluminum flash in the headlights of his truck and swings the gun toward Andy, and pulls back the hammer.

Andy can see Mike drawing back on the trigger as the bat reaches its apogee over his head and begins its downward arc toward Mike's head. He thinks of Ashley and all that she gave him, including Lilly, the little girl he never knew he had, never knew he should mourn. He thinks of the life Ashley gave him that he could have taken advantage of, but didn't because he thought instead she had taken it from him. He thinks of Abby, and how this step toward Mike, this swing of the bat, this step into the unknown will give her the mother Mike is trying to take away. He thinks of Scarlett, screaming behind him, screaming NO at the top of her lungs, and how she seemed willing to give him a new life, too. And he realizes as the gun flashes and the bat crashes down onto Mike's head that this step forward, this swing of the bat, this is his new life, short as it is. That after seventeen years of paralysis, of others making the choices for him, of being only able to react to those around him, that he has at last made a decision, taken an action for himself, and determined his own fate. No more waiting for others to make their choices for him.

The blast of the gun silences the cicadas, and Andy feels an entire star explode inside of him, turning his chest into heat and light expanding outward. The bat seems to continue down under its own power, striking Mike's head with a sickening thunk, and Andy can see the gun smoking and held awkwardly as Mike falls backward and glazed-eyed onto Scarlett's car. Andy looks at Scarlett as he begins to fall against her house, trying to comprehend both the feeling of openness in his chest – of air actually passing through it – and the feeling of warmth rushing out of it. As he falls, the sound of the gunshot still echoing in the suddenly silent night air, he thinks of his sister Sally, saving him from drowning in the canoe when they were kids, when all he could think was that it was supposed to have been Ashley that saved him. It turns out, he thinks, that it was Ashley that had saved him after all. All of them had, really, each in their own way. And that let me save myself, tonight, here on Scarlett's porch, he thinks. And finally he knows why Sally pulled him out of that water, why he had lived when there had never seemed any point to it. It was for this: This moment, this one leap into the air was the very reason he had been born.

He remembers that once, on Ashley's porch, he felt he was falling away into nothing, that the world was an emptiness taking him. This time, as he lay on another porch, Scarlett standing over him, unable to move, unable even to scream, he realizes it isn't nothingness at all he is falling into, but a sound, a sound that resonates from the molecules of the air itself, a sound that rings across the universe and into his very being, making him one with the Song, one with everything that is and ever was. The Song wasn't between him and Ashley – it was between him and this moment, this place where the river of his soul moves and swirls into the sea that had been calling him to her endless arms and, at last, peace. And as the supernova in his chest continues to blast outward, he hears another voice in the Song, a smaller voice from inside Scarlett; different, but the tiny boy's voice is instantly familiar. My part of the Song will continue after all, he thinks.

Nearby, in the shrubbery, a lone cicada begins to sing, and soon, his song is taken up by others in a great chorus that rises and falls in the muggy night air, a living, shimmering resonance that is only interrupted by the shrill sound of sirens, and Scarlett at last remembering how to scream out her grief.

©Callie Cwiakala

ABOUT THE AUTHOR

Dan Stockman is an award-winning journalist and a writer
in Fort Wayne, Indiana, where he lives with his wife, two children
and two dogs in a house that seems in need of constant repair.
He has Bachelor's degrees from Western Michigan University
and a Master of Fine Arts degree in Creative Writing from
Fairleigh Dickinson University.

Follow him on Twitter @DanStockman or join him on Facebook at
www.Facebook.com/dan.stockman2

NickelPlatePublishing.com